Aleister Crowley MI6
The Hess Solution

To the memory of my mother Lynne Munn
(aka Maud Agnes McNeff: 1924-2022).
How sweet the moonlight sleeps upon this bank!

Aleister Crowley MI6
The Hess Solution

Richard C McNeff

Mandrake

First Edition

By the same Author
Fiction: *Aleister Crowley MI5*
Satire: *The Dream of Boris*
Memoir: *With Barry Flanagan: Travels through Time and Spain*

Published by
Mandrake
PO Box 250
OXFORD
OX1 1AP (UK)

Contents

Prelude 7

Part I England 1941 11
Chapter One Commander Fleming's Proposal.......................... 12
Chapter Two The Nazi Sky At Night 21

Part II Crow's Last Nest
Chapter Three Netherwood 50
Chapter Four Room 13 57
Chapter Five Fortune, Lady Frieda & The Mage 64
Chapter Six The Birthday Party 71
Chapter Seven Castle Interlude 82
Chapter Eight The Birth Pangs of the Aeon 90
Chapter Nine Professor Butler Visits 98
Chapter Ten The Devil and Doctor Fast 109
Chapter Eleven Symonds & Gleadow 115
Chapter Twelve The Comintern Couple 121
Chapter Thirteen Latin Lesson 131
Chapter Fourteen 'The Z File' 136
Chapter Fifteen Knight's Black Agents 157
Chapter Sixteen At the Customs Station 161
Chapter Seventeen A Good World to Leave 164

Part III Pasadena 1952 175
Chapter Eighteen Pioneers.. 176
Chapter Nineteen Jack Blows It...................................... 187

Part IV London 1965 191
Chapter Twenty Year Zero 192
Chapter Twenty-One Soho Haunt 200
Chapter Twenty-Two The Sonneteer of Moabit 207
Chapter Twenty-Three The Secret of the Bug Hotel 221

Dramatis Personae 233
Further Reading 246

Prelude
Reception Committee

It is a fine Saturday night in May 1941. A prince and a spy are in the Kennels, an outbuilding in the grounds of a Scottish stately home called Dungavel. The Kennels is on loan to the International Red Cross and thus outside the jurisdiction of any state. This is vital as the visitor they are expecting holds a very high rank in the command structure of a hostile power. Neutrality means he can land, parlay, and return to his own country without fear of arrest.

That morning Rudolf Hess has risen early. The day is sunny, clear, and perfect for flying as the weather forecast confirms. After breakfast, he takes his son and the family's four dogs for a long walk along the path of the river that flows past his house on the outskirts of Munich. He lunches with a fellow minister of the regime, then changes into a blue shirt, blue tie, breeches, and flying boots. Ilse, his wife, is not feeling well. He goes to the bedroom. She is pleased he is wearing a blue shirt rather than his customary white one. She is reading a book by the first pilot to fly over Everest, a pre-war present from British friends. Hess leans over and gazes at the photo of the author, the Marquess of Clydesdale, now the Duke of Hamilton. He remarks that he is very good looking. His wife agrees. There is a letter from Hess to the duke in the small suitcase in the boot of his car. He tells her he is going away and will return by Monday evening. She does not believe him.

In the late afternoon he is driven to the Messerschmitt works an hour from his home. Hitler, his closest friend, has forbidden him to fly, but he managed to have the ban reduced to a year. This has now elapsed. Waiting for him on the apron of the hangar is a twin-engine Messerschmitt-110, with grey-green camouflage above and a blue-grey underside. He has had it customised and added two extra fuel tanks. In the administration building he dons a new tailor-made Luftwaffe captain's jacket and pulls a fur-lined flying suit over his

7

clothes. He returns to the plane, watches the tanks being filled and checks for himself that none of the guns are loaded. It is crucial to arrive unarmed. After climbing into the cockpit, he switches on the engines and gives the thumbs-up for the chocks to be pulled from under the wings. The plane taxies away up-wind. It is a quarter to six. The plane's designer, Willy Messerschmitt, is among those who watch him fly away.

The first news reaches the Kennels just after ten p.m. The source is the man whose picture the visitor has admired that day. The duke is in command of an aerodrome 54 miles north-east of Dungavel. His message is relayed to the prince by a girl in ATS khaki hunched over a wireless receiver. Hess has just flown into RAF Turnhouse, the sector the duke oversees. The Observer Corps has identified the plane as hostile. The duke rejects this on the grounds that the type of aircraft specified has insufficient fuel capacity to return to its base. The plane's status remains "unidentified". The rule in such cases is not to open fire. The aircraft, however, has not responded to challenges and ignores requests to show the colours of the day. It is on course to Glasgow Sector, which has been devastated by recent bombing raids. There is a "flap" in the control room and a call for fighters to be scrambled. As it moves through the sights of two heavy AA batteries, the duke faces down the consensus that they should open fire.

The spy waits impassively, but the prince paces nervously back and forth. He is a fine-looking man dressed in the uniform of an air commodore, with a gold-braided cap and a broad gold hoop on both lower sleeves. It is a recent promotion, but the rank, like the rest of his existence, is largely ceremonial. In the years leading up to the outbreak of hostilities he conspired with his German cousin, also a prince and an intimate of Hitler, to avert the coming conflict. In this, he had the full support of his family, who view the war as a tragic folly.

Hess is of the same opinion. He also feels he has been relegated to the sidelines. He is Deputy Führer in name only. Hitler has made Hermann Göring his successor. Hess heads any number of committees charged with administering the Reich, as well as the prosecution of the war — but the real power lies elsewhere. He believes a peace treaty can restore him to favour with Hitler, whom he worships.

Just before eleven, the prince and the spy hear an approaching plane. The engine whines like a dentist's drill, a noise typical of enemy fighters. They go outside and wait beside the landing strip that runs alongside. The plane flies overhead but returns a few minutes later. The other ATS girl stationed at the Kennels switches the landing lights on. The plane lines up with the runway and begins its descent. There comes the more familiar drone of a British aircraft. A Defiant night fighter is at twenty thousand feet. The Messerschmitt-110 shoots past, so low that the prince and the spy can make out the black crosses on wings and fuselage and the swastika on the twin tail fin. The plane zooms over the hangar beside the strip, in which the fuel tanks for the return journey are stored, with the night fighter in pursuit. The engines fade, leaving the not-quite silence of the Lanarkshire night. Eighteen miles from Dungavel, The Messerschmitt goes into a fatal nosedive. At nine minutes past eleven, burning fuselage lights up the northern sky.

Part I
England 1941

"Sir, If it is true that Herr Hess is much influenced by astrology and Magick, my services might be of use to the Department, in case he should not be willing to do as you wish."
Letter from Aleister Crowley to Naval Intelligence, 14 May 1941.

Chapter One
Commander Fleming's Proposal

The Cavendish Hotel, Mayfair: Monday, 19 May 1941

Though neighbouring Bond Street and Hyde Park, the Cavendish has the musty air of a run-down country house. Abandoned polo sticks litter the front hall. In the adjacent dining room, blotches deface the peeling mirrors and cobwebs of shrapnel-generated cracks the French windows. Fleet Street dubbed the hotel's owner the Duchess of Jermyn Street in her heyday. Now silver-haired and stooped, Rosa Lewis pauses solicitously by a pair of diners draining a 1929 Romanée Conti. They crave tobacco more than food, having left the *consommé aux ailerons* untouched. One of them resembles a giant crab, with shaven head and staring eyes. He is dressed in a gaudy green tweed suit with plus fours and a floppy bow tie.

'Winston,' Rosa purrs, 'so good of you to come.'

After a lifetime spent accumulating aliases, it has come as a relief to the Great Beast to capitalise on his resemblance to the current prime minister. He takes a drag on his Corona.

'That is if you really was the young scapegrace who nicked eclairs when I cooked for 'is pa. You're that beastly fellow the newspaper Johnnies are always 'arpin' on about. I don't give a 'oot if you're Satan's representative on Earth as long as you're not a bloomin' writer. Last one 'ere couldn't stop blubbin' 'is wife 'ad left 'im. 'e'd only gone and put 'er in a book!'

'All I write are cheques,' beams Crowley.

'I wrote one for a billion quid once, but nobody could cash it. Talkin' of which, didn't I once shop you for an unpaid bill?'

The Beast draws a practised veil over his moonlight flit in 1932 and the not inconsiderable sum of £24 he still owes her.

'Ah well, people only comes to the Cavendish to bounce cheques and pee. Peculiar company for you to be keepin', Admiral!'

Rosa is renowned for mixing up the actors of the First World War with those of the Second. In fact, the gold embroidery on the shoulder boards identifies the craggy-faced diner as a Royal Naval Reserve lieutenant-commander. The uniform is a sham. He is Personal Assistant to the head of Naval Intelligence and as such a spy. He removes the black-and-silver Asprey holder that clasps a handmade Morland cigarette.

'War makes for strange bedfellows, Madam.'

' 'ope you ain't thinkin' of getting up to any of that malarkey 'ere! It is against the law you know, except when Tredegar stays. 'Course, 'e's a lord and filthy rich.'

'Filthy *and* rich,' agrees Crowley. 'A fine bugger of a man!'

Rosa emits a peal of raucous laughter. 'The viscount knocks about with the oddest types. You must be one of 'em!'

A distant explosion rattles the windows. A bomb dropped on May 10, the heaviest night of the Blitz, when 500 bombers rained fire on London and devastated the House of Commons chamber, has finally got round to exploding. The blast alarms the flower girls around Eros and the camel paraded through Mayfair to advertise a well-known cigarette brand. There are casualties on Shaftesbury Avenue.

'Such a bloomin' nuisance this war,' sighs Rosa, grimly foreseeing another night shovelling incendiary bombs into buckets of sand on the roof. 'Don't let the consommé get cold, duckies! I put the last of the sherry in it. My word did the old king lap it up like that!'

A beauty in her youth, Rosa was Edward the Seventh's favourite cook as well as alleged mistress. May is cold and dull with abundant rainfall. Coal is rationed and wood in short supply. The Cavendish makes do with boot and shoetrees abandoned by well-shod guests. A maid lifts one onto the fire. Flames lick at the boxwood. Rosa shuffles across the chipped parquet floor to chat with a pair of Wren officers lunching by the windows.

Crowley scrutinises his fellow diner with an eye well versed in winkling out human foibles. Ian Fleming can be cheerful, exuberant even. He is debonair, a hit with women. The broken nose earned at Eton gives him a raffish air. Yet in repose, wreathed in tobacco smoke, he looks morose. The Beast's old chum, Augustus John, who has painted and bedded the Flemings' beautiful mother Val on three occasions, puts this down to younger brother syndrome.

Peter Fleming, the eldest, has dazzled the age as adventurer, soldier, and writer. On New Year's Day 1940, he even published a bestseller. Hitler is shot down over England while gloating over the destruction wreaked by his air force. The Eagle Führer becomes such a laughing stock that the British pack him off back to Germany. On 14 May, a *Times* leader flagged up the uncanny parallel between the book and the mysterious arrival of Rudolf Hess.

'Does your brother have second sight?'

Fleming chuckles. 'Peter has always led a charmed life but to anticipate Hess's jolly really takes the biscuit. *The Flying Visit* is flying off shelves, as fast as paper rationing allows.'

'Perhaps your brother's success gives rise to that fashionable affliction, an inferiority complex?'

'Oh, tosh, don't throw Adler at me!'

'I met the shrink in Berlin, you know. I advised him to psychoanalyse the Kaiser if he wanted to make a bob or two. '

'That must have been 1931. You were in Portugal before that?'

'With Hanni Jaeger: a cauldron of shame to die for.'

'Which you proceeded to attempt at Boca do Inferno.'

'The mouth of hell? My suicide? Just a little publicity stunt.'

'Everything you've done is on record.'

'I hope it's a very magical one.'

'To get slung out of Italy and France is quite a feat.'

'I am much misunderstood.'

Is it that or is Crowley truly evil? His pitted cheeks, and the white that rings the irises like Mussolini's, lend him an appropriately sinister air. Yet 'M' laughed off the whole Beast of the Apocalypse display as just an act when he tossed Fleming Dossier 666 one drizzly autumn afternoon in 1939.

The first section bore stamps of British Intelligence before it split into MI5 for UK-centred affairs, and MI6 for matters abroad. The yellowing pages reported on the Beast's first mission in 1898 after his recruitment at Cambridge University. This was to spy on the Golden Dawn, an occult order that included subversive Irish Republicans and Jacobites in its ranks. Relocated to America as a pro-German agent provocateur, 666 helped spur the entry of the United States into the Great War.

Throughout the Twenties and early Thirties, he crisscrossed Europe. His reputation as a sex-and-drug-crazed diabolist was perfect. Who could believe the Service would employ such an outrageous figure? The Abbey of Thelema he founded on the Sicilian coast made an ideal vantage from which to spy on the manoeuvres of Mussolini's navy. Translated to Berlin, he snooped on German communists for MI6 and Special Branch. In June 1936, he played a pivotal role in the London-based operation to expose Wallis Simpson as a German agent and avert the Abdication, a fiasco that rankles with 'M' to this day.

Just after the outbreak of war, 666 offered his services to Naval Intelligence. The Division summoned him for an interview. They were particularly interested in utilising his celebrated powers of hypnosis in the interrogation of enemy prisoners.

'Your brother only wrote about a flying visit. You made it happen.'

'If only. The truth is we did everything in our power to lure a top dog like 'Z'-'

' 'Z'?'

'Sorry, old boy! Hess's code name. The squaddies call him "Jonathan", but I find that overly familiar.'

'His flight was willed.'

'By you prancing around Ashdown Forest in your wizard's outfit stabbing effigies of the Nazi High Command?'

Fleming had staged Operation Mistletoe during the summer solstice of 1940 to convince the occult-fixated enemy they were under magical attack. The commander's fondness for entertaining bizarre schemes was well-known: a chain of heavily fortified Allied icebergs in the North Atlantic; frozen clouds moored along the coast as a platform for anti-aircraft guns. Recruiting a magician to crack the Deputy Führer was par for the course.

'Our operation lured Hess. I'm convinced of it.'

'I'd like to think so too, old chap. Sadly, it's far more likely that black propaganda we seeded concerning Churchill's imminent downfall did the job. A high-ranking Nazi dropping out of the sky with a treaty and, abracadabra! — hostilities would cease. Our ruse, however, wasn't a patch on the baloney from a Swiss astrologer called Krafft about the terrible fate in store for Hess's beloved boss that only an act of pointless bloody lunacy could avert. The stars all pointed to 10 May.'

This excites Crowley. A horoscope he cast back in March predicted a great change on that very night, itself remarkable for an incredibly rare alignment of six planets in Taurus. On 9 May he had a vision of colossal crimson and cream-robed Angels directing the war. They wanted him at their side, robed as a warrior.

Fleming leans closer. 'There was a Reception Committee waiting for 'Z' at Hamilton's Scottish pile, helmed by a figure of such eminence I would roast in hell if I so much as whisper the name. That was the icing on the cake as far as 'Z' was concerned. He's hopelessly starstruck.'

'Churchill?'

'Mum's the absolute word, old boy.'

'It always seemed fishy that Hess would desert his beloved Führer on the off chance of bumping into the duke.'

'Quite right, but that's the official line. Of course, 'Z' baled out a few miles from Dungavel and tried to pass himself off as Hauptmann Alfred Horn. Short of applying thumbscrews and the rack, MI6 have done everything to crack him but have drawn a blank so far. Given his addiction to the dark arts, someone of your expertise might just be the solution.'

'I offered as much in my letter.'

'"M' is all for it, but the other chiefs are hardly ecstatic to have you on board after the Abdication debacle. It will take all my powers of persuasion. In the interim, you'll receive a standard letter of rejection.'

'Don't they appreciate mine is the loyalty of Bill Sikes's dog?'

Such patriotism puzzles Fleming. Is it just another pose, or does the old devil really love his country?

'Tom Driberg will vouch for me.'

'The Labour MP? One of 'M's' boys, isn't he? Racy private life and all that. Not sure how that will go down with the chiefs.'

'Colonel Carter?'

'Of Scotland Yard? That would certainly boost your credibility. It will also help matters if you do a bit of prep.'

Fleming reaches down and extracts from his calf leather attaché case a large buff envelope which he hands across.

'Inside you'll find a translation of the diary of Albrecht Haushofer, 'Z's' chief assistant and bosom chum of the Duke of Hamilton. He's the catalyst. All the background you need.'

Crowley's nose wrinkles as though detecting a bad smell.

'Any relation to "Hitler's Merlin"?'

'General Karl Haushofer? Albrecht is his son. Do I detect a whiff of envy?'

'One likes to keep abreast of the competition.'

'You'll be relieved to know all that guff about the general being a magician schooled by levitating lamas in Tibet is black propaganda put out by us and Pee Wee. Not that he isn't dangerous. He's the architect of *Lebensraum* after all, which gives the ghastly crew licence to invade anyone they bloody like.'

'There was some hullabaloo about a Jewish wife.'

'The general was 'Z's' teacher and hid him after the failed putsch in 1923. 'Z' adores him almost as much as he does the Führer. He exempted Martha Haushofer and her sons from the Nuremberg Race Laws. Albrecht, the eldest, is the link with the Swiss astrologer. His father threw petrol on the flames with a dream of 'Z' sealing peace between two great nations in a castle with tartans hanging from the walls.'

'Stars and dreams!'

'The main drivers of 'Z's' flight. Right up your alley if I may say so. If you do get access to laughing boy, you'll find him very hard to read. One minute he's all sunshine and smiles; the next, rambling, depressed. The squaddies call him "Death's Head" because he's such a moody bugger. Every day they tot up his value. He's down to about half a crown at the minute. It's very hard to know what he's on about, he spouts such mumbo jumbo.'

'Making me the perfect choice?'

The thin smile. A man of cool passions. 'It's your lingo.'

'Not all that far removed from your own. Take your boss, Admiral Godfrey, or 'C' of MI6. Don't they resemble Secret Chiefs? Hidden, recondite, communicating by signs and cipher; invisible until they need you. Yet you do their will.'

'If you say so,' splutters Fleming, queasy at the thought of Godfrey finding out who his luncheon companion was. The explosion from his irascible boss would be all the greater should he bring Crowley to the office, Room 39 in the Admiralty, looking out onto the garden at 10 Downing Street and the barrage balloons on Horse Guards Parade. Crowley could expect a similar reception from 'C', amidst the worn-out carpets and bare lightbulbs of Broadway Buildings, MI6's seedy headquarters beside St James's Park tube station. Only 'M' of B5(b), an autonomous section of MI5 devoted to ferreting out homegrown traitors, would welcome him to his menagerie in Dolphin Square — along with all the other beasts.

'Our worlds really aren't that different,' continues Crowley. 'There's a long tradition of their meeting. Consider Doctor Dee, court magician in the reign of Elizabeth. Scryer. Cuckold. Intelligencer.'

'Isn't that the old word for spy?'

'The Virgin Queen called him her eyes. His cipher was 007 on account of his pince-nez.'

'My word, that's interesting!'

Fleming glances at the Wren officers, now tucking into pudding. One is pretty, the other elegant. He imagines humiliating the latter. He has a cruel streak which manifests itself in scattering bondage photos around his Piccadilly flat in the hope of corrupting girlfriends.

"Tomorrow 'Z' is moving from the Tower to a country house in Surrey that's been specially fitted out for him. He'll be under round-the-clock surveillance by his "Companions", a crack team of German speaking MI6 operatives. I'm flying to Lisbon then on to the States for a month or so. 'M' will be running you, but it's MI6's baby. Word is 'Z's been out of the loop for a while. His flight was a frantic attempt to claw his way back into favour. Broadway's convinced he's in possession of vital intel pertaining to the invasion of our green and pleasant land. Hitler's itching to have a bash at Russia as well. 'Z' may well know the invasion date.'

'A war on two fronts?'

'Sounds far-fetched, doesn't it? Adolf and Uncle Joe have been cooing like lovebirds for the best part of two years, but there are reams of intel that indicate an attack is imminent. 'Z' bottles up or speaks in riddles when asked. There'll be something in it for you. Can't say precisely what. Don't expect a knighthood!'

'Better food perhaps.'

'Yes, I do apologise, this game pie-'

'Still has beak, shot and feathers in it!'

'Keep your voice down! Rosa may well charge extra. I should have taken you to Quaglino's.'

'Or that Hungarian place where Dennis Wheatley stood me a sublime banquet.'

'He frequented your séances, along with 'M', I hear?'

The Wickedest Man in the World did not do séances but was long accustomed to having his practices confused with things they were not.

' 'M' is seriously on the path, but Wheatley just wanted to leech for his black magic potboilers.'

'Well, they've made him a very wealthy man. Now he's gone and wangled a position on the Joint Planning Staff. The news doesn't seem to have you brimming over with glee.'

'My own prospects would be significantly improved if you took the r out of crash.'

'Or the r and t out of drought,' laughs Fleming, quick to catch on. 'Of course, that will all change if you really are the Hess solution.'

Chapter Two
The Nazi Sky At Night

Torquay Express: Monday, 19 May 1941 (evening)

The fiend with the toothbrush moustache was beaming at him.

'Welcome to my modest chalet,' purred Adolf Hitler. 'I'm so delighted you could come.'

They were standing beside the red marble fireplace Mussolini had presented to the Eagle's Nest. Adolf grasped Crowley's arm, ushered him across the heated floor and out onto the terrace, with its panoramic view of the Bavarian Alps. Far below, the roofs and church spires of Berchtesgaden nestled on the plain.

'If we said our prayers, which of course we don't, you'd be the answer to them,' continued the Führer effusively. 'A new age of magical interpretation of the world is coming, focused on will not intelligence. We will supply a translated edition of your sublime *The Book of the Law* to every ministry, school, barracks, hospital, library, and hotel in the Reich. Such a pity the Soviets and the Allies do not do likewise! We would have world peace, which, as everybody knows, is my heart's desire.'

It was very rare to find someone who esteemed the Beast more highly than he did himself. He was quite overwhelmed.

'The Soviets are in dire need of a spiritual path. Atheism and materialism are a road to nowhere.'

'*Absolut!* A complete dead end! A thousand thanks for your gift of the swastika as well.'

Crowley basked in this acknowledgment of the ancient rune he had urged on Hitler's crony General Ludendorff. Glancing down, he noticed a vast multitude cramming into the streets and scrambling like ants up the mountain slopes.

'Heil Beast!' their massed chant rose.

Hitler wrapped a chummy arm around his shoulder and grinned. Was it his imagination or did the Führer have horns and Dracula teeth? 'Love is the War!' hissed Adolf.

Goebbels and Goering had sidled up behind them.

'Splendid chap!' declared the corpulent Reichsmarschall, slapping Crowley on the back.

'You are the saviour of the Reich,' agreed the propaganda minister with an oily smile. (It was extraordinary how well they all spoke English!). 'We shall have you broadcasting to the British Isles in no time. Lord Haw-Haw has become shrill and lacks the gravitas you so obviously possess.'

'You can call me Lord Horus, Warrior-Lord of the Forties.'

This tickled the Nazi bigwigs pink. They are still chuckling when the jolting of the carriage wakes the Beast. He is travelling second class on the six twenty-seven from Paddington, taking him to Torquay and the latest in a long line of temporary lodgings. Still suffering the after-effects of the game pie, he burps loudly as he opens his case and takes out his red Morocco leather-bound diary. He scribbles down the details of the dream in the five-minute window before they vanish. A fashionable theory contends that dreams foretell the future. The prospect fills him with relish.

Replacing the diary, he pulls out the buff envelope and removes the file. He recalls the other things Fleming has told him about Albrecht Haushofer. A professor of political geography at Berlin University, the German speaks near perfect English, has excellent contacts in both chambers at Westminster, and is the Nazi's leading authority on all things British. He is a poet and playwright with an ambiguous love life. Like his father, he is a student of Nostradamus and astrology. The file is festooned with red TOP SECRET stamps.

The Beast is gratified by these sigils of intrigue. The express is pulling into Reading. The signal from the gods could not be clearer. He instantly obeys.

The Diary of Albrecht Haushofer
(November 1939–May 1941)
Monday 13th November 1939

Is Karl Ernst Krafft the new Nostradamus? Do we finally have a soothsayer who really can read the future in the stars? Yet, with his greased back black hair and pasty features, the squat man in a paper collar summoned to our office in Wilhelm Strasse this morning reminded me of a Swiss gnome. Except, his pitch-black eyes are deep and hypnotic, evoking the steely-blue Führer's eyes that so mesmerise the German Folk.

Krafft is a functionary of Section VII of the SS, devoted to freemasonry and the occult. On the second of this month, he sent his immediate superior a warning that Hitler's life would be under threat from assassination by explosives between the seventh and the tenth. Every 8 November Hitler and the Old Guard attend the reunion at the Bürgerbräu beer hall in Munich to commemorate the failed putsch of 1923. This year fog was forecast, so the decision was taken to return to Berlin by rail instead of plane. Hitler cut his speech in half and left early, along with Hess. Thirteen minutes later a bomb hidden in a pillar directly behind the speaker's rostrum exploded, killing seven and wounding 63. The next day Krafft addressed a telegram to Hess at the Reich Chancellery, crowing over his prophecy.

'You went directly over the head of your superior,' snapped my boss, a stickler for protocol.

'Doctor Fesel considers astrological speculations relating to the Führer improper. He would not pass the memo on.'

'The doctor behaved impeccably. Was the source of your tip-off indeed Herr Hitler's horoscope?'

'My method takes account of correlations between cosmic cycles and human affairs, planetary periodicities such as the conjunction of Jupiter and Saturn, as well as recent discoveries I have made regarding the behaviour of sunspots. If you see my telegram…'

'I have. So has Herr Hitler. He read it aloud to Doctor Goebbels at lunch.'

Krafft beamed with pleasure. He had attracted the attention of the big shots. 'My approach is entirely scientific, Herr Deputy Reichsführer. I have proven beyond doubt that human destiny is a dance choreographed by the cosmos. I studied many thousands of horoscopes to reach this conclusion. It is all in my treatise on astrobiology. It would be an honour to furnish you with a copy. I must also warn you. The peril is not past!'

'Herr Hitler is the greatest man to appear in the last thousand years of German history. Sadly, there are those who wish him ill. We are ever vigilant.'

'But do you know the time or place in which assassination attempts could occur? I can pinpoint them for you.'

'In doing so you would be performing an inestimable service for the Reich. But a word of caution. Some do not believe the cosmos affects destiny and will actively seek to discredit you. Heydrich is one, Bormann another. The Führer himself is deeply sceptical about the influence of the stars. He wonders openly why identical twins do not share the same fate. Is the threat current?'

'I have been out of action for several days, held by the Gestapo.'

'They had to establish that you weren't party to the plot; the downside I'm afraid of this second sight of yours.'

'I am a scientist. My methods are rigorously empirical. Do not lump me with yellow press stargazers or old crones who read tea leaves!'

The Führer has such incredible luck it makes you wonder if a malignant force scores human destiny. This was the thirteenth assassination attempt he has survived. Almost all of them have been carried out by Germans, including the latest. It seems a communist carpenter working at the beer hall was responsible.

'We're blaming the English,' said Hess.

'They would not do something as craven as assassinate the head of a foreign power,' I said. 'The Russians might.'

'We are at war with the wrong enemy!' declared Hess. 'What possible interest is Poland to the British? They are in the grip of Churchill and his bloodthirsty clique.'

'But the Reich will prevail!'

'Is that opinion or prediction?' I asked.

Krafft glared at me. Such revulsion is something I have schooled myself to rise above. It is well known I am a *Mischling*, a quarter-Jewish on my mother's side.

Hess frowned. 'It is true we are carrying all before us, but our destiny lies in the East; there is our space to breathe, our *Lebensraum*. When interpreter Schmidt read out the British ultimatum on 3 September, Hitler turned to me and said, "My entire work is undone. My book was written in vain. No sacrifice is too great in winning England's friendship". There must be a way we can inch back from the abyss.'

His fierce glance reminded me of the conversations we'd had on this theme.

Wednesday 6th December 1939

Hess decided Krafft was too unstable to be offered a job. Besides, the Swiss only wants to devote himself to his own 'world-shaking' projects. Apart from promoting his book, *Traits of Astrobiology*, and developing his crackpot word-play theories, he wishes to compile a compendium of all the leading astrologers and occultists in the Reich, a *Who's Who in Borderland*. Meanwhile, Goebbels has given our sorcerer a highly paid job in the propaganda ministry. The

Reichsminister intends him to edit the quatrains of Nostradamus and produce pamphlets to embolden our troops and deflate our enemies. Depressingly, it seems the Renaissance seer was a fledgling Nazi, who foretold total victory for the Reich.

Thursday 7th March 1940

More news of the indefatigable Krafft. He attended a party at the Grunewald home of Arno Brekker, sculptor of those looming monstrosities depicting "Nordic" men and women that glower down at you in the Reich Chancellery. Bernard Rust, the science minister, went. Like me, he fails to share the widespread enthusiasm for the cold-blooded Swiss. We met last night on Kurfürstendamm. Over glasses of Asti Spumante, he related how Elli Ney, the concert pianist, paused her recital when Krafft entered. Hans Frank, the repellent Governor General of Poland, introduced the guest of honour as the man who had accurately predicted the attempt on the Führer's life. How sweet must be such public recognition, especially for a man so hungry for it as the Swiss! The gnome showed the guests something he called a "Dynogram", a graphical representation of the astrological factors that would influence Germany during 1940. For victory to be achieved, he told them, the war must be over by the winter of 1942.

Tuesday 18th June 1940

Hess is suffering from stomach pains, but this does not account for the state of near hysteria he was in after meeting Hitler today. Something the Führer has resolved to do has deeply upset him. He would not divulge what it was. He kept repeating it was more vital than ever we make peace with Britain. I think he has an inkling he is in eclipse. According to Bernard Rust, Hitler pities Germany should Hess ever lead her. Crafty Göring is the successor these days; Hess they call "a flag without a pole". As his power wanes so, worryingly, does the protection he extends to my family.

Monday 23rd September 1940

Well, I've done it and must hold my breath until (when or if!) a reply comes. Hess talks of nothing but a peace offer, but I've convinced him that going through former appeasers in embassies or the Cabinet in Whitehall is futile. The Führer has squandered all trust when it comes to the British. Nobody believes a word he says. A more circuitous route must be taken and who better than my old friend the Duke of Hamilton, steward of the king with the ear of Churchill? Hess needed little convincing. He has been in awe of Hamilton, the first pilot to fly over Everest, ever since the duke came to the Berlin Olympics where we met. He insisted I mention his own victory in the annual air-race round the Zugspitze, the highest peak in Germany. I assured him I would at some - much later - stage.

This is the second letter I have written to Douglo. The first was in July last year while I was on a cruise off the west coast of Norway. In that I alluded to Hitler's *idée fixe* that his life will be short, which explains his haste. I predicted war could break out at any time from last mid-August onwards. I was only a couple of weeks out. Perhaps I should set myself up as a rival to Krafft?

I sent the letter today. Hopefully, it will reach Douglo via neutral Lisbon. I conveyed my condolences for the death of his father and that of his brother-in-law, Northumberland, who lost his life near Dunkirk. I suggested we meet in a neutral zone on the outskirts of Europe, perhaps Portugal, with the caveat that I understood he might not be awarded leave. I proposed he send his reply in a double closed envelope, inside addressed to "Dr A H" (if it's intercepted, they might think it meant for Hitler!), outside to the Lisbon address used by the Abwehr as a posting station. Admiral Canaris, the head of military intelligence, is in the loop. I think Hess will tell the Führer about the letter. A fool's errand, no doubt, but what is the alternative? I press my thumbs for luck.

Wednesday 23rd October 1940

In wartime, a letter sent from Britain should take three or four days to Lisbon and a further two or three to get here. I have been waiting a month. Did I write too early or too late? Was my letter seized? My thumbs ache. I long to stop pressing them!

Friday 15th November 1940

Nothing from Lisbon. Meanwhile, death is having a field day. Last night the Luftwaffe razed Coventry. Please Douglo, lift that treasured Montblanc and write to me!

Tuesday 24th December 1940

I have stopped pressing my thumbs. In this season of hope, so much dread!

Tuesday 7th January 1941

Against all the odds, a letter reached me today, forwarded from Lisbon. It was typed, but the signature was Douglo's. He apologised for not responding earlier. His duties prevent him from meeting. However, if I could be in Portugal on the twenty-fourth of this month, I would learn something of great benefit. That was it. Not the barest hint of who might be waiting for me. I thank the Gods of Olympus and of Tibet! I will fly to Lisbon on the twenty-third, travelling incognito. A tourist destination provides perfect cover.

Friday 24th January 1941

Lord Byron described Sintra as the most beautiful town in Europe. I have little way of knowing if he was right. Rain is lashing the window of the café I am writing this in. It is almost impossible to make out anything outside, though every so often I catch a glimpse of poor souls dragged along by wind-upturned umbrellas. The turrets of the fairy-tale castle, brooding over the town from a rocky promontory, are almost completely obscured by cloud. Despite all this, I am the happiest tourist in Portugal after the momentous encounter that finished but an hour ago.

The designated meeting place was the Lawrence Hotel, the time just after three. With its English-style décor and wood panelled walls, the bar must look much the same as when the "mad, bad, and dangerous" lord was a guest. It took me only a moment to recognise the balding middle-aged man with the kindly face at the table furthest from the counter. He was in the company of an attractive young woman.

'May I present my secretary, Miss Jenkins,' he said, rising at my approach.

I bowed and clicked my heels like a Prussian officer, a silly thing to do in the circumstances. The barman, who was polishing glasses, didn't seem to notice, but then they're trained not to. We shook hands.

'Delighted, Mr...?'

'Fairclough.'

I suppressed a smile, for of course I knew his real name: Frank Foley, who ran the Passport Control Office for the British Embassy in Berlin in the early Thirties. In that capacity he had furnished thousands of Jews with papers so they could flee the inferno. This at great personal risk, for Foley did not enjoy diplomatic immunity. From time to time, he had enlisted my aid when up against particularly obstinate officialdom. Foley, I also knew, was a high-ranking officer in MI6. Whether he knew I knew I knew not. Such halls of mirrors are our modus operandi.

I sat down and ordered coffee and a couple more of the delicious custard tarts he and his secretary were enjoying. We exchanged pleasantries and grumbled about the weather. Foley's German is fluent, but in such surroundings, it seemed more appropriate to speak in English. He asked about things at home. I told him they were diabolical. The Wehrmacht's victories were producing very high morale and support for Hitler. He appreciated the irony.

We moved on to what the English call the 'nitty-gritty'. The peace party in Britain are in a much stronger position than I had hitherto believed. They share our conviction that the two white master races must immediately cease hostilities and turn their guns on the real enemy — the Soviets. The party enjoys the support of Queen Mary, her sons the Dukes of Windsor and Kent, the bulk of the aristocracy, as well as bishops, industrialists, press barons, and government ministers like Rab Butler and Lord Halifax. Convoys sunk, armies vanquished, and the pounding of the Blitz drive home to the British their terrible predicament. What is needed, Foley told me, is for a representative of the Nazi high command, the higher ranking the better, to come over with peace proposals that would demonstrate that Germany has no territorial designs on Great Britain or her empire but instead extends the hand of friendship. This would provide the impetus the peace party needs to send Churchill packing.

'Göring offered to go to England. Hitler almost accepted.'

Foley did not know this and did not like it, either.

'He may be a war hero in Germany, but when not despising him for destroying their homes, my countrymen view Göring as a figure of fun: fat, unpleasant and sleazy.'

The last word was new to me. I asked 'Fairclough' what it meant.

'Sordid, corrupt, immoral!'

'That's your man,' said I.

'You need someone clean and respected that would add lustre to the peace party, not diminish it. Moreover, that person must be of the highest rank and have the ear of Hitler himself.'

In other words, a Parsifal, a holy fool. I could think of only one candidate, but the thought was preposterous! Foley leaned over and whispered the name of the chief of the Reception Committee. What a moment before had seemed absurd was suddenly inevitable!

Monday 27th January 1941

I conveyed everything I had learned from 'Fairclough' to Hess. He was thrilled. As I had suspected, his eyes gleamed when I mentioned who would be waiting to receive the envoy.

'We can learn to hope again. Preparations must begin in earnest for such an epic journey!'

A grin furrowed his cheeks. I badgered him about who the envoy might be, but this lover of mystery was happy to leave me with the riddle.

Friday 14th February 1941

Through my letter box, the strangest thing: a postcard-sized pamphlet titled 'Napoleon Bonaparte'. I could not see the point at first. Then, as I read it, the parallels hit me like thunderclaps. A former corporal wielding absolute power over a country he had not been born in. (The latter true as well of Macedonian Alexander and Georgian Stalin). One, furthermore, believed invincible by his people, who claimed he only wished to restore his country's natural borders and then waged war to create an empire. Yet this warning from history puzzled me. Is the Tribune about to open a second front, even though *Mein Kampf* expressly outlaws it? I recalled my boss's agitation back in June last year. How is it that I, a high-ranking adviser to the foreign ministry, am in the dark about all this?

I was heartened by this act of rebellion. Not the first, I may add, for I heard of a previous subversive pamphlet delivered anonymously through hundreds of letter boxes - though not through mine - to the great vexation of the Gestapo. There are still some not scurrying like rats to the precipice, maddened by the piper's tune.

Tuesday 18th February 1941

Today in the refectory at Friedrich Wilhelm University a lanky Luftwaffe officer approached me. His blue-eyes and chiselled features marked him out as a poster boy for the regime. I am usually the target for contempt from such paragons. There was no Hitler salute, however, instead a firm handshake, warm smile, and friendly tone as he introduced himself. I recognised the name instantly. Distinguished Prussian stock. His great uncle built the Kaiser's navy. The officer is a student himself but has been called upon to deliver seminars in the foreign policy department, due to the number of assistants who have been sent to the front.

He had a favour to ask. An exceptionally gifted student, his best listener as he put it, would greatly benefit from a transfer to my department. The student in question is the son of a professor from Dresden. He is also a member of the party and the Hitler Youth. Normally, such details are added in a reverential manner, but the officer's tone was wry and, most unexpectedly, he winked. He invited me to a party he and his wife are hosting on Carnival Monday. I told him I had no costume, but he said not to worry, only masks would be worn. I would be provided one. Again, the rueful smile as he added, "after all, that is how we have to live these days".

Tuesday 25th February 1941

Last night I took a taxi through blacked-out streets to the plush residential district of Neu-Westend near the Olympic Stadium. Carnival does not feature greatly in the life of Berliners, being more a custom of the Catholic south, where the Nazis have tamed the Lord of Misrule. In Nuremberg, a papier-mâché Jew swings from a bar on a model mill as if on a gibbet. In Cologne, a float carries men dressed up as Orthodox Jews beneath a banner saying, "The Last Ones Are Leaving". In the same city, a celebrated Carnival speaker makes a Hitler salute and quips: "Looks like rain." He is thrown instantly into jail.

The typical rumbustious music of the festival played on brass instruments was coming from the light, airy penthouse where the officer lives. A masked woman, his wife, opened the door. At the end of the corridor, I glimpsed the lounge in which the party was in full swing. She ushered me through the Japanese-styled foyer into a parlour and handed me a Janus mask bearing two faces, one tragic, one comic. She raised her own mask and revealed an earnest, pretty face framed by light brown hair cut short as is the fashion. She comes from old Prussian aristocracy even more illustrious than the lieutenant's people. Göring gave her away at their wedding in the family castle. She turned and gazed out of the window at the dark roofscape beneath a moonless sky.

'It is so peaceful now,' she said, 'but only two nights ago, I snuggled up with my husband on the divan and we watched as the British planes rolled in. He says we're just as safe here as in the shelter. The searchlight beams clustered together then parted in a sort of dance; the flak-jinxed sky turned ochre as the bombs exploded. Isn't it strange how war can be so beautiful?'

She told me to wait as her husband wished to speak with me. In the meantime, I browsed his bookshelf. Several works were Bolshevik tracts, possession of which is a capital offence. Copies of *Pravda* and *Izvestia* lay casually strewn on a coffee table. Two masked figures entered. One was the officer. I recognised his voice. He noticed my surprise because he wryly informed me that access to such illicit works was a "privilege" of his job, which was evaluating the foreign literature and press on air armament.

The officer was wearing a golden mask with a bald head that I later learnt was called "The Hangman". He raised his mask as did his companion, a youth in his late teens with a guileless, freckled face. I asked my prospective student why he wished to move to my department. The youth told me he aspired to become a diplomat. "Not sure I can recommend that," I said, "in times like these." The officer asked what I thought of their postcard. This confused me until memory struck, like a ship an iceberg, the Napoleon pamphlet.

'It was you?'

They both nodded, proud of their creation.

'It seemed far-fetched,' I continued. 'The Axis-Soviet pact is rock solid.'

'On the contrary,' the officer told me, 'our desks at the Air Ministry are piled with aerial photos of Leningrad: railway junctions, depots, ports, all targeted for bombardment. Each Gauleiter of the future conquered regions has been appointed.'

'So, you conceived the pamphlet...?'

'To stop the bloody thing in its tracks!'

It seemed foolhardy to believe a homemade tract could derail a war machine. I had not reckoned on the extraordinary individual before me. He was adamantine in his determination to end our nightmare. I felt transfigured by his presence. He told the youth to go and enjoy the party. When alone, I shared my misgivings about the futility of words against the deafening drumroll of the zeitgeist.

'We've done more than that,' he said. 'We've warned the Russians.'

I was astounded. This was *Landesverrat*: high treason. The mask was an omen. The hangman's noose beckons. But there are dark times when all the best heads swing from a rope. This was a line I could not cross; but he was of different mettle. He wished to unify East and West, to find a middle ground between capitalism and communism. In the early Thirties he had published a magazine, *The Adversary*, that proposed exactly that. The magazine was banned. He was tortured by the brownshirts, which gave birth to the vendetta. I asked if he had really thought things through. Consider Stalin, the show trials, the gulag, the mass starvations. Were they any better than what Hitler was doing?

'We are informing the Allies as well,' he said defiantly. 'The Russians want us to stop sending out pamphlets. They believe it is too dangerous. I have refused. We wish to create a counter-public who will swim against the tide and overthrow the Nazis.'

"We" turned out to be a loose network of more than 150 individuals, busily doing all they could to subvert the regime: creatives mainly, actors, dressmakers, artists, musicians, writers, though there were other Luftwaffe officers and ministry functionaries involved. A joyful image arose of an ever-widening crack in the foundations that would topple the whole rotten edifice. My metaphor pleased him. Having taken me into his confidence, it seemed only fair to take him into mine.

'In working for the regime am not I, a *Mischling*, betraying my own people? Wouldn't it be better to flee abroad and volley broadsides against the evil from afar like Thomas Mann?'

'Not at all,' he reassured me. 'When they scarred and mutilated me and pulverised my kidneys, I resolved to retaliate from within. Real subversion begins at home. If you can't join them, beat them.'

Now he was subverting catchphrases. We smiled for a few seconds, like the sun in winter bursts through hurtling cloud in the Frisian archipelago. I told him the greatest chance had already slipped through our fingers in '38 when a powerful clique of generals stood poised to stage a putsch should Hitler invade Czechoslovakia. Chamberlain and his silly bit of paper scuppered that. The officer refused to indulge my gloom.

'Even if we are devoured,' he said, 'it is a grand adventure. The seed bears fruit. If heads roll, the spirit nevertheless forces the state. Believe with me in the just time that lets everything ripen!'

I felt no compunction in divulging the current state of the resistance. I spoke of Carl Goerdeler, ex-mayor of Leipzig, and his conviction he only needs an hour alone with the Führer to convince him to resign. The officer chuckled and began to fill his pipe. He asked about the Kreisau Circle: distinguished elder statesmen, wrangling over the new constitution in a never-never land in which Hitler likewise obligingly abdicates. We discussed the Admiral at the helm of our spies, who loathes the current order but is too vacillating to do anything other than to tantalise the British with titbits of intelligence. I revealed the details of an assassination plot in progress, but dejection crept into my voice again. So many conspiracies have failed. Why should this one be different?

'Our lives may be lost but that is a trifle,' he said. 'Even if we don't live to see it, we shall succeed. But enough chit-chat. Let's join the party.'

So, we went and mingled with the revellers. They were good people: sane, noble, deserving of a better destiny. I moved amongst them like a brother. They did not care I was a Jew. A woman in a grey-green cape and leotard, with a skeleton painted on it, performed a dance called "Last Man Standing", whose theme was death on the battlefield. She was the maker of the masks and has a studio in Adolf-Hitler-Platz. Often, she's touring through France and Holland, entertaining the troops. It was she who told me the name of the officer's mask.

'And me?' I asked. 'Why have you given me two faces?'

'Because that's what you wear, like all of us. One for the regime; the other for the resistance.'

Wednesday 23rd April 1941

Yesterday I attended the third in a series of lectures Krafft has been giving. About sixty people were crammed into the hall of a music school in Nürnberger Strasse for "Nostradamus as a Prophet of Greater Germany". The first lantern slide showed the famous woodcut portrait of the seer; the rest quatrains, the cryptic four-line prophecies. I had heard from an Abwehr contact that Krafft was behaving in his usual headstrong fashion. Apparently, when under investigation by the Gestapo, he had signed an undertaking not to discuss astrology or Nostradamus in public. You might as well demand of a zebra that it change its stripes.

He began by referring to the remarkable prediction made by C. Loog, a Berlin postal official, in his 1921 edition of the prophecies: a critical situation in Poland would coincide with Britain's last and gravest crisis. This would occur in 1939! The book was now in its fifth edition, its longevity no doubt attributable to such a stunning bullseye. According to Krafft, a great deal more could be read into Nostradamus that spelt total victory for the Reich. He deployed the hundredth quatrain of the Second Century in support of this depressing assertion:

"Within the isles so horrible a tumult,
One will only hear total war:
So great will be the insult of the predators,
That they will be ranged against by the great league."

"The isles" are Great Britain, and the "predators", the piratical inhabitants of that beleaguered place. One has only to contemplate the citizens of London, cowering like rats in cellars and underground stations as the bombs rain down for evidence of "tumult" and "total war". Ever since Dunkirk, the British have made feverish preparations to resist invasion and are now entering a state of total chaos and societal breakdown. Nevertheless, they persist with the "insult" in solitary defiance of the Reich. Consequently, Germany and the rest of the Axis - "the great league" - is left with no choice but to annihilate them. Krafft finished by boasting of an edition of the quatrains with his commentaries that is about to appear throughout Europe.

The audience filed out sheepishly, as though aware something not quite right had been going on. As the seer gathered up his papers, I approached him on the rostrum. There was the usual disdain. I asked what we could expect from the rest of the year. He told me there was a significant conjunction of Saturn and Jupiter coming up on May 10. Six planets would be in Taurus simultaneously, coinciding with a full moon. Along with other stellar dispositions in the spring, this heralded a very difficult, not to say malefic, period for the Führer. 'In early summer,' he continued, 'there will be large-scale military operations in the East. This will tip the balance against us, perhaps decisively. The lesson of Napoleon's retreat from Moscow seems to have been forgotten.'

I wondered again if this is what has been preoccupying Hess since last June. I had made a similar prophecy myself when news of the Soviet-Nazi pact reached us on 22 August 1939. Because of such things they call me Cassandro, the bird of ill omen. I was standing at my desk with two students, the *Times Atlas* map of the Soviet Union open in front of us. "Now they have concluded a friendship, but in four weeks at the latest we shall have a war," I said, unwisely adding; "then the madman in his drunkenness will overrun the West: he will gorge himself in the Sarmatian steppes and it will be the end of Europe." One of my favourite students, Wolfgang Hoffmann, shouted, 'You damned pessimist!' Hoffmann was shot down over Kent in February and burnt to death in the wreckage.

A couple of stragglers stood by the exit. They were probably out of earshot, but it felt risky, so I invited Krafft to a nearby bar on Augsburger Strasse. His look of horror hurt even a quarter-Jew who has grown accustomed to what Shakespeare called "the slings and arrows". It was only later I found out the Swiss shuns alcohol, fearing to lose his rigid self-control. I took my wallet out and pressed a 100 Reichsmark note on him, anticipating he would be too proud to accept. Instead, he said the donation would help pay for the hall. I warned him it was dangerous to go on with such public talks.

'Nothing at all will happen to me,' he said pompously. 'This lecture has been registered with the police. Certain very important and powerful people know all about the subject matter.'

Saturday 26th April 1941

Hess's villa at Harlaching on the fringes of Munich is getting bigger.

I counted spaces and pumps for ten cars in the garage, as our driver parked the Mercedes that had transported my father and I from our family home in the city. It was a little before noon. We passed the recently built telephone exchange and made our way through the house to the dining room, also enlarged to accommodate meetings with the Wehrmacht. Hess was upstairs, playing with his son Wolf, who's nicknamed "Buz". At the boy's naming ceremony, earth, and water from every region of the Reich was sprinkled over him. He was called Karl, after my father, and Adolf after... — no prizes for guessing!

We sat at the table with Ilse Hess: a once attractive woman, now a little run to fat, with a homely, down-to-earth attitude. She poured us green tea and told us that her husband spends most of his time at home recently, playing with their son. He claims it is a subtle way of educating the boy.

'But Buz's just three and a half. It seems too early,' she laughed. 'Magda Goebbels tells me her husband wants their son to be a politician, but I think it's rare for father and son to prosper in the same field — the child is always overshadowed by the father.'

'Are you in my shadow, Albrecht?' demanded my father, his tone jovial.

'Naturally, there are exceptions,' Ilse added quickly with a blush. She was clearly embarrassed. I came to her rescue.

'I may also be an expert in geopolitics, but I assure you I will never be a major-general. In fact, my father has frequently berated me for my lack of martial spirit and criticised my artistic pursuits.'

This was a cue for her to gesture at the upright Bechstein near the window: 'Will you play for us later?'

Above the piano was a painting of a hunting scene, revoltingly kitsch as were the hideous series of prints of the 1936 Berlin Olympics lining the rest of the room. Jesse Owens, the black American athlete, was conspicuous by his absence. Hess's appalling taste had so disgusted Hitler after a visit that he designated Göring as successor. The failed art student, who spends more time with Speer designing the dream metropolis of the thousand-year-Reich than he does waging war, knows what a great art lover his Luftwaffe chief is. Göring collects so much of it!

'It will just be the four of us for lunch,' she added, *'en famille.'*

Like her husband, Ilse is a strange mixture of parts. The couple adore Hitler and are convinced Jew-haters yet treat all of us, including my mother, as family. Hess himself, who is steeped in Goethe and Mozart, was a seasoned street fighter who frequently turned up at my father's lectures bruised and in bandages.

We all rose when he came in, not our usual custom, but today is his forty-seventh birthday. He shook our hands warmly, giving us that famous goofy grin that has so endeared him to the German Folk. My father presented him with a model battlecruiser, an addition to the Battle of Jutland set he devotes hours of play to with Buz. I gave him something he requested a while back. Executed by my students, it is a copy of the escape maps allied airmen carry should they be forced to bale out in hostile territory. Inscribed on a silk handkerchief, the map shows an area of south-west Scotland where Hess told me he wants to build a hunting lodge when the war is won. He is a shy man and adopts an alias when flying: Hauptmann Alfred Horn. This was stitched at the bottom. The first versions of the map came out fuzzy but adding a sugar acid called pectin to the mix sharpened definition. He thanked me in English, a language we sometimes practise when together.

We lunched on bio-dynamic beans, seeds, pulses, with black rye bread and elderflower-infused water treated under special light. We finished with cake — sugar, gluten, and flavour free. We toasted his day and then, at Hess's insistence, the Führer's, whose fifty-second birthday occurred just six days ago.

The afternoon was cloudy but mild. We took a stroll across the tidy lawns, lined by clipped rhododendron bushes and meticulously pruned fruit trees. I had been aching to tell him what I had learnt from Krafft, mentioning first the malign portents for the Führer, mumbling the words as you never know who's listening. Hess told me he was already aware of this. Steps were being taken to avert the threat by those who loved the Tribune.

'Moreover, I've already been briefed me on the conjunction and planetary dispositions of May 10,' he said.

This must have come from Schulte-Strathaus, a high up in one of Hess's culture ministries and his adviser on astrology. Krafft's prediction of a military offensive in the East did not surprise him either, though it shocked my father, who said, 'Opening a second front could spell disaster for our project. What possible reason could the Tribune have for even considering it?'

Ever loyal, Hess played devil's advocate. 'It could stop the British holding out and end their naval blockade of our northern ports. The Führer believes we are fighting a new sort of war in which even victory on two fronts is possible. Consider the speed with which our Panzer Corps have smashed their way across Western Europe.'

I knew him well enough to say, 'You don't sound convinced,' and repeated Krafft's allusion to the disastrous precedent of Napoleon in Russia.

Hess sighed and wrinkled his nose. 'It makes it even more tragic that we are not standing shoulder to shoulder with England against Bolshevism. That is why the Führer allowed the English army to escape at Dunkirk. He did not wish to sabotage the prospect of a treaty. Can you really imagine cool, calculating England running her neck into the Soviet noose, instead of saving it by coming to an understanding with us?'

'The English regard the Führer as the devil's deputy on Earth.'

Hess did not reprimand me.

'By that you mean Churchill and his band of terrorists, but we know the king and his brothers want peace. It only needs a little prod, and George will invoke his reserve powers and banish the warmonger to Canada.'

I could not bring myself to explain yet again that the British monarch's role is almost entirely ceremonial. Like Hitler, Hess takes the Kaiser as his model and endows George VI with the powers of a medieval ruler. It is an unshakable mindset. Perhaps, there is romance in it for them. "The English have a constitutional monarchy," I once told them. "How can that be when they do not have a written constitution?" barked Hitler, a gleam in his eye — he likes his triumphs small as well as big.

Hess began clicking his fingers. 'The British ambassador in Madrid...?'

'Samuel Hoare,' I prompted.

'Only last week we heard that Hoare is predicting the imminent collapse of Churchill and his own recall to form a new government. There are terrible scenes of devastation and chaos in the British Isles. Looting, sabotage, furious mobs! The whole country is having a collective nervous breakdown. I am sure you will hear much more about this in Geneva.'

On Monday I am due to meet Professor Carl Burckhardt, a leading light of the International Committee of the Red Cross. It is the latest in a long line of back routes to peace. Significantly, Burckhardt has already conveyed greetings from "our friends in England". I will wear my Janus mask and represent Hess and the resistance. At the end of January, I went to Stockholm and met the King of Sweden, who has been lobbying for peace. Nothing came of that overture. I was not surprised but then I am Cassandro, harbinger of doom. '*You damned pessimist!*' Will I ever be able to forget Wolfgang burnt to cinders in the blazing fuselage?

My father is well known for having prophetic dreams. During the First World War, he acquired a reputation for refusing to take trains that invariably crashed or came under bombardment. Hess is very intrigued by such second sight. Most recently, my father dreamt about the Deputy Führer signing a peace treaty in the tapestried hall of a castle. On the drive up, I asked what purpose such an intoxicating image could serve. He replied that Hess, who is as close to him as I am - he did not say this - was rumoured to be about to personally embark on a peace mission. The dream was a ruse to get at the truth. After relating it, which I could see greatly gratified our protector, my father bluntly asked if such an adventure was on the cards. Hess looked put out but did his best to maintain his composure.

'The flying ban the Führer imposed has expired. He has gifted me a wonderful Messerschmitt of the latest type, but I have no plans for foreign travel. Perhaps I will need you, Albrecht, to make such a journey.'

I was not sure if he was joking.

'In that case I would require strict guidelines and cast-iron guarantees from the very top.'

I meant Hitler must be in the picture and approve.

Only a year and a half ago Hess had described the conflict as "a little thunderstorm" but he has woken from that illusion. 'In my mind's eye,' he told us, 'I keep seeing - in Germany and Britain alike - an endless line of children's coffins with weeping mothers behind them, and then the coffins of mothers, with their tearful children behind them.'

On the drive home, I covertly observed my father. With his walrus moustache, beaky nose, and rigid frame, he already resembles the statue he hopes to become. He is widely viewed as the principal architect of the Third Reich. For four and a half months in 1926 he visited Landsberg Gaol every Wednesday and schooled the conspirators. "Prison was my university," Hitler declared. My father taught them that a nation is an organism and has full licence to grow without hindrance, just as ivy scrambles over a garden wall and invades a neighbour. This *Lebensraum* justifies the utmost brutality and deceit in the service of blood and soil.

The general is very rich and garlanded with honours. It is easy to speak of Faust, but another image comes to mind. In China all the evil genies were imprisoned at the bottom of the sea. One day a fish came and ate them, but it too was caught. A fisherman raised the wriggling creature in his net and asked himself if he should throw the fish back or keep it and unleash the evils expelled by its mouth. My father gave succour to the breath.

Sunday 11th May 1941

It does not seem that this will be a restful Sunday. The Legation Secretary at our embassy in Spain wired that I am scheduled to give a lecture at the Madrid Academy of Sciences tomorrow! Why such short notice? Is it a mix-up? The secretary is a former student of mine. He is also our link to Sam Hoare. I have been hoping to arrange talks with the ambassador for a very long time but supposed I would have more time for preparation.

I imagine Hess is strolling with his son and their Alsatians by the river. Otherwise, I would call him. I start packing. The phone rings again. It is my mother. She sounds fearful. The Gestapo called last night and demanded my Berlin phone number. "It made us think," she says. I ask to speak to my father. He wants to know if I have heard the latest. "Tomodachi has flown to Scotland!" 'Tomodachi', the Japanese for friend, is our nickname for Hess. We call Hitler 'O'Daijin', leader or great spirit. I remember the undisclosed secret that seemed to have burdened my boss these last many months, the cryptic utterances, the map inscribed upon a silk handkerchief that he requested. The last piece of the jigsaw is in place. "Does he want to return like a motorised Parsifal with the grail of peace to redeem himself with O'Daijin?" I cry. My father sighs: "He is a man at war with himself. He cannot stomach the atrocities in the east, or the daily murders in Germany; yet neither can he turn against O'Daijin whom he adores. Flight is his escape route from the unbearable." We all need a bit of that, I think. A commotion in the background. Harsh voices barking orders. "The Gestapo have arrived," my father hisses. He and my mother are being placed under guard. In the house there are copies of my letters to Douglo and the peace proposals I helped Hess draft. In the wrong hands they will be viewed as treason. With luck, I can post this diary to "Fairclough" via Lisbon before the Gestapo get here.

To you my secret readers, stirring in the shadows, in universities and field headquarters, in factories and chancelleries, who have not been bewitched by the piper and conspire to silence the malevolent tune; forgive us, we know not what we do. And PERSEVERE!

* * *

The compartment door slides open. Crowley looks up from the diary he has just finished. A young couple peer back at him. Their giggling cuts off, and the man slams the door shut in alarm. A vicar, a ticket inspector, a pretty nurse, and an old lady with a face dried up like a raisin have all done the same. Why have none of them come in, ponders the King of Depravity? As the train pulls out of Taunton, his baleful eyes, which have hypnotised horses and small children, swivel beneath the intimidating dome of his shorn head, on the prowl for a solution.

The compartment is certainly shabby, with worn dust-layered cushions and a bent luggage rack, but such neglect is true of almost every railway carriage in the kingdom. He fidgets in his glaring knickerbocker suit. The sickly pungency of Abramelin oil envelops him. His fingers, with their claw-like nails and huge talismanic rings, drum the windowsill. His other hand grips a meerschaum pipe which emits a foul and lethal column of smoke in sympathetic magic with

the locomotive ahead. Why nobody should want to share his compartment remains unfathomable.

Truth is, he is lonely like a frightened child. His nerves are on edge
due to lack of flesh: a man or woman's, it does not really matter. He
has founded a second Abbey of Thelema at Barton Brow, the rented
house to which he now is heading on the outskirts of Torquay. To
date, he has one follower: a neurotic beanpole of a woman with whom
the wand no longer casts a spell, despite sound birchings, given and
received, and frantic bouts of cunnilingus. A cow streaks by at 60
miles an hour. Grey fields, a muddy sky: the perfect landscape for a
god of suffering and remorse. What hope for an abbey of unbridled
Will amidst such bleakness? If only his American followers could
spirit him away to California. He could bask in the sun as they adore
him. But the war and his sinister reputation with the FBI prevent this.

His credit is exhausted with grocer, vintner, and candlestick
maker. The landlord of his previous lodgings in Torquay is chasing
him for back rent. This, despite the premises being destroyed in an air
raid. Some people lack all shame! There are still attacks every night,
dogfights that thrill the boy in him, and plane crashes on the moors.
Twice, close by, people have been blown apart by bombs jettisoned
in dejection from wounded planes. Lady Frieda Harris is still remit-
ting two pounds a week, despite his fury when she ditched his
catalogue for the exhibition of Thoth paintings, planned for Oxford
in June. The taint of his name could scupper the whole business. She
did not say this. She did not need to.

None of his schemes have come to anything: the Black Magic
Restaurant serving up his scorching curries; a boardgame called
Thelema; his Elixir of Life pills, thoughtfully laced with his own
semen. Even Amrita, his course of sexual and bodily rejuvenation,
available for a snip at 25 guineas a week, has no takers. He sees
himself shunting endlessly between shabby rooms in coastal towns.
Fleming's proposition is a lifeline. The only one he's got. According

to Albrecht Haushofer, Rudolf Hess is a man in thrall to occult arts and magical thinking. The Beast has preyed on many such.

Part II
Crow's Last Nest
(February 1945-December 1947)

Chapter Three
Netherwood

The telegram declared the new guest would be accompanied by a consignment of frozen meat. As rationing was strictly enforced, the Post Office had passed this information on to the Food Ministry. This accounted for the two inspectors on the north-side driveway. With them were the middle-aged couple who ran Netherwood, a guesthouse standing in four acres of grounds on the Ridge, a long narrow hilltop 500 feet above Hastings, with views of the Norman castle, the town centre, and the Channel. The man wore a jaunty cravat and had a friendly, inquisitive face. As longstanding couples do, the woman in her fawn coat resembled her husband and radiated the same warmth.

'Here he comes,' said Vernon Symonds as an ambulance turned into the drive, adding in a stage whisper, 'the Wickedest Man in the World!'

'Oh, I don't care about that,' replied his wife.

The ambulance rattled to a halt in front of the stone steps. The driver helped out a man in a tattered tweed coat, soiled oversized corduroy plus fours, stockings, and shoes clasped by silver buckles. Compared to the bulky figure who had lunched with Fleming only four years before, Crowley was shrunken and frail. It was as though a tent had collapsed and a much smaller figure had crawled out. He had a goatee beard and watery eyes that took in his new home, a three-storey ivy-covered pile with a battlemented tower on the north-east corner. Netherwood seemed to startle him, though this in fact had become his fixed expression.

'Do what thou wilt shall be the whole of the Law,' he intoned in a nasal voice that was not endearing.

'Oh, I'm sure we will and have a great deal of fun while doing so. I'm Vernon and this is my wife.'

'Call me Johnnie,' said the woman, 'everybody else does.'

It occurred to Crowley to introduce himself as Alys, his female alter ego, but he decided this could wait until he knew them better.

'And you must call me Crow,' he said.

The ambulance driver had started to drag out the new arrival's one item of furniture, a wooden chest, which Vernon went and helped unload. Next came several parcels that they transferred to the foot of the steps. The food inspectors began sniffing around.

'Is this the meat?' barked one.

'Indisputably,' retorted the newcomer.

'We're from the ministry,' said the other. 'You're welcome to see our credentials.'

'I'm sure they are as impeccable as mine.'

The inspectors unwrapped a parcel each and began rifling through them.

'There just seem to be books,' said one.

'Ah, but if you only dare to open a volume, you'll find the beef: life, existence, the cosmos, everything.'

The taller of the inspectors extracted a buckram-bound book and peered at the spine. *The Equinox of the Gods*, he muttered.

'There's a lot of meat in that one.'

'This one's in Latin!' exclaimed his colleague, holding up a slim white volume with the title stamped in gilt on the cover.

'Highly nutritious fare that you could really get your teeth into.'

'Are you telling us that all you have are BOOKS?'

The inspector waved at the thirty or so parcels scattered on the gravel.

'And paintings, ceremonial robes, wands, Tarot cards, oils, unguents, yarrow stalks, sacramental wafers, talismans: the tools of the trade.'

'And just what might that be?'

'Magick.'

'What, like a conjuror? You entertain kids and suchlike.'

'No, I summon winds and tempests, converse with angels and demons. I am the scribe and messenger of the gods.'

'Gor blimey!' exclaimed the inspectors, exchanging helpless looks before trudging off with a defeated air to their van.

'Soon you'll need a permit just to breathe,' said Vernon. 'I thought it was freedom we were fighting for. Instead, we're being strangled by red tape. Anyway, never mind them. We always welcome new guests with tea in the lounge. We have a boy who can take the stuff up. Rooms 7, 13 and 15 are free at the minute.'

'Oh, 13 will suit me perfectly.'

'Thought you'd plump for that one. Pretty mild, isn't it, after the sleet and snow we've been having?'

Crow followed Johnnie up the steps, with Vernon bringing up the rear. The porch gave onto the lobby, with a telephone in an alcove adjoining a staircase to their left. The hall table sagged beneath a Bradshaw edition of railway timetables, blotters, unopened letters waiting for already departed guests, a brass-and-mahogany collection box for Dr Barnardo's Homes, and sheets of blue-and-white notepaper headed with Netherwood's motto, "The World's a Stage".

Vernon steered them right, past the bar, and along a corridor lined with posters of plays put on by the Court Players, a local repertory company he was an enthusiastic member of. The recently redecorated lounge boasted pastel green wallpaper and chintz curtains beside tall windows that looked out onto the rolling grounds. There was a new fireplace, with a copper jug and two Delft bowls on the mantelpiece. A coal scuttle and set of fire tools stood on either side of the hearth in which oak logs were gradually burning. Vernon waved Crow onto the armchair nearest the fire. Johnnie lowered herself onto an adjacent sofa.

A sprinkling of guests reclined on armchairs reading newspapers. *The Times* reported Hitler's defiant last speech in the ruins of Berlin,

The Daily Telegraph, the Soviet torpedoing of a German military transport ship in the Baltic, with the loss of 9,400 souls. Vernon disappeared and returned a few minutes later with the register and a card that he handed to Crow. He joined Johnnie on the sofa.

'All the paperwork this bloody war requires! Have a gander at the house rules while I find the right place!'

Crow handed over his brown identity document and peered at the card. It requested guests not to tease the ghosts; to be as quiet as possible while dying of fright; to take breakfast at 9 a.m. should they survive the night; to not dig graves on the lawns but make use of newly filled ones under the trees; to not cut down bodies from the trees. Should they require it, Hastings Borough Cemetery was five minutes' walk away (ten minutes if carrying a body), but only one minute as the ghost flies. A certain amount of used clothing was available for purchase from the Office, the property of guests who no longer had any need for earthly raiment.

'Much jollier here than my previous abode,' said Crow.

'Where was that?' said Johnnie.

'Bell Inn, Aston Clinton, Buckinghamshire. Good food, dismal company. The most frightful collection of drudges and wastrels it has ever been my misfortune to rub shoulders with!'

'You won't be saying that here. Johnnie's cooking is the best in the county. You won't believe the distinguished personages who've slept beneath this roof.'

A maid hovered over them. Her luxuriant lips, tight curls and wide nostrils spoke of exotic blood, but the skin of her nearly beautiful face was pale, her cheeks pitted with adolescent acne. Crow did nothing to conceal his admiration.

'How do you take your tea?' asked Johnnie.

'With a very large brandy.'

Vernon was a thirsty man himself and seemed delighted. 'I've got a first-rate Hennessy laid down before the war. I think I'll join you. Maria, would you fetch two cognacs from the bar?'

Crow pursued the swaying black dress that was just a little tight. He sighed.

'C.E.M. Joad of *Brains Trust* fame was here just before Christmas. He gave an enthralling talk on the latest psychical research.'

'A fraud and impostor!'

Unabashed, Vernon attributed this remark to Crow's eccentricity, of which there seemed to be vast funds. 'We had Julian Huxley, the esteemed scientist, who gave us the latest gen on evolution.'

'Knocked around with his brother Aldous in Berlin. Dry, listless fellow, far too brainy for his own good, though I opened his eyes to a thing or to.'

'My husband doesn't want Netherwood to be a common or garden boarding house,' said Johnnie. 'We offer bed and board on a complimentary basis to distinguished intellectuals in return for talks to our very own Brains Trust.'

Crow was never one to miss an opportunity. 'You could have my Gilles de Rais. I was supposed to give the lecture at Oxford, but the dons banned it. Can't for the life of me think why!'

'Gilles de Rais,' repeated Johnnie doubtfully.

'Black magician, cannibal, and killer, it is alleged, of over 500 children. The original Bluebeard, though my take is he was slandered by the church.'

'Might be good for Halloween if you're still with us,' said Vernon.

'As we hope you will be,' from the wife.

'In every sense,' her husband added hastily.

Maria had returned with a tray bearing tea and two generously filled balloon glasses. She was followed by a boy in his mid-teens, with green eyes, floppy red hair, and an open freckled face. His overalls were spattered with dried mud and paint.

'I've put all the parcels and the chest in Room 13,' he said.

'Thank you, Will. Our neighbour's boy,' Vernon explained to Crow. 'He's been helping out.'

'And what is he planning to do afterwards?'

'Going to a Catholic seminary. Wants to be a priest.'

Crow's mouth wrinkled at the corner.

'And after that?'

'Well, he'll become a cardinal or the second English pope, I suppose.'

And then?'

'He'll die and go to heaven.'

Crow peered at Will. 'How's your Latin?'

'That's the bit I find the hardest,' the boy said in a friendly voice.

'You may find being cut off from the pleasures of the flesh a bit of a challenge as well. I'm a Trinity man. I can help you with your Latin. What time do you knock off?'

'Around five.'

'Come after that and we can work on your declensions.'

'Are you sure it won't be too tiring after your journey?' said Johnnie.

'On the contrary, I need something to occupy me.'

'I think you're going to be quite an adornment to our little community,' said Vernon.

Crow drained the last of his cognac. 'My life has always been at the service of others.'

They made their way out and collided with an extremely flustered postman in the lobby, carrying a very large box wrapped in brown paper.

'Delivery for a Mister Crowley,' he said. 'Needs to be signed for.'

'Does it say anything about meat?' asked Vernon.

Johnnie leaned forward and read out the packing note: 'Cigars, wine, brandy, chocolate, bonbons.' Then she blushed because she felt she was being nosy.

'It was sent from that American base in Welford,' said the postman. 'Overpaid, oversexed, and over here if you ask me.'

'I don't believe anybody did,' said Vernon.

Chapter Four
Room 13

Thursday, 1 February 1945 (evening)

The first thing that overpowered the visitor to Room 13 was the molasses reek of the Beast's Perique tobacco. The second was the lurid paintings and drawings which the Ulema of Thelema had wasted no time in plastering over the walls. Rendered in garish primary colours, grotesque faces peered out from landscapes that seemed the creations of a very disturbed child. On the largest canvas, red-cowled monks trudged across a snowy plain towards a castle on a misty mountain, carrying a black goat. Will asked what it was about.

'The Himalayan expedition in search of the Buddhist dream-kingdom, home of the adepts,' Crow explained. 'Those aren't monks but Soviet spies.'

'It exists?' said Will.

'They didn't find Shambhala, nor has anyone else. That's why the painting's called *Across the Snow to Nowhere*.'

They were facing each other across a rickety table. A few feet away there was a divan bed. Beside it, a small table supported an empty tin that served as an ashtray, bottles of medicine, a pipe, and a box of hypodermic syringes. A chest of drawers, a wardrobe, and a small coffee table took up the remaining space. Butts of highly aromatic Weinsberg Special cigarettes lay strewn across the floor. Water gushed constantly from the hot tap of the washbasin to compensate for the radiator not giving out enough heat. Books lined the shelves along the wall and rose in towers from the floor. Many of these had been written and published by the new guest, though there was a complete edition of Shakespeare, a King James Bible, and the Latin primer now being used to run Will through his declensions.

'It does seem a bit of a waste,' sighed Crow.

'Shall I go through it again?

'I mean your vocation not the vocative. You're a good-looking chap. I think Maria's got her eye on you.'

Will crimsoned. 'You sound just like my father. He was horrified when I said I wanted to be a priest.'

'The Aeon of the slave God is over. You might just as well become a lamplighter or hansom cab driver.'

Will rose to the bait. 'Jesus was the greatest gift God gave to man. Nothing could be finer than a life spent in his service.'

'Gawd, you're smitten. I expect he wants you for a sunbeam. It would surprise many to know that I went through a similar phase in my early teens. Then it occurred to me to ask who is this Jesus everybody loves so much? December 25 also marked the birthday of Mithras, the god of the Roman legions. He had 12 disciples and was resurrected. Did your Jesus really exist or was he just another fertility god?'

'Miss Clarke says you're the anti-Christ.'

Crow snorted. 'People call me all sorts of things. I never hated Christianity by the way, just the zealots in my own family. We're on the threshold of a new age primed with promise for the young like you. You should devote your energy to that. Has anything out of the ordinary ever happened to you?'

The question was one he invariably posed. The unseen, after all, was his stock in trade. Will reflected for a moment.

'I saw a ghost when I was ten.'

'That's promising.'

'The house I live in with my father is just along the Ridge. I often came here to play with the guests' kids. One evening there was a game called "torchie" in progress in the grounds. One boy went up to the second floor and shone a torch from a corridor window. The idea was to hide from the beam in the garden. The minute it caught you, you were out. It was dark and very shadowy. I darted into a glade. There was a child standing there. He was about my age.'

Crow seemed very interested. 'What was he wearing?'

'A ruffled shirt, a jacket with tails, and tight white breeches.'

'Mmm, eighteenth century.'

'There was a patch of red on his sleeve. I assumed it was blood. He smiled at me, but I scampered away in terror.'

'What do you think this boy was?'

'Maybe something my mind produced. There wasn't much light. A trick of the shadows perhaps. I was very excited. It was easy to imagine something.'

'Or perhaps, just as insects get trapped in amber and remain frozen for millennia, certain images are indelibly stamped upon a scene where something epic happens: a murder or suicide, for example. This building is Victorian, isn't it, so whatever manifested itself must relate to what stood in these grounds before. I don't suppose you know the history of Netherwood, or any local legends. No? Well, no matter. It does indicate you have the gift. People like you with red hair and green eyes often do. You're obviously a Celt from way back. Any other strange occurrences?'

'When I was eight, I was crossing the clifftop just west of the town when a breath that wasn't mine seemed to inhabit me. It transformed everything. There was surpassing peace, ecstasy, a sense of closeness to God. That's what I'm looking for from the Church.'

'I'd be surprised if you find it there, though they do have a name for it: the Holy Ghost. My church calls it the Knowledge and Conversation of the Holy Guardian Angel. It can happen naturally but also can be attained by artificial means.'

There was a tap against the door. Will went and opened it. The housekeeper hurried in with a tray bearing a plate of curried sardines on toast. A look of disgust stole over her shrewish features, inspired by the fug of tobacco, the messy room, and most of all its occupant.

'Set it down on the divan, will you Miss Clarke? I'll just finish running Will through this grimoire, which is very like the cookery books you use, dear lady, except instead of raising flour it conjures devils.'

'Upon my word!'

'Oh, come now! There's no need to feign ignorance. I can see you're a great adept of the black arts. I expect you can't wait to jump on your broomstick for your tryst with Old Nick.'

Miss Clarke scuttled to the door with a stricken look as Crow fired his parting shot: 'And do check with Johnnie! Should it be before or after midnight?'

Emitting a strangled cry, the housekeeper was too flustered to close the door properly. Crow rose, propelled his withered frame across the room and pushed it shut. He shambled over to the chest, raised the lid, and extracted a small package which he handed to the boy. 'A present for Maria. Don't tell her where you got it!'

Will cradled the soft bundle. His father had taught him not to accept gifts from strangers. But was Crow still a stranger?

'I should leave you to your tea.'

'No, stay awhile!' There was an unexpected pleading. 'I can munch away while you run through the other cases. There's a passable bottle of red that's been warming by the radiator. Open it will you and fill two glasses!'

'Alcohol doesn't agree with me.'

'Nonsense! You should be less argumentative and learn to agree with *it*.'

After Will had poured the wine, Crow raised his glass and clinked it against his pupil's.

'Here's to Maria! She reminds me of toothsome Blowzabella, of well-formed bust and dusky latitudes, who sucked me to the gates of paradise in Rotting Hill.'

Will blushed as Crow gulped down a third of his glass and then made one of the abrupt detours that were becoming a habit: 'I should have been awarded a knighthood. But hush-hush, so mote it be.'

'You did something in the war?'

'A very great something! But there's a thorny bush called the Official Secrets Act which will not let a glimmer of light leak out. Maybe in a hundred years or so my exploits will be celebrated. In that chest is something that would merit the Victoria Cross if people only knew. In the meantime, I have to content myself with the idiocy of my so-called followers and their Californian love cult.'

Crow was referring to the sole remaining bastion of the religion he had founded.

'Each faith can be summed up in a word. In the case of Buddhism: resignation; in Islam: obedience. With Christianity it is...'

'Joy?' suggested Will.

'Penitence! It's an abject doctrine that makes slaves of its followers, but I suppose there's no convincing you. The word of my religion is "Thelema", that's Greek for "Will".'

Crow recounted how in 1935 an English follower, Wilfred Talbot Smith, had founded the Agape Lodge in Hollywood. As he spoke, the conviction grew on Will that this was a self-glorifying fable spun in the old dreamer's brain. It seemed absurd that the feeble and impoverished figure before him could really be the founding father of a new religion.

'Two years ago, I did Smith's astrological chart and made a remarkable discovery: he was a god.'

This was blasphemy and an obvious fiction, but Will still asked, 'What god?'

'How should I know? The chart wouldn't tell me, though going by the way Smith carried on I would think a minor sex god: he'd hump a sheep if you let him! I ordered him to take a magical retirement in the desert and find out himself. In the meantime, the Lodge moved to Pasadena and a new man took the helm: Jack Parsons, a rocket scientist.'

Will felt pity for the ancient scribbler. His imagination was obviously failing him. The notion of a scientist heading a magical order was frankly ludicrous.

'I was very pleased with Parsons at first. He invigorated things. Subscriptions grew. I made him my magical son. But it turned out he was a reckless romantic, a weakling, and a sex maniac to boot. He took up with his wife's sister, a half-demented alley cat called Betty. His wife Helen ran off with Smith. They're all diving in and out of each other's beds. It's like a French farce.'

This sounded more promising: sexual shenanigans sold books.

'Miss Clarke says you have a reputation for that sort of thing yourself.'

'I never abused my position to get anybody into bed. That's what Smith does. He should exalt science, art, philosophy, not the oily pangs of lust. Now it seems Smith and Helen have returned to Pasadena and are staying with Parsons, who does whatever the last person he talks to tells him to. He has all the conviction of a marshmallow sundae. Even had the cheek to accuse me of egotism and pedanticism. Can you imagine it? You'd be hard put to find a less likely candidate for such failings. I quickly put him right. Had he travelled the globe? Was he on first name terms with scores of world-famous Personalities? That shut him up.'

Crow must believe the characters he dreamt up had independent existences, Will supposed. Perhaps it helped him realise them better. The Beast gave him a slim volume from which he set a short poem to be translated for homework.

'It's by Catullus,' he said. 'Number 21 in the catalogue of saints.'

Will was studying just such a list in preparation for the seminary. He could recall no such name.

'Was he a martyr?'

'Only to the cruel and lascivious demands of Lesbia.'

'He seems an unlikely candidate for sainthood.'

'I meant the Gnostic Saints: Lao Tzu, Nietzsche, Gauguin, To Mega Thêrion, Sir Aleister Crowley etcetera.'

'But the last one's you!'

'And the one before that. Your church doesn't have a monopoly on everything, you know. We also have a creed, baptism, last rites, and don't forget the Gnostic Mass, where a priestess officiates with the priest. I composed that while touring Russia with the Ragged Ragtime girls back in 1913. Two nymphomaniacs, two dipsomaniac nymphomaniacs - the worst kind - and two prudes as sunk in depravity as Betty May. Only a saint could compose a mass in such company.'

There seemed no boundary to the flights of fantasy of the tenant of Room 13. Feeling he could digest no more, Will left. He met Maria coming out of her box room at the foot of the stairs. Wine had made him brave. He thrust the package at her.

She looked confused. 'It's not my birthday.'

'That doesn't matter. I just wanted to give you something.'

'That's very sweet!' She had lovely teeth, dainty and pearl white.

A further adventure awaited him in the lobby. Miss Clarke was in a huddle with Vernon. Johnnie emerged from the bar. The house-keeper glared at her.

'It appears that the lusty old goat in Room 13 is intent on an assignation,' said Vernon.

'Whoever with?' replied his wife.

'Why, you! He wants to know if it should be before or after midnight.'

Johnnie's infectious laugh was her most attractive asset. 'I asked him to do my horoscope. He wants to know my time of birth, that's all.'

Chapter Five
Fortune, Lady Frieda
& The Mage

Saturday, 17 March 1945

Steam billowed from the funnel of the London train as it chugged into Hastings Station. Will hovered at the ticket barrier, nervous lest he miss Crow's guest. 'You'll know her right away,' the old reprobate had muttered, refusing to furnish any further leads. In their shapeless demob suits and utility dresses, the passengers spilling onto the platform were a sea of greys and blacks. Then a tall woman, sporting a velvet cape in a patchwork of colours and a large brass sun medallion that flapped against her chest, stood out. Almost every finger bore a ring Will noticed as she handed in her ticket.

'Mr Crowley sent me,' he said.

She glanced around furtively and quickly handed him her case. As the taxi climbed Elphinstone Road, he learnt the lady's name was Dion Fortune and she had travelled from Glastonbury via London. Will wondered what had enticed her to make the journey, especially as she breathed with difficulty and her pallor was deathly. He tried to make small talk, but she responded with monosyllables and then lapsed into a silence he found aloof. Did she take him for a servant? At the top of the road, they took a left opposite the cemetery, passing Saint Helen's Church and the gabled Victorian house Will shared with his father. There was a green Bentley parked in the forecourt of Netherwood. A chauffeur in peaked cap and grey uniform was lounging by the gate, savouring a Capstan Full Strength.

Will showed the woman up to Room 13 only to find the Beast already had company: an elderly woman with a pinched yet lively face dressed in a mink coat and patent leather shoes. She and Crow were peering at three canvases propped up on the bed. Crow turned round. His shock mirrored the newcomer's. When they had first met at a public talk Dion was giving, Crow had been physically intimidating, the Great Beast of legend; the woman stately and imposing, compared by some to a Valkyrie. The intervening years had withered them both. Crow recovered quickly and patted out his standard greeting.

'Love is the law,' the woman in the mink responded.

The new arrival sighed.

'I know there will come a day when I must hail the New Aeon, but you must let me choose the time for that. I thought it literary honesty to confess my debt to you in my Qabalah book and got howls of outrage in return. It was as though I had praised Beelzebub himself.'

'You flatter me,' said Crow.

'Miss Thelema is a very harsh mistress,' said the other woman, whose name was Lady Frieda Harris. 'She almost cost me my marriage.'

'Oh gawd, here we go again! What would the yellow press have to write about without the King of Depravity to hang out to dry? I think it's time for Demon Crow to prey on that sausage-lipped renegade Victor Neuburg and terrify the wits out of him and his dusky wife. I wonder if he's still in Steyning.'

'He died in 1940,' said Lady Frieda.

'Typical! He'd do anything to frustrate me. I'll have to find someone new to persecute. Turn up the heating, dear boy!'

Such services were quid pro quo for the lessons, an expression Will had picked up during one of them. The heating for once seemed to be working. The newcomer removed her cape. Underneath she was wearing a tan blouse and a jacket with suede panels.

'Are those the Thoth paintings?' she asked, indicating the canvases. 'I saw a couple in the Atlantis Bookshop a few years back and thought them very fine.'

'Yes, we had a display there,' responded their creator, Lady Frieda. 'These are rejects. We thought we'd take another look in case one or two could be used.'

'For the tarot pack?

'No, an exhibition. We'll have to wait for the war to end to bring them out as cards. We had a devil of a time publishing the *Book of Thoth* last year. Had to pretend it was in the *Equinox* series and classed as a magazine to get enough paper.'

Dion smiled for the first time.

'You wrote a lovely inscription, Crow. Mine was the ninth copy.'

The Beast also smiled. 'Zoroaster held the number sacred and the summit of all philosophy.'

'We want the Royal Mint to produce the cards. No one else could do them justice. I'm Frieda Lady Harris by the way.'

Crow interceded. 'I'm quite forgetting my manners, which should come as a surprise to nobody. May I present Dion Fortune, Artist of the Word, High Priestess of Selene, fresh - if that is the word - from her Fraternity of Inner Light at Glastonbury. Perhaps Sorority would be more accurate but now's not the time to quibble.'

The ladies exchanged a conventional "How do you do!".

'Night after night, Dion and her flock invoked the Bornless Ones in their magical Battle of Britain against the Black Brothers. My own contribution was hardly less significant. Yet who will remember what we did or even thank us? By luring poor Horn over I performed a great service for the nation.'

'Is that a hunting or drinking horn?' queried Frieda.

'Aha!'

'You always insist on being so mysterious!'

'It's my job.'

Miss Clarke bustled in bearing a Royal Doulton tea set on a tray. This was reserved for distinguished visitors, despite Vernon's socialist misgivings. She solicitously handed Frieda the first cup. 'Here you are, your ladyship,' she simpered.

'Soon be Imbolc. Expect you can't wait to smear yourself with datura and soar off with the bats, eh, Miss Clarke?'

'Filth,' she spluttered, turning on her heels and exiting.

'You can't get the staff these days, or the followers for that matter. Flocking to the vales of Avalon, are they, Dion?'

'The war concentrated minds. We had quite an upsurge at the beginning. More recently we're seeing more of the young.'

'They're heeding the call of the New Aeon. By my latest reckoning, 1965 will be a critical juncture for the Child Horus.'

'I'm afraid I'm not going to be around for that. I got the results of some tests in London yesterday.'

Lady Frieda clucked sympathetically and wondered if she should revise her first impression of Fortune, whom she had up to now found self-important and tiresomely mysterious. Crow took a large gulp of brandy and a deep drag from his pipe. A racking cough ensued.

'It seems we'll all be on our way soon,' he rasped stoically.

Lady Frieda tutted. 'I do worry about you so. We'll get you a nurse if I can convince Percy to fund one.' Her husband was Chief Whip of the Liberal Party. 'You haven't taken that pipe out of your mouth since we came in.'

'Doctor's orders,' wheezed Crow.

'Doctor Faustus, I shouldn't wonder.'

'Speaking of doctors, would you pass Pandora's box, it's just beside the bed? That's a good chap, Will.'

Crow opened it. Removed a hypodermic syringe. Took off the plunger. Added hot water from the jug Miss Clarke had brought. Shook a pink pill out of a small medicine bottle. Crushed it against the table with a spoon. Scooped the powder into the chamber. Replaced the plunger. Agitated the hypodermic until the powder dissolved. Rolled up his shirt sleeve. Used a garter as a tourniquet. Clenched his fist. Fumbled for a vein. Pressed the plunger. This had all taken a couple of minutes. A couple more, and his eyes grew bright and glassy.

'It's getting harder and harder to get a prescription. I wish you'd put in a word, Frieda.'

'Not sure it's good for you.'

'I need it for the asthma. That stuff I used to get from Germany worked wonders but along came the war and supplies dried up. Otherwise, I agree heroin is a dubious ally.'

Crow turned his attention to The Universe, The Moon, and The Empress leaning against the wall. The vibrant colours and geometric designs, the gods, goddesses, and heraldic beasts anticipated psyche-delic art by twenty years. There were also secrets for those with the eyes to see them: the periodic table of chemical elements in the lower part of The Universe; the phallus flanked by pharaonic attendants hidden in The Moon.

'I told you, Frieda, practise without cease and when caught by stray mist on a hillside or the hues of a ripple in a stream, ask yourself what is this message that has rolled across the centuries uniquely to me? Do this continually with great love, and one day when you least expect it the sacred breath will fill you. This tarot will be the compass of the good ship Magick for the next two thousand years. Better make that a rocket ship in honour of Jack Parsons. I just wish you'd done as I suggested and made your women more...'

Crow frowned as he scrutinised the two miserly brushstrokes that sketched the face of the Empress.

Lady Frieda exploded. 'Know what you *won't* do shall be the whole of my Law! I can put up with a lot, lumbago included, but I will NOT draw like Aubrey Beardsley'.

'Do you really think you should be addressing your Holy Guru in that petulant fashion?'

Lady Frieda nodded in Will's direction. 'This poor boy can't have a clue what we're squabbling about. Does he even know what the tarot is?'

Crow grunted. 'It's the devil's picture book as far as he's concerned. He wants to be a priest.'

'Well, don't let this old beast put you off, young man. The tarot is a symbolic portrait that maps our relation to the universe.'

'Also called the tarot of the Bohemians,' added Crow. '*Boem* is old French for sorcerer.'

'I didn't know that.' said Dion.

'I often wonder why a repository of useless wisdom such as I is relegated to obscurity by the Great British Public. Surely, I should be gently levered into national treasure status as poet and seer. My doom is to be vilified. Yours, sweet ladies, is to have never realised your true Will. You would both have made excellent Scarlet Women.'

'Didn't most of them turn to drink or go mad?'

'It's true several weren't up to scratch, Frieda.'

'Which is exactly what they wanted to do to you.'

Crow looked rueful. 'Some of them did.'

'I find the companionship I've attained with Percy a very peaceful dwelling.'

'Is that why he spends his time in London and you in Chipping Campden?'

'The Great Work requires solitude.'

'Bah, the way of the Tao is to be open to everything that comes your way; to immerse yourself in the hurly-burly of existence.'

'I didn't marry until my thirties,' said Dion flatly. 'My husband left me.'

As far as physical love went, hers had been a pauper's table. Purity and abstinence were paramount in her Fraternity. Nevertheless, she suspected sexual energy was a pathway to very high magic, and Tantra and Crowley had drawn the maps. It had been left to her well-received occult novels if not to feast on flesh, at least to take a nibble. But that was fiction. In life she was intimidated by the forbidden that reeked like Ruthvah from the Beast.

That morning Will had found a note in the pigeonhole in the lobby where the Symonds left scribbled lists of his daily tasks. It instructed him to come at four if he wanted to see his present. Taking leave of Crow and his visitors, he bounded down the stairs and hovered outside the box room. It was Maria's day off. He wondered if the Holy Ghost would descend and plead with him to not go in, but instead, as the grandfather clock in the lounge struck four muffled chimes, he tapped on her door and softly turned the knob.

She was lying on the bed with her back to him. The dim bedside lamp played on her suspender belt, glossy satin knickers, seamed stockings and black stilettoes. The stockings were his present, their source Crow's unlikely fan base at the U.S. army camp. Maria's breathing was light and regular. She seemed to be asleep. The paleness of her skin never ceased to astonish him. Her body odour mingled with cheap scent was hopelessly arousing. He crossed the Rubicon, stumbled forward, and ran a finger up one seam.

'Window shopping only!' she objected.

Chapter Six
The Birthday Party

Saturday, 16 June 1945

The Ridge was enjoying respite from the cool and damp that had characterised the month so far. The first fortnight had been changeable, but on the fifteenth the fine spell had started. Bees gathered pollen from lemon balm and comfrey in the kitchen garden. Kamikaze wasps divebombed glasses of ginger beer beneath the parasols on the terrace. A party of four played croquet on the lawn, while Vernon mowed the long grass that fringed the shrubbery. Hikers had set off early and were rambling in the lovely walking country of the Firehills and the Glens. For once, Maria and Will's day off had coincided, and they were sharing a blanket in a glade ringed by brambles and rhododendrons at the edge of the grounds. The maid was due to visit her mother, who lived in Saint Leonard's, that afternoon.

'She's a seamstress now but used to be a dancer.' Maria sniggered. 'At the Windmill.'

'Isn't that where...?'

'Yes, the girls are naked,' Maria seemed quite proud, 'and as frozen as statues. If they so much as twitch, they get the sack. But mum was a proper dancer. She even appeared before King George and Queen Mary at the London Palladium. She was also a Bluebell girl in Paris for a while. God, I envy her that! What thrilling times she must have had! Paris is where she met my father.'

'I'm sure you'd be a fantastic dancer.'

'My hands and feet are all over the place. I'm just cut out for scrubbing dishes, I reckon.'

'I'm sure you're wrong. Where's your father now?'

'Search me! He was a bandleader from Cuba. A real charmer they say. He put her in the family way and then pissed off.'

The crudeness made Will flinch.

'Your mother brought you up alone?'

'She got arthritis and gave up dancing. Had to pass herself off as a widow to stop people talking. It was hard. People are always judging you when you stand out from the crowd.'

She had a gap tooth that made her smile endearing. Will felt he owed her.

'My mum died while she was having me.'

'That's awful! I'm so sorry.'

'My dad never met anyone else. I don't think he really tried. He's an accountant but hates it. His true love is theatre. He directs for the Court Players.'

'That's where Mr Symonds acts.'

'They're friends. That's why I'm at Netherwood. And you know, there's nowhere else I'd rather be.'

He was fishing for a kiss but landed a frown instead.

'Mrs Symonds is fretting about her husband.'

'Drink?'

'Getting more noticeable, isn't it?'

'Crow downs brandy for breakfast, but it doesn't seem to have any effect on him.'

'Miss Clarke says he's a dope fiend. Doesn't your father mind you having lessons with him?'

'Dad's a freethinker. He despises the yellow press and thinks Crow's been hard done by. He's like Vernon - I mean Mr Symonds - in that regard. Sometimes I think Crow's evil reputation is all smoke and mirrors. He's just an old Tory gent at heart. He'd be horrified if Labour won the election.'

'That won't happen. Winston's bound to walk it.'

Will wasn't so sure. The poll was only a month away. There was talk the returning soldiers were on the hunt for a new Jerusalem. Maria was wearing a tight chiffon top that did little to disguise her bust and a flowing skirt that had ridden up above her knees. Her sunlight-dappled body was very close. He peered between the leaves that ringed their patch and spied picnickers on the lawn. He was sure they could not be seen. He rolled over, grateful she didn't move. The pressure of her breast against his shoulder was dizzying.

'Talk of the devil!' she said.

Crow was ambling across the lawn in a most peculiar way. As though dodging an invisible obstruction, he weaved sideways, then walking on he bowed or lifted his hand in greeting, smiling as if at old friends, though there was nobody there. The Beast's costume amplified the performance: a turquoise robe ringed by a cummerbund, with the jewelled hilt of a dagger poking out of it. A turban bound his head. Enormous rings made from lumps of uncut turquoise hooped his fingers. Alongside him was a man in an olive drab uniform. Another figure in a striped summer blazer and straw boater was lagging just behind.

'Whatever is he up to?'

'You better go and find out.'

Will rose and began heading in the direction of Crow's party. 'Don't mind me!' Maria called out. This abrupt counter-command caused him to waver, but curiosity impelled him to catch up until he was level with the man at the rear, who possessed an enormous beak of a nose and bushy eyebrows. Removing his pipe, the man introduced himself as Major Knight.

'You must be Will,' he said in a warm, plummy voice; 'Crow's star pupil. Ah yes, I've heard all about your lessons. As a matter of fact, I'm a student of his myself.'

'Are you learning Latin too?'

'No, I'm studying a tradition. Dates back all the way to Egypt. Crow probably knows more about it than anyone alive. Keeps me coming back. I've always felt there's more to life than meets the eye.'

'Why is he weaving about like that?'

Knight smiled. 'On leaving the house, Crow invoked a tree-spirit who contacted all the elementals in the area to let them know a magician was abroad. The satyrs, nymphs, and fairy folk of the woodland are flocking to pay homage.'

'But there's nobody there.'

'Ah, you can't see them because you're not an initiate of the higher grades.'

Will was half-expecting a wink, but none was forthcoming.

Crow had had a fair number of visitors since arriving at Netherwood. Augustus John had been discovered comatose on a sofa in the early morning by a scandalised Miss Clarke, sleeping off heroic quantities of brandy. There was an intense German woman who always brought flowers. Two impeccably dressed and well-spoken gentleman who visited separately, a Mr Yorke and a Mr Wilkinson. There was the swarthy American company commander with the drooping moustache, currently marching ahead and talking about a book the magician wanted.

'Lady Harris just wouldn't send it when I asked her to in London. I don't have a clue why not. It was like I'd asked her to do something dirty or dangerous. I had to post it from Germany. Sorry it still hasn't arrived.'

Crow, a man who had nobly borne many wrongs, emitted a sigh. 'Frieda is an adorable angel and the most devious, scheming harpy it has ever been my misfortune to have crossed paths with. It won't surprise you to know she exhibited the Tarot paintings without telling me and tried to pass them off as her own.'

'She did *paint* them.'

'A mere technicality. Every design was accomplished according to my precise instructions. She was the executor, but I was the creator. Is she wicked or merely insane I ask myself?'

'Her husband's a swell guy though. He showed me around parliament and gave me lunch on the terrace. Said lots of my ideas on economic dynamism made sense.'

'As indeed they do, my dear Louis. They call Percy Harris the "chamber pot" because his mind-numbing speeches empty the Commons so quickly. Don't know how he puts up with Frieda. Living apart must help. Any word of 210? I haven't had a squeak for ages.'

Frater 210 was Jack Whiteside Parsons, the man who had introduced Louis to the Agape Lodge in Pasadena.

'He wrote me a mail full of baloney. Said I should go to Brittany and watch by moonlight for the Shadow Queen, beware of the Death Star and listen out for the bells and the Whispering Druid. Jesus, the bells! They're jangling away in his belfry along with the bats. Jack's drunk on witchcraft and voodoo. He invokes banshees and demons like you and I down coffee. Doesn't care if they come from the pits of hell itself as long as they put in an appearance.'

'That is worrying. The bulk of black magic is gibberish, the bit that isn't is meaningless filth. But it certainly works and has terrible repercussions on its practitioners. The problem with Jack and the American lodge is that they're obsessed with sex.'

'You can say that again.'

The American was still bruised from the break-up with his wife after she slept with Parsons in the sexual free-for-all of the Lodge. Crow, for his part, had discovered that the advancing years had unchained him from the sexual maniac of his youth and were fostering a prudish condemnation of the fiend.

'The gods didn't anoint me as their chosen messenger just to spawn a love cult. Speaking of which, how's my rehabilitation progressing?'

'If we only had an official declaration that you were working for the British Government in the Great War. That would clear the air regarding everything else.'

'I shall pester 'C' at Broadway and Carter of the Yard. Pity we can't enlarge as well on my sterling role in the latest conflict.'

'You mean the "V for Victory!" sign?'

'A fairly minor contribution compared with other feats that I sadly am not at liberty to disclose.'

'The BBC said the Belgians invented it.'

'What have the Flemish and Walloons ever come up with but chocolate, mussels, and beer? Find those old *Equinox* photos of me in my hooded robes. I'm sure I'm flashing it. Why, there's an edition of *Magick* from the Twenties with a V sign and a swastika on the cover.'

'The swastika might not be such a good idea.'

'I should never have mentioned it to Ludendorff: hammer of Thor and all that bunkum!' Crow came to a standstill, wheeled around, and glowered at the major. 'Max, isn't it time my wartime exploits bask in the glare of publicity they so richly merit.'

'Mum's the word, old chap.'

'Ahead of my time as always,' sighed Crow, resuming his walk.

'We have to use the most up-to-date methods,' urged the commander. 'Headquarters in a choice London location. A bevy of secretaries working round the clock. A director to manage the operation and get the press on side.'

'I look to you to manage that.'

The American shook his head. 'I'll be back in Germany very shortly. We need someone eminent to represent you and tell it like it is. "So, what if the Beast took every narcotic under the sun," they'll say. "They were experiments conducted for the betterment of humankind".'

'How well you understand me! Such a pity you can't do the job.'

'All that bullshit about crucifying frogs and drinking cat's blood!'

'We better keep a lid on the hashish and menstrual blood in the wafers of light as well, until such time as the masses are ready, hee-hee!'

'It's down to you to contact some of the greats you've known for testimonials. Rodin ...'

'Dead as bronze sadly.'

'That writer with the weird name.'

'Somerset Maugham? Owes me a huge favour. I still regret not suing him for his libels in *The Magician*. The point is to keep the campaign as simple as possible. The hoi-polloi will run a mile from anything they perceive as clever. I reckon I've hobnobbed with about eighty world famous Personalities.'

'Hey, you don't suppose some dame is going to crawl out of the woodwork and start dishing dirt?'

Crow stopped walking and wheeled round.

'Like that demented harlot Nina Hamnett. Have no concerns on that score! Johnnie Public admires a man for putting it about a bit, even if they pretend not to.'

This did little to console the American. 'If we can get you to the States, we may be able to junk all this.'

Crow perked up at the prospect. 'You've no idea how dreadful things are around here: freezing winters, draughty rooms and rationing, not to mention the appalling company!'

'Rancho Royal is in the southern California desert. Climate's warm and dry. Do wonders for your asthma. Hey, I don't suppose you've kept a record of the money orders I've been posting you.'

'Far too busy working on *Aleister Explains Everything*, dear boy. If memory serves, you own twenty-five percent of the gross sales. That should be a tidy sum.'

'I'm very grateful, Master.'

Crow peered over his shoulder.

'I see no masters here,' he said.

Beachy Head emerged through a gap in the wind-bent trees as they walked on. The Beast halted, allowing Will and Major Knight to catch up.

'I was the first to scale that headland back in 1894. Chalk is the most dangerous and difficult surface there is. You sort of ooze or trickle up it. You see that pinnacle just below the corner of the cliff. That was the route I took. It's called the Devil's Chimney.'

'How apt,' smiled Major Knight, tilting his gaze upwards. 'There's not a cloud, not even a white trail of vapour from a fighter plane. One got so used to them. Let's hope we won't be spotting any more.'

'Did you see action?' asked Will.

'I was based in London throughout the hostilities. You should come up and visit. The number's Pimlico 2000. Not so hard to remember. I have parrots, monkeys, snakes, and a tame bear called Bessie. My, whatever's this?' he reached into his pocket and pulled out a pale brown lizard. 'May I introduce Cyril the Chameleon?'

He held it up above his head. The lizard's colour began to change, morphing into a medley of greens. They turned back towards the house, retracing most of the way in silence which Will broke by asking the major how he had met Crow.

'A mutual friend called Dennis Wheatley introduced us. You must have heard of him. He's had huge success with his black magic thrillers. We also worked together.'

'Crow doesn't look like a soldier.'

'There are different sorts of battles.'

'He told me he did something really important in the war but won't let on what it was.'

The major frowned. 'Crow's greatest failing is an insatiable urge for the limelight. It can make him highly indiscreet. People quake in their boots at the sound of his name, but more fool them. The horror stories in the yellow press are for the most part hogwash. I mean look at these kids. They're not scared of him.'

They had come to the north-west corner of Netherwood's four acres, just beside the road that ran along the Ridge. The going rate for the wisteria-festooned cottage that stood there was two and a half guineas a week, while the main house was four guineas, inclusive of full board. The current guest was holding a birthday party for her daughter. The girl's name was Lucy. She had bonded with Crow over their mutual admiration of Johnnie's pet white rabbits, the "chrysanthemums" as the Beast had dubbed them, who loped about on the lawn outside the main house.

A crowd of boisterous children and their mothers were clustered around a long, rickety table laden with watery lemonade, sliced bread thinly coated with jam, and humble cakes boasting an occasional raisin. It was the best that could be mustered in wartime. The children could not start on the food until after the entertainment. This had arrived in the form of Crow, who they greeted with a cheer and the hope he would get on with it.

A tubby woman greeted the newcomers. This was Lucy's mother, who had enlisted the Beast's services. A method actor to his fingertips, Crow raised his arms in a hieratic gesture and commanded the children to sit in a circle around him, which they did with shiny, expectant faces. The magician turned to each of the four points of the compass, muttering spells as he did so. The children seemed amused. He glared at them. They chuckled. The glare became a simpering smile. They laughed even louder. He pulled the dagger from his cummerbund, crouched down, and drew a circle in the soil, then pointed the blade at a faun-like boy with black curly hair and full lips. The boy leapt to his feet, bounded forward, and stepped cockily into the circle. Crow let loose a stream of Enochian spells. He gestured to the child to vacate the circle. The boy smirked, raised his right foot, moved forward, but came up against an invisible barrier. With a look of gathering consternation, he strained and pushed, but nothing could release him. The children gasped and squealed and flapped their hands. Crow went up to Lucy and ordered her to stand up and step out of the ring of children. As she did so, the boy stumbled forward, free of the circle. The children shrieked and cheered. Major Knight made his way through them until he was standing in their middle.

'Once you know what things are called, you can always identify them,' he said in the soothing tones of a kindly uncle. 'You gain command off them. Who can tell me the name of the tree behind us with the smooth grey bark and majestic branches?'

'Is it an elm?'

'Spot on, Lucy! To be precise, it's a wych elm. That doesn't mean it's home to women in pointed hats flying around on broomsticks who you probably imagine are good friends of that gentleman there.' He nodded in the direction of Crow, who was casting shadow-silhouettes on the tablecloth with his talon-like fingers. ' "Wych", you see, is spelt w-y-c-h. Now, who's noticed that butterfly fluttering about? It's called a white-letter hairstreak. When it was a caterpillar, it bred on the elm. There's a bird singing in the branches. The notes are like liquid. You can almost imagine them dripping from the leaves. It's called a willow warbler.' The major dropped to one knee and picked up a dark grey twig. 'This fell from the tree. You can tell because it's covered in coarse hairs and the bud on it is hairy, purple-black and squat.' He peered at the ground again. 'My word, what do we have here? I've just found some tracks. Do come and look!'

The children scrambled to their feet and crowded round him.

'Careful, you don't want to rub the tracks out with your heels. Let's see if we can find out any more about the animal that made them! If we follow the tracks, we should be able to discover in which direction it was heading. We may even come across its prey; that means the animal it was hunting.'

The children approached the horse chestnuts and Austrian pines that lined the Ridge. A green double decker with cream stripes rumbled by. The driver honked his horn.

'If the tracks suddenly peter out,' continued the major, 'you may find their maker became food for another animal. There might be physical clues of a struggle. If that's the case, what might have taken it? How big could this creature have been?'

'There are some new tracks here,' said a sandy haired boy.

'Wizard! Can you find more signs? A branch that has been broken off; the husk of a shell of a nut that's been eaten; the bark of a tree nibbled or scratched in a certain way.'

The children scoured the area.

'I still can't get over the stunt Crow pulled with that kid in the circle,' said the American officer, now alongside Will. 'That was real magick!'

'Indeed.'

It was an excellent word, satisfying the conventions of an occasion without contributing a thing. It could mean "I agree" or "I understand" or whatever the listener chose to understand. Will omitted the fact he had seen Crow whisper instructions to the curly haired boy that very morning and seal the conspiracy with a sixpence.

Chapter Seven
Castle Interlude

Friedrichshof Castle, Hesse, Germany:
Friday, 3 August 1945

An MI5 major is ascending the backstairs of a castle in the Taunus Mountains, 424 miles from Netherwood. His name is Anthony Blunt, and he is wearing an army captain's uniform as disguise. With him is a bald, kindly faced Home Guard Commander called Owen Morshead, Royal Librarian to George VI.

They are taking the backway because that morning, in the grand panelled hallway at the front, the waspish American captain in charge refused to admit them. Their visit bears no relation to the castle's current mission of providing rest and recreation for senior military staff. That the British king has sent them does nothing to sway her.

Undaunted, they call on Princess Margaret of Prussia, exiled to her estate manager's house just outside the castle gates. She has lost three sons in two world wars and had Hitler to tea while the swastika flew from the battlements. Over half the German aristocracy flocked to the Nazis, the "new Teutonic knighthood" of the SS being a particular draw. She is not happy to see them. It requires all their charm to persuade her to disclose their current route. "Your family papers have become exposed to the eyes of the inquisitive and fingers of the acquisitive," Blunt tells her. Though his German is fluent, they speak in English, her strangulated vowels very like those of her cousins, the British royals.

At the top of the stairs, Blunt and Morshead come to a small door framed by fifteenth century Venetian stonework posts. Using one of the keys Princess Margaret has given him, Blunt unlocks it. They enter a richly furnished Renaissance-style library, with massive brass chandeliers hanging from the solid oak recesses of the rosetted ceiling. Busts, antique bowls, and Roman vases line the tops of the five-shelved bookcases that run round the apartment. The first case they come to is filled with volumes dedicated to the Empress Frederick, known as "Vicky", the first occupant of the castle after it was built in 1893 and daughter of Queen Victoria. The books in the next case are inscribed to her husband, Emperor Frederick III, who reigned for only 99 days as King of Prussia, dying after a grisly battle with disease in 1888. It isn't until they come to the case nearest the window that they find what they are looking for: 4,000 letters Queen Victoria wrote to her daughter and Vicky's replies. They stack the leather-bound volumes on a mahogany table conveniently lit by sunlight.

'Shouldn't you take a gander before we pack them up?' says the major, his tone deliberately offhand. His companion frowns. Morshead routinely archives innumerable dreary accounts of shooting, fishing, and balls.

'Did you notice how jumpy that American captain was?' he says. 'I reckon she's got her hands in the till and thought we were on to her.'

'Looting's rife all over Germany. Looks like we got here just in time.'

'Well, we might as well oil our pipes while we're at it.'

Morshead has spotted a decanter and set of crystal balloon glasses on a nearby shelf. He goes over, extracts the stopper and sniffs: a prime aged brandy. He pours, handing one glass to his companion. 'King and Country!' They touch glasses.

'I'm going to have a gawp at the paintings,' says Blunt.

'Don't know why it's taken you so long, dear boy.'

Above the bookshelves, an Adoration of the Magi takes up an entire wall. Blunt immediately clocks it as a copy of Meister Stefan's altar piece in Cologne Cathedral. He begins to languidly stroll the length of the apartment. It is important to show no urgency, to display a connoisseur's appreciation of the sketch by Titian and the Piranesi engravings of Rome he finds along his route. He is less taken by the portraits of the Hesse family who own the castle, with their dutiful, unimaginative faces. There are cases as well, displaying bronze medals and the autographs of most of the European royal families. In the glass he catches his reflection: the pinched, upturned nose and haughty features. Another bookcase is lined with works on the kings and queens of England. The castle is often called the German Balmoral, he reflects.

When nearly at the end of the apartment, he comes across the bureau. Another borrowed key unlocks the drawer. It is crammed with letters. An envelope on top bears an English stamp and post-mark. He lifts it out. It is addressed to Philipp, the current Prince. Raised by an English nanny and schooled at a home counties prep school, Philipp showed an early enthusiasm for the Nazi Party and joined in 1930. He became Hitler's art dealer, a fact that resonates with Blunt. More pertinently, he was a key channel between the Nazis and the appeasers in England, being cousin to two of the foremost: the Duke of Windsor and his younger brother the Duke of Kent.

The major lowers the desktop and sets down the glass of brandy on the leather writing surface. He peers into the shadowy recesses. There are ink pots, blotters, nibs, sheets embossed with the rampant lion of Hesse, but no more letters. He glances at the other end of the apartment. Morshead is still absorbed in his reading.

Gathering up the letters, Blunt bears them into an adjoining waiting room. It is in the style of Louis XV1 with slate-coloured silk hangings. A rosy-cheeked girl smiles down at him. He clocks her as a Reynolds while placing the stack on the walnut table beneath. He begins sorting through the letters. The first is dated 21 April 1941 and was sent from Fife via neutral Sweden. With a shudder of grief, he recognises the beautiful handwriting.

Ever the methodical and punctual correspondent, Prince George, Duke of Kent, extends warm greetings to Cousin Philipp. Several lines of family gossip ensue. The queen is "grinning Liz", and the king

"Bertie". He mocks them as little more than "civic functionaries" and scoffs at the king's habit of investing money. The prince himself thinks nothing of splashing out on snuffboxes, diamonds, expensive China, furniture, and paintings, having inherited from his mother, Queen Mary, an artistic bent and love of collecting.

Nobody seeing the royal family together would have twigged the duke disliked the king and queen so much, Blunt muses. Kent was as charming as a jewel but at the same time treacherous. He'd happily sling you to the lions or damn you with faint praise. "Oh, go and ask Anthony, he knows absolutely everything about absolutely fuck all!" He was sorry afterwards of course. Everything was done for him, but nothing did. He knitted incessantly to calm his nerves. He gave wonderful Christmas presents and sent recipients the bill. He was insanely bored, and his shenanigans with men were a burden to him. Not the acts themselves but the concealment. The letter concludes by requesting that Hauptmann Alfred Horn be assured that all necessary arrangements have been made for his reception.

Blunt recalls the fatal night at Dungavel. The duke talking rapidly and irritably as the long minutes ticked by. It was supremely vital to him. He had felt cramped and frustrated for so long. At last, circumstances were poised to give scope to his supressed and manifold gifts. Then the circling plane. The touchdown the night fighter aborted. The flash on the horizon that spelt calamity.

General Sikorski, the Polish prime minister in exile, was due to land at Prestwick the next day and be ferried to the Kennels. Making Poland, the *casus belli*, a signatory would legitimise the treaty. A German speaking clerk from the Polish consulate in Glasgow was already on site. Kent instructed him to find out what had happened. He returned just before dawn with news of disaster. The Home Guard had captured Hess. MI6 was on its way to collect him. The duke ordered the two ATS girls back to base. The delegates of the Link and the Anglo-German Fellowship so far not interned who were due the next day, received telegrams to abort. The attendees from the House of Lords were slipped notes with the kedgeree in their Glasgow hotels telling them not come.

Also disbanded was a squad of Knight's black agents, as the spooks of B(5)b called themselves, a phrase borrowed from the Scottish play. The next morning, they checked out of their B & B in Strathaven, the closest town to Dungavel, and headed back to London.

Blunt rapidly scans the rest of the correspondence. He reaches into his khaki jacket and pulls out the slim Leica Minox his Soviet Controller has given him. Normally, he delegates the copying of files, such as those he stealthily borrows for a night from the MI5 Registry. Not possible now. It takes 35 minutes to photograph the letters. He considers hanging onto the missive from the duke as a keepsake but thinks better of it and tears it up. He crams the shreds into an envelope which he stuffs into his pocket. He saunters back to find the Royal Librarian chuckling over his catch.

'What a livewire that Vicky was! I mean just listen to this: "I cannot do the simplest thing without its being found to be in imitation of something English, and therefore anti-Prussian. I feel as though I could smash the idiots; it is so spiteful and untrue." '

'The Prussians thought she was a spy.'

'Well, they were right. Agent Vicky is sending oodles of secrets to her controller, Queen Victoria.'

'A liberal Englishwoman in regimented Prussia. Quite the fish out of water.'

'Her husband was a liberal as well. To think they were Kaiser Bill's parents. Just imagine if Frederick hadn't been stricken with throat cancer. No world wars! No Hitler!'

Futile! Futile! As pointless as dreaming that the Messerschmitt-110 had touched down on the runway alongside the Kennels. Just over four years had elapsed since then, entire countries and races had disappeared; fifty million had died, many of whom could still be alive. Tolstoy held that history rolled on like a wheel, grinding down armies and dynasties; great men like Alexander the Great or Napoleon were specks of mud thrown up by its revolutions. It wasn't true. A decision might be taken, or not be taken, that transformed the world in the batting of an eye. A birth or death could fell an empire.

'Are you all right, old chap? You look quite green around the gills.'

People frequently compare the major to Leslie Howard, but he looks more like a sea horse.

'It's hellish stuffy in here!' Blunt is well versed in attributing his behaviour to a cause other than the true one. 'I think these are what the king was after.'

He plonks the stack of letters onto the table. Morshead picks the top one up and begins to read. When he looks up, his face is ashen.

'I often saw Prince Philipp and Prince George huddled together at the palace, scheming to avert the war. They even got the backing of the king. But I never imagined they'd keep at it once the balloon went up.'

'The letters from Windsor are even worse. He urges bombing London to bring matters to a quick conclusion. He also gives the allied battle plan away.'

'That must be why the Germans changed their attack from Belgium to the Ardennes, which, of course, went very well for them.'

'This could doom the monarchy!'

Morshead purses his lips and emits a very long sigh. 'I am the Royal Librarian. I must consider future generations.'

'Posterity can take care of itself. Look at the others if you don't believe me!'

The librarian reads a few lines and then flings the sheet from him as though it were a red-hot coal. 'Windsor's eager to assume the throne when Britain is defeated. This can never come out! We must burn them in the grounds.'

'Not safe. Too many GIs wandering around on the lookout for plunder.'

The major removes a silver case from his pocket, extracts a Passing Cloud and taps the plain tip against the metal. He transfers it to his lips and fires it up with a Gold Dunhill lighter. As he does so, he gazes at the spacious fireplace midway along the wall. A Prussian eagle is painted on the front of the projecting chimney-cover of Istrian stone.

'Funny thing to do in August,' mutters Morshead.

'Nobody will notice. It will be a very small fire.'

Morshead gets to his feet, gathers up the letters, approaches the fireplace and dumps the sheets onto the hearth. The major follows, extracts the envelope from his pocket, and lights its edge. When the flame has taken, he lets it float onto the pile.

'You were quite thick with the duke at one time, weren't you?' says Owen.

Blunt strives to remain impassive. A faint blush crimsons his cheeks as the plummy voice he would rather not be hearing goes on: 'Prince George was a rum cove, wasn't he. Loved interior design. Even played a bit of music. Who would have thought it in such a family? Spot of bother, wasn't there? Got mixed up with that Happy Valley set in Kenya. There was an American heiress, "the girl with the silver syringe" the yellow press called her. Got him hooked on drugs.'

'His brother Edward helped wean him off.'

'Yes, dashed good of him! Windsor gets such a bad press these days. Then there were those rumours Kent batted for the other side. Noël Coward was a special chum if you know what I mean. They used to go around togged up as gals.'

An image springs unbidden into the major's mind. The prince sprawled on the divan, a trim, perfumed, sun-worshipping nude, sharing a post-coital Craven 'A'.

'Not something I'd know anything about,' he says.

'Of course not, old chap. Don't know what's got into me.'

'Too much of that!'

Blunt jabs in the direction of the half-empty decanter.

Chapter Eight
The Birth Pangs of the Aeon

Netherwood: Monday, 6 August 1945

Will was making his way through the lobby when Maria waylaid him. They had hardly spoken since the day in the glade. He had begun to hope things would stay like that. But she still ambushed his thoughts, most uncomfortably on waking.

'Are you going to keep pretending that I don't exist?' she said, her nostrils flaring.

'Please try to understand. I'm going to be a priest. There are vows and suchlike.'

'Then why do you spend so much time with that old devil?'

'He's helping with my Latin.'

'I'm Latin, too — anyway, half Latin American. You should see how he looks at me. Just like the way that posh friend of his looks at you!'

'The major? But he's married.'

'Means less than you think.'

Her grey maid's uniform was drab, but everything else about her was vivid and rousing. He imagined undoing the buttons on her starched blouse.

'It's the Symonds' wedding anniversary. They asked me to play for them.'

'Don't let ME stop you!'

'Maria, don't take it like that.'

'It's just I'd love to hear you do it myself.'

'Some other time. I'll stand beneath your balcony and play just for you.'

'I don't have a balcony.'

Vernon appeared from outside, on the lookout for him. His eyes were slightly out of focus and his voice was slurred. 'It's our troubadour. Come on! Everybody's ready.'

Will followed him down the front steps and along the path that skirted the lawn to the Dance Hall. There was applause from the 60 or so guests and neighbours sitting in the rows as they entered. Crow was next to Johnnie in the front, a brandy in his hand. Major Knight was on his other side. Will went and sat on the straight-backed chair that had been placed on the small stage, took the guitar out of its case, blew an E on the pitchpipes, and began tuning the bottom string. He had mild stagefright, but this did not turn tuning into the drawn-out embarrassment it sometimes became. He started with 'Greensleeves', a piece he knew so well it served for making any last-minute refinements to the pitch. He went on to play some Bach and Rodrigo and a medley of country and western as well as swing tunes. He finished with Arthur Smith's 'Guitar Boogie', a great hit that year and special request from Johnnie. After the applause had died down, Vernon, Crow and Major Knight crowded round as he put away his instrument.

'Chapeau!' declared the major in his avuncular tone. 'That's French for hat. It means bravo. You play very well. Must have started young?'

'When I was ten. Dad found a classical guitar teacher in the town.'

Don Romero had severe arthritis. Each time he plucked a chord or strummed his crooked fingers across the strings was a triumph. Yet under his tutelage Will had acquired the makings of a good musician.

'Ever tried jazz? No! You should! There's no freedom like jazz. I played clarinet and sax in a band in the Roaring Twenties. I still like a blow from time to time. When you visit me in Dolphin Square, we could have a jam. God, I'm really talking another language, aren't I? I mean we could improvise together.'

'Is that sort of thing still allowed?' asked Crow glumly.

'Just because the socialists won the election doesn't mean they're going to ban jazz. They love it in Russia.'

'I suppose you're right. Atlee looks more like a grocer than a Gestapo officer with that silly moustache of his.'

'Scaremongering like that is precisely why the Tories lost,' huffed Vernon. 'Our boys were sick to death of seeing Winston puff on a fat cigar when they'd been hard put to find a decent fag in the hellholes they'd been sent to. The age of forelock tugging is over. That's why the first election we poor serfs have been permitted for ten long years went the way it did.'

'I hear the Soviets are over the moon,' said Major Knight drily.

Vernon ignored this. 'We're going to build a fairer society. Health, coal, water, transport, owned by the people for the people, instead of by a few wealthy parasites getting rich off the backs of everybody else.'

'It's our anniversary,' said Johnnie. 'Let's not get all het up. Politics always brings out the worst in people.'

'Politics is just what people need.' Vernon was a few decibels short of shouting. He was a man of sweet temper, but alcohol rendered him belligerent.

When they returned to the lounge, the minute hand on the grandfather clock showed it was just before noon. Vernon weaved across to the radiogram, a state-of-the-art EKCO in a walnut-veneered cabinet, and pushed in one of the five pre-select knobs on the front panel. The rousing strains of 'Imperial Echoes' announced the news, followed by the presenter's cut-glass tones.

'A United States aircraft has dropped the first atomic bomb on the city of Hiroshima, an important Japanese army base. According to President Harry S Truman, the explosive was 2,000 times stronger than the largest bomb ever used and harnessed "the basic power of the universe". An American B-29 Superfortress, the Enola Gay, released the device at 0815 local time. The plane's crew witnessed a tall column of smoke billowing 20,000 feet above the city and powerful fires springing up. So far it has not been possible to make a precise audit of the destruction because of an immense mushroom cloud of dust obscuring the target.'

Johnnie broke the silence. 'What a dreadful way to mark our anniversary!'

Vernon's Dutch courage had been holed like a dam. His eyes were glistening. 'There must be thousands upon thousands of dead.'

Major Knight was steelier. 'The war will be over that much sooner. It will save millions of lives in the long run.'

'We are in the inclement straits between two Aeons, suffering the tempest of the equinoxes, with much more tumult to come,' said Crow. 'This new bomb must be the War Engine you'll find prophesied in the book I gave you, Johnnie.'

That morning Crow had presented her with a copy of *The Book of the Law*. On the title page he had written: "To Johnnie: — not to be surprised, or shocked, or put in fear by the horrors which encompass us about on every side. These are no more than the birth pangs of the New Aeon."

Once Will had seen the newsreels of the destruction of Hiroshima and Nagasaki, the mushroom cloud bursting above the cities would seed his dreams. Blast waves, radiation sickness, the shadows of the dead etched on the walls of gutted buildings would wake him in a state of terror that transmuted into a resolve to prevent the unthinkable.

***

The Symonds had a farm in the West Country that supplied the rarest of wartime commodities: chicken. Equally hard-to-get vegetables and potatoes were grown in the kitchen garden. These made up the menu for the anniversary lunch held in the panelled new dining room next to the lounge. Vernon supplied a few bottles of white Bordeaux he had acquired before the war. It was a second glass of this that emboldened Will to ask the major what he did.

'I'm sort of between the War Ministry and Scotland Yard,' Knight trotted out his stock answer. 'But I'm branching out. I'm in talks with the BBC about doing some broadcasting.'

'Will you be revealing state secrets?' teased Crow.

'Only if you count which species of deer - red, fallow or roe - scraped the bark from a tree. I'll be hosting nature programmes.'

'Did you write that piece on the cuckoo for *British Birds*?' said Will, a keen birdwatcher.

Major Knight was delighted. 'My word, we do seem to have a lot in common.'

'Max is a cuckoo himself,' said Crow. 'He insinuates his change-ling eggs into the nests of dupes.'

Knight looked reproachfully at his guru. 'Many things that seem worlds apart are in fact very similar. A naturalist pries open the secrets of animals and plants; a secret agent, those of an enemy state or of enemies hiding within his own. You, Crow, probe another set of mysteries: the magical dimension that underpins reality.'

Will glimpsed Maria hovering at another table, ladling bread sauce onto chicken. She moved towards them bearing the tureen. She dished sauce onto Crow's and the major's plates but as the ladle hovered over Will, Crow startled her by hissing, 'Love under Will'. The sauce cascaded down onto Will's lap.

'Jesus Christ!' he exclaimed.

'Won't help you with that one,' said Crow, delighted. 'I was merely saying grace.'

Will rose, but instead of going out to the shed and changing into his gardening trousers, he made directly for her room. She had little to protect, and the door was unlocked. He had not long to wait.

'I can only stay a couple of minutes,' she said.

She had hurried like him and was still panting as she undid his belt. His trousers slid down until they crumpled over his scuffed suede brogues. He felt ridiculous standing there in his underwear.

'You need to take those off as well,' she said.

She moved closer, the pressure of her breasts against his chest becoming intolerable. He strained for her lips, with their coating of cheap Woolworth's lipstick, but she turned her face away as her hand went to work.

* * *

By now the guests had finished off Mrs Symonds' celebrated plum crumble. Crow and the major had transferred to the lounge for brandy and cigars. Knight had been cheerful during lunch but now seemed morose.

'The new chief's a chap called Sillitoe,' he said.

Crow looked blank.

'Formerly, Rhodesian police. He's been chief constable of half the counties in Britain. Stickler for discipline and going by the book. I fear we won't get on.'

'And the Reds?'

'Oh, they'll be having a field day. Sillitoe thinks it's preferable to have two or three traitors in the office rather than breach anyone's civil liberties. Two or three! There are at least five moles in British Intelligence.'

'Despite your warning?'

In 1943 Knight had circulated a report entitled "The Comintern is not Dead" which exposed Soviet penetration of MI5. It had been resolutely ignored, even when it made its way up to Churchill, who was determined not to upset his ally Stalin.

'We infiltrated Tom Driberg into the Communist Party, but he was expelled.'

'Someone blew his cover?'

Knight nodded. 'An art historian pansy currently doing a very hush-hush job in Germany for the Royals. An old informer of ours, a woman as it happens, identified another Soviet spy in the ranks. Naturally, he's a chum of the art historian's. They were all up at Cambridge together. That's what I hadn't realised. The Woolwich Arsenal spies were trade unionists. Made sense they wanted a worker's revolution. But Centre infiltrated the universities as well back in the Twenties and Thirties, recruiting some of our brightest and best. Left them in place as sleepers, sometimes for a decade or more before activating them.'

'What about the informer?'

'Sadly, our canary in a coalmine has a reputation for spreading false accusations. I'm sure she's right though. Everything's topsy turvy if you think about it. All the Nazi spies dropped into Britain were turned by Foley and the Double-Cross Committee. Meanwhile, the Abwehr was plotting against Hitler. Canaris was even feeding secrets directly to Menzies.'

' The Ipsissimus of MI6! 'C' himself!'

'That's how Broadway had advance warning of the Hess debacle.'

'It's all water under the bridge.'

'If only! British Intelligence is practically a branch of the Soviet Secret Service nowadays. How long is it going to take for a traitor to give Centre the blueprints for the atomic bomb? Our head start will evaporate. The Nazis were just a short-term problem, but the Soviets are in it for the long haul. Fighting communism is like breaking the tail off a lizard: it simply grows another!'

Crow took a deep swig of his brandy and looked sternly at his interlocutor. 'Pity you can't do that yourself, Max.'

'Whyever should I want to?'

'Because you don't face up to things, come clean, take it like a man.' Crow dissolved in a bubble bath of giggles.

'Discretion is the better part of valour.'

'No, it's better to hide in the light than under a bushel. But I suppose for you just another secret hardly tips the scales.'

'It is against the law, you know.'

'You don't follow the law, Max. You're above it, exempt.'

'The law could still follow me, Crow.'

'Oh, have it your own way!'

Chapter Nine
Professor Butler Visits

From the professor's diary: Tuesday, 1 January 1946

Dread clawed at the pit of my stomach as the train pulled in. The overcast sky was dense and yellowish, presaging heavy snow. The cold was so bitter that I seriously contemplated staying aboard and returning to Charing Cross. Why on earth was I, Schröder Professor of German at Cambridge University, on my way to meet the Wickedest Man in the World? On New Year's Day of all days! Steel yourself, Eliza Marian, I told myself, though you walk through the shadow of the valley of death yours is a noble crusade.

There is nothing gloomier than a resort out of season. Hastings looked drab and scruffy as the taxi climbed the steepening incline to the Ridge. Netherwood, however, an ivy-draped Victorian pile, struck me as clean and cheerful. Vernon Symonds, the owner, was charm itself as he welcomed me in his festive jumper and jaunty cravat. A red-haired boy, carrying a pile of logs to the lounge, made me a friendly bow. My apprehension abated only to reignite a hundredfold but a minute or so later when the most sinister apparition appeared at the top of the stairs and began to monstrously descend, stooped and seemingly on the point of complete disintegration. Encumbered by a baggy tweed suit, in such a threadbare and moth-eaten state that the Salvation Army would reject it, he seemed far older than his seventy years. His yellow skin was crumpled like old parchment, and he was wearing thick eyeglasses with a perpetual tear in the corner of his eye. Worst of all, however, was the voice that greeted me, a grating whine such as you can imagine a demon using when inducting the fallen into hell. After patting out his stock "Do what thou wilt", which I firmly put him in his place by ignoring, he came out with a more conventional "Happy New Year". This I echoed. Then he displayed that infamous second sight of his and divined my deepest fear.

'You may have more time than you expect for your research. There will be a blizzard!'

My white knight, Mr Symonds, instantly came to the rescue.

'Don't worry our guest like that, Crow! It's been years since the Ridge was cut off.'

'And years since we had a winter quite as cold as this one. You should welcome the custom.'

'Oh, I'm not staying here,' I said. 'I'm expected at Chellows.'

'Didn't you read my letter? I told you what an excellent establishment this is.'

The Beast's peevishness only strengthened my resolve not to spend a single night under the same roof as him.

'All our rooms are centrally heated and boast hot water,' said Mr Symonds, adding chivalrously, 'but I'm sure you'll be perfectly comfortable at Chellows.'

'I'll be taking all my meals at Netherwood, except breakfast,' I said by way of compensation.

'The food here is the finest in the county.'

'Crow is very kind, but I'm sure Professor Butler hasn't come all this way just to sample our table. I'll leave you-'

'Not just yet!', interrupted the Beast. His eyes were swivelling left and right; sweat was glistening on his Neanderthal brow. He seemed to be in urgent need of something. 'I'll rejoin you after lunch.'

Mr Symonds smiled amiably at the fiend's departing back. When out of earshot, he said, 'Asthma is a great trial. He has gone to take his medicine.'

One did not need to be a professor to read between the lines. The Beast is a dope fiend! I searched for a parallel amongst his more illustrious peers. Nutmeg was reputed to have inspired Nostradamus. Accounts of Doctor Dee refer to the fumes of a magical herb, probably cannabis. Madame Blavatsky chain smoked cigarettes laced with hashish. That was the best I could muster.

Mr Symonds and his wife, who joined us at luncheon, were cordiality personified, despite her insistence I call her Johnnie, which struck me as most peculiar.

'Since your visit was first mooted,' she said, 'we couldn't help wondering what a professor in your discipline would want with Crow.'

'The pursuit of German studies in the twentieth century can have brought mental serenity to few,' I replied. 'I've been drawn, instead, to the history of magic. I'm working on a book on the key events that distinguish the life of a magician: a miraculous birth, for example. Sounds a little dry and academic you rightfully object. What better last chapter than an interview with the leading contemporary practitioner of the craft?'

We set to on beef that was as succulent and tender as any I've enjoyed at the University Arms. And the portions! It seems they have not heard of rationing at Netherwood being, delightfully, in possession of their own farm. There was a scrumptious treacle pudding for afters.

'You mustn't mind Crow,' Mrs Symonds said. 'All the fire and brimstone are a bit of an act. He's a kindly old gent in many ways.'

Just to prove her wrong, the Beast seemed even more diabolical when he joined us for coffee, wielding a bottle of what was admittedly a fine old cognac. There was an aura of physical putrefaction such as I have never witnessed in another human being. Was it possible to imagine anything more repulsive than his fretful voice? The Symonds amazed me by the amiable attitude they displayed to this most loathsome of guests. Just before two o' clock, Mr Symonds went and switched on the radiogram, and we listened to the news on the Home Service. Japan's Emperor Hirohito has dumbfounded his subjects by revealing he is not descended from a Shinto sun goddess. Consequently, he is not a "living god" himself!

'So few of us left these days,' sighed the Beast absurdly.

'He's trying to save his own skin. It's quid pro quo for the Americans not putting him on trial,' said Mr Symonds.

This, of course, was not the case in Germany, and the focus of the next piece was the Nuremberg Trials. The weather forecast was especially grim. There seemed no end in sight to sub-zero temperatures and howling gales. It occurred to me again to cut my visit short.

After the news, Mr Symonds shuffled back to the radiogram and did something terribly clever that made me long to get just such a model for myself and Isaline, my companion. The knobs must be preset for different stations, for he pushed one in on the walnut façade and Vaughan Williams started playing at a suitably muted background volume. The conversation turned to Nuremberg and in particular Rudolf Hess, who claims not to recognise his old secretaries or comrades when confronted with them. Mrs Symonds was sure that he was faking. More charitably, Mr Symonds considered such amnesia genuine. We asked the Beast for his opinion, but with typical self-centredness he took us off on a tangent.

'Did you know that Churchill paid a secret visit to Hess when he was a prisoner in Surrey?'

'How did you hear of that?' piped up Johnnie.

'Because I was there!'

The Symonds chuckled, but I could not help noticing how the Beast turns every conversation to his favourite topic — the glorification of his foul and fetid self. I was relieved nobody asked for my opinion. Magic may be a recent addition to my academic repertoire but is not so removed from my core subject. A deep-seated fixation with myth and the occult sealed the Faustian pact Hitler made with his people. Valkyries, the Pied Piper of Hamelin, the Twilight of the

Gods are just a few examples of the bewitchment by the irrational that spawned Nazism.

After coffee, I was left in the lounge with Crowley. Invigorated by frequent nips of cognac, he insisted on lecturing me on the Law. On and on he droned in that frightful voice. 'The Khu is in the Khabs, not the Khabs in the Khu,' he said with a complicit stare, as though imparting the secret of the ages. Well, I never! Such gibberish! Whatever was he rambling on about? I felt sorry for the young honeymooners near us on the sofa. I could see from their peeved glances that the Beast's pontificating was most disagreeable and hoped they didn't also hold me - its innocent victim - responsible. Very soon they got up and flounced out. The foreign looking maid that had served luncheon came in. Instead of enquiring if we wanted anything, she collapsed onto the recently vacated sofa. Ever since the Labour victory, servants act as if they own the place! She had with her a magazine and a pair of scissors and began removing a section with a look of total absorption on her vapid face. Crowley's drivelling was driving me to distraction. I grew so desperate that I called across to the silly girl and asked what she was doing.

'I'm cutting out a photo of Princess Marina. I've got quite a collection,' she replied in her common way. 'So sad what happened.'

I could vividly picture the debris of the flying boat strewn across the Scottish hillside after the crash: a photo that all the papers carried. The summer of 1942 if memory serves.

'The poor Duke of Kent. He was so handsome, and they were so in love.'

'More to that crash than meets the eye,' wheezed Crowley, whose every breath must engender mystery. He resumed his insufferable monologue.

A few minutes later the red-haired boy came in and hovered around the sofa, ogling the maid as though she were Helen of Troy, not a brainless nincompoop. Didn't they have any duties to attend to?

The Symonds captain a very lax ship! Crowley was bleating on about how he had crossed the abyss and become an Ipsissimus. How do his hosts put up with him? Perhaps he knows something about them, I conjectured, a baleful secret, that keeps them in his thrall. I could stand it no longer.

'You must get me a taxi. I will go the sea.'

'The sea ... the sea,' he repeated as though the word frightened him.

'I need to clear my head. The breeze will do me good. I must have a taxi.'

'There are gales I hear,' but he rose and went out, leaving the door ajar. He must have the run of the place for the next thing was I heard him on the telephone.

'The professor must go down to the sea again, to the lonely sea and sky.'

He came back looking very pleased with his joke. The minutes ticked by. I grew more and more convinced he had only pretended to call. 'Crowley's Cars never come,' I muttered, but as the grandfather clock emitted three chimes, Mrs Symonds poked her head around the door and informed me my taxi had arrived. Crowley was so wrapped up in his impenetrable bunkum that he paid no heed and was still spouting drivel as I left.

The wind shook the cab during the descent, bending the trees lining the road. I still had my overnight bag, so the driver, who was going very slowly, must have assumed I was leaving.

'Good thing you're going,' he told me. 'Looks like the Ridge could be cut off for days.'

I countermanded my original instruction to drop me on the promenade and told him to make directly for the station. However, by the time we reached it, the wind had dropped. It seemed a pity not to take a last look at the sea. The promenade was five minutes' walk away. It was blustery. Waves crashed against the supports of the pier.

Icy spray stung my cheeks. Girding myself against the gale, it struck me as faint-hearted to abandon my quest. Apart from a smattering of sympathetic professors in European and American universities, the study of magic is looked on askance by my peers. A notorious figure like Crowley might just open the door to a wider readership. My resolve reforged, I took a taxi from the stand outside the ersatz-Turkish White Rock Theatre and returned to do battle.

Powdery snow was falling in flurries thick enough to settle as the taxi reached Netherwood. The gale had blown up again. The cold cut through my camel hair coat like a scimitar, far worse than on the seafront. My misgivings were further stoked when Johnnie informed me the Beast was expecting me in his room. She insisted on escorting me up the stairs and along the corridor. Room 13! Where else? She tapped gently on the door and that quavering whine, which I had longed so fervently to never hear again, summoned me in. I turned the doorknob and was met by a scene of incalculable horror.

The fug of tobacco, infused with a sickening stench of what most certainly was hellbane, made me pant for breath as I recoiled from the atrocious daubs hanging crookedly on walls stained a grisly yellow by nicotine. Executed in colours that actively loathed each other, these, for want of a better word, pictures depicted leering figures with diabolical squints. The nightmare hallucinations of delirium tremens were transparently the inspiration. The Beast was perched on the edge of his tumbled divan bed sucking ravenously on his meerschaum pipe. 'My own creations,' he pompously wheezed. Apart from his artwork, which was almost enough to make one wish humankind had never put a brush to canvas, there was a battered writing table, a worm-eaten chest and sagging bookshelves A tap he had obviously forgotten to turn off was gushing steaming water on to the cracked enamel of the washbasin. An interloper had crept up behind me unawares: the boy I had last seen mooning over the dusky maid in the lounge.

'Not tonight, Josephine,' the Beast called to him.

Who did he think he was? Napoleon? Then a more sinister explanation insinuated itself into my thoughts. The residents of Netherwood must assume nicknames borrowed from the opposite sex to while away the tedium of their provincial lives. Could this in turn lead to darker, nay unimaginable goings-on? The growing conviction that my presence had forestalled the most unspeakable depravities was a trifling consolation, for the boy said, 'Tomorrow then,' to which the Beast replied, 'As long as the professor won't still have need of me.' Fat chance, you jumped up, pedantic bore, I thought, and almost vomited as I imagined the pair of them coiled in the sin against the Holy Ghost. How could the Symonds allow such reprehensible goings-on under their roof unless Vernon and Johnnie - the giveaway? - were also willing participants in the Beast's sex-magic rites? I resolved to inform the authorities just as soon as I had escaped.

'Do push the door shut behind you,' said Crowley, 'and we'll make a start. Cognac?'

Against my better judgement, I accepted. He wished to take my coat, but I refused to part with it. He waved me onto an armchair. Snow was swirling against the window.

'The drifts can be as much as ten-feet high. You probably won't be able to return to Chellows.'

I ignored the provocation; his words only spurring me on to expedite my mission. I asked him about his birth. Disappointingly, no signs or portents attended the Beast's deplorable arrival on this planet. His father, who he claimed to have adored, died when he was ten. If it hadn't been for that, it is possible to imagine his life taking a very different course. His identification with the Beast of Apocalypse was sparked by a desire to outrage his family, whose Plymouth Brethren fundamentalism repelled him.

Moving on to initiation, he seemed truer to the archetype, relating in hushed tones how he had been admitted into the Order of the Golden Dawn on 18 November 1898. The next box to tick was far-flung wanderings, and of course he had trotted the globe. He launched on a long-winded anecdote about sacrificing a black goat to Kali in an Indian temple, but I cut this short by moving on to the next prerequisite: a revelation and/or holy book. He claimed *The Book of the Law* had been dictated to him by a preternatural entity in Cairo in 1904. He grabbed a copy from the bookshelf and was on the point of reciting the whole thing, but I put a stop to this by barking out the next yardstick: a contest with a rival magician. He replied there was nobody in the present age of sufficient magical standing to oppose him. That went without saying. How silly of me to have asked! Undaunted, I pressed him further. He muttered something about 'agents of the black lodge', but as they were invariably 'dipsomaniacs or perverts' all such attacks had failed. It was of course premature to ask about the final defining acts in a magician's life - a poignant and dramatic send-off; a violent or mysterious death; a resurrection and/or ascension - though I'm sure he could have come up with the goods in spades.

'Why magic?' The scorn of colleagues had alerted me to how out of kilter its study, let alone its practice, is in our so-called modern world.

'It put me in a blue funk when I realised what death really meant. Nothing...the void...emptiness! Was it just for that we were put on Earth? I searched for the Elixir of Life and even dabbled in black magic. After that I never strayed from the path of goodness as chosen prophet of a new religion.'

This was his cue to reach across and pluck another book from the shelf. 'I am the flame that burns in every heart of man, and in the core of every star,' he read. Despite my revulsion, I could not doubt his sincerity. Tears were streaming down his cheeks. 'It was a revelation of love,' he murmured.

He seemed shattered after this. Going by his edgy glances at the medical clutter on the bedside table, I felt sure he required another shot. Fearful of witnessing the abominable mechanics of his solitary vice, I made a hasty getaway and went down to dinner carrying a pamphlet he had given me. It was a printed list of his enemies, along with prophecies of the terrible fates in store for them. He had begun to compile it 20 years before. Scrawled in his spiderish handwriting, annotations in the margins detailed the actual date and manner of passing of several of them. This was indeed significant. The eighteenth-century magician Cagliostro had compiled an identical list. I told the Beast as much when he joined me.

'I was Count Cagliostro in a former life,' he enlightened me and embarked on an exhaustive list of his previous incarnations that included a female Greek temple dancer, Doctor Dee's crystal-gazer Edward Kelley, and the French magician and priest Eliphas Levi. He concluded with an account of his running into Merlin on a Clapham omnibus.

I was exhausted by now. Fortunately, there were only a few flakes of falling snow. Wrapped in a black cloak with a black cat lapping at his heels, he escorted me to my guesthouse. As he bade me goodnight, he looked at me gravely. I remembered he had been considered handsome in his youth. 'Magic is not *a* way of life,' he murmured, 'it is *the* way of life.'

I rose bright and early the following morning with the firm intention of avoiding him, as I still had to go to Netherwood and settle for my food and beverages. Imagine my dismay when Mr Symonds informed me the Beast had paid for everything! Seeing my discomfort, he added that I shouldn't feel too bad as the old devil was funded by "admirers". Even the fine old cognac hadn't cost him a sou.

The weather was much calmer. When I went back outside, the red-haired boy was crossing the driveway bearing a pile of kindling. Sighting me, he set it down, ran over and held the taxi door open. How sweet, I thought, more resolved than ever to release him from sexual servitude and the ghastly clutches of the despicable Beast. I said, 'Why thank you awfully, Jo-Jo-Josephine!'

Chapter Ten
The Devil and Doctor Fast

April 1946

During the war, the military had requisitioned Hastings Pier, cutting out two sections to prevent it being used as a landing stage for the enemy. On the shoreline next to White Rock Gardens, two huge storage tanks gravity fed oil to a pipeline laid under the pier. This enabled small naval vessels to refuel alongside, but also, in the event of invasion, would allow oil to be discharged over the surface of the water and set alight — a line of defence hidden from the locals.

The pier theatre had reopened on 8 June 1945. The two productions so far, a J.B. Priestley play and an adaptation of *Little Women*, had received a lukewarm response, with the theatre rarely more than half full. This was a new experience for the Court Players. Despite shoddy sets that sometimes collapsed and a soiled red chintz cloth that served as a tablecloth in one play and a curtain in the next, pre-war productions had invariably sold out. 1946 was too hand-to-mouth for such enthusiasm. No longer could dance bands like "Allan Green" attract a thousand dancers nightly. A lot was hanging on the Court Players' third play of the season, *The Devil and Doctor Fast*, and not just Maria's attributes.

It was a blustery day with the mercury never rising above 45 degrees Fahrenheit. Except for a diaphanous robe and silver stilettos, Maria was naked, her fulsome breasts and trim belly an object of veneration for actors and stagehands alike. The latter comprised Will and Roger, a gangling man with bulging eyes who had recently been released from a lunatic asylum, a stint in the theatre being considered good for his rehabilitation. Maria had goose bumps all over. She shivered then sneezed.

'Do that again and they'll close us down!' came a frenzied bark from the stalls. The speaker was the director overseeing the rehearsal,

Will's father Robert, a thickset man with a flowing salt-and-pepper beard.

'I just can't keep still for this long,' Maria snapped back. 'I'm not made of blooming wood.'

'I told you this wouldn't work!' Robert turned and glared at his expert adviser: Crow, who was sprawled behind him in the second row. It had been the Beast's idea to have Maria represent Helen of Troy in the Court Players' modern take on Marlowe's *Doctor Faustus*. The gruesome paintings lining the set's backdrop, with their malevolent imps and lost souls, were a further contribution from the generous-hearted mage.

'Talking of wood, couldn't we use a ship's figurehead instead?' continued the director. 'There's one in the props department.'

'Then your production would be completely wooden,' objected Crow.

'I thought you were our consultant on all things hocus pocus, not the set designer!'

'Belittle magick at your peril or it will belittle you!'

'Are you threatening to turn me into a toad?'

'How can I perform an operation that has already been accomplished? I have the gravest fears for your future in the zoo infirmary.'

'Gentlemen, this bickering is not progressing matters.' Vernon Symonds stepped out of the wings. He was wearing a lab coat, with a stethoscope hooped around his neck. The director had decided to make the protagonist a medical doctor rather than the alchemist of the original, despite Crow's protestations that he was on first name terms with several current practitioners. 'Crow has a point: Maria's presence can only enhance the production.'

There was a murmur of agreement from the crew.

'As long as she keeps perfectly still.'

'How do you expect that when it's so bleeding cold.'

'Language, Maria! The weather can't stay like this much longer. It's spring.'

'Yes it bloody well can. It's England!'

'Kindly don't answer back. You can go and get dressed. Vernon, your cue!'

'Right, I've seen the face that launched a thousand ships so what other marvels can you show me, Mephisto?'

This was addressed to a beanpole of an actor in an ill-fitting black suit and fedora. He had a mournful face.

'What wilt thou?' he responded in a sepulchral voice.

'Cut out the archaisms!' from the director.

'Nothing wrong with those,' muttered Crow.

'What would you like to see?'

'Hell.'

'You only need to look around you. The boundaries of hell are infinite except where heaven is. I have gazed on the face of God, which is lost to me evermore. Where I am is hell.'

'There's no mistaking you are a sombre fellow. Have you nothing more cheerful to tell me?'

'I am here to do your bidding, Doctor Fast, but must warn you to back off while you still have time!'

'Bah, why should I when I can have paradise now?'

'You will have all eternity to regret it.'

'Does your master know you're such a reluctant salesman? Summon Alexander the Great! I've always wanted to see that formidable conqueror.'

'By great Lucifer, Satan and Beelze-'

'No! No! No! You'd never use the names of the big chiefs at this point,' interrupted Crow. 'You invoke step by step, going gradually up the infernal chain of command. At the current juncture you should summon Samael, Asmodeus, and Belial.'

The actor did so, adding, 'I invoke thee.'

' "You" not "thee",' snapped the director.

'You're addressing the princes of hell not a crew of removal men,' said Crow. 'You cannot possibly conjure spirits without "thee" and "thou". It's disrespectful.'

'Do you think the audience will give a fig? We don't want to drive them away by being old-fashioned.'

Having employed more modern pronouns to complete his invocation, Mephisto raised a bowl from a table sited centre stage, inserted his hand and began sprinkling drops of dark liquid around the stage.

'What's that?' demanded Crow.

'Ribena.'

'Blackcurrant squash! Nothing less than the blood of a freshly slaughtered ox will do at this point. You'll never raise any spirits like that, let alone the audiences. Not even at the matinee!'

* * *

On opening night, the cast were gratified to see more than two-thirds of the seats occupied. There were appreciative "oohs" and "aahs" as devils and imps pranced across the stage. Maria, in all her semi-naked glory, was greeted by a communal intake of breath and the titters of a group of sixth formers from the local grammar school brought along by their well-meaning English mistress, now trying to hide her blushes. Vernon, who regularly fortified himself with shots of rum backstage, only needed the prompter twice. Right up to the last act he seemed to be making a go of things. The critic from the *Hastings and St Leonards Observer* was rehearsing "enthralling" and "tour de force" for his review.

At the climax, remorse so overwhelmed Doctor Fast, now wearing a white wig to signal the dire consequences of his truck with demons, that the stage directions indicated he should pluck his eyes out, a straight steal from Donald Wolfit's *Oedipus Rex*, which the director had caught at a wartime matinee in Drury Lane.

'Get behind me Satan!' he cried. 'I will never gaze upon your works or see the shape of hell.'

He raised the bowl from the table, now brimming with ox's blood, splashed the contents over his face, ran into the wings and grabbed the first thing that came to hand. This happened to be the stagehand working with Will. 'My eyes! My eyes!' shrieked Vernon. Roger screamed back at him, ran onto the stage, and leapt with flailing arms into the stalls. Pandemonium rippled along the rows giving way to thundering applause. "The avant-garde is alive and well on the pier. Hastings is the new Left Bank," the critic furiously scribbled.

After the audience and most of the cast had left, Will escorted Maria out of the theatre. Spring had turned balmy. Wispy cloud hardly veiled the winking stars. A man with a Ronald Colman moustache and a flashy tie was loitering outside the art-deco foyer. It was unusual to see anything other than demob suits, so Will was impressed by his smart navy-blue blazer and paisley pocket square. He produced a red box of Du Maurier which he opened and thrust at Maria. She giggled and saucily extracted two cigarettes, one of which she pressed on Will. The man leaned forward and lit hers with a silver Zippo he had won at poker from a GI.

'You was ravishin',' he said.

'But I didn't do anything. It wasn't real acting.'

'You didn't need to.' He handed her a card. 'Gimme a ring! You're a dead cert for the big time.'

Will and Maria sauntered on, past the abandoned American bowling range then through the pier's entrance, with its still disused tollgate, closed café and arcade, over which the neon strip lightning was now switched off.

'Aren't you man enough to smoke?' teased Maria, passing Will her cigarette. He pressed the smouldering tip against the end of his, inhaled and coughed his lungs up, much to her amusement.

She went up to London on her free day. She came back sporting a new pink beret and lipstick that came from Paris. She seemed sullen yet excited. Johnnie told Will she had handed in her notice. She was going to be a West End actress. "Soho more like", he heard Vernon mutter. She invited Will to her room the night before she was leaving. He found her prone on the bed with her back to him, just like the first time. One stocking was laddered and she was not wearing knickers. Under the suspender belt, the top of her rump merged into a single line.

Chapter Eleven
Symonds & Gleadow

Friday, 3 May 1946

'I'm not going to say a word about how I got wind of him. He would accuse me of being in league with the enemy.'

The speaker was a thirty-three-year-old man with long oily hair, an aquiline nose, and a strident expression. He was sitting in a dowdy compartment of the nine twenty-seven to Hastings. It was a sunny day, but the window was shut against the brisk wind blowing in steam from the soot-blackened locomotive. His companion was a few years older, with dark good looks that were starting to fade. His angular face jutted forward thoughtfully.

'How so?'

'Do you remember those digs I had in Swiss Cottage?'

'With that bluestocking landlady?'

'God was she peculiar! Had the hots for D.H. Lawrence but a total frump and stickler for convention! No girls brought back to the room in her lodgings! All the more surprising to find books on magic on her shelves. Turns out she was the widow of Victor Neuburg.'

'Have to help me with that one.'

'Poet, fairly minor, verse editor of *The Sunday Referee*. First person to get Dylan into print. He was also our sorcerer's apprentice. They got up to all sorts of magical hanky-panky in Paris and the Algerian desert.'

'You don't say!'

'Then they fell out big time. Just like everyone seems to do with he they call the Beast. When I told the landlady I wanted to commission Crowley to write a piece for *Lilliput,* she warned me off. Said it had taken ten years for Neuburg to shake off the curse.'

'Which was?'

'Crowley turned him into a camel, apparently. Of course, I ignored her, especially after a mutual friend told me I should look up the Beast. Said he'll die soon, and I'd lose my chance. Offered to have him sent up to London for me, as if he were a fine old vase.'

'Instead, the mountain's going to Mohammed.'

Beneath a poster of Norman knights, they hailed a taxi that took them up to the Ridge. The ivy-festooned walls of Netherwood emerged between the trees. Despite the gaily painted swings and see-saw in the play area by the lawn tennis court, the Beast's lair seemed sombre and brooding, an impression inspired more by Crowley's reputation than the place itself. They were admitted by Nancy, a chirpy local who had replaced Maria and made up in character what she lacked in looks.

'Said for you to wait in the lounge. He's probably brewin' potions in his den. Sure do smell like it!'

A series of hunting scenes, portraying scarlet-coated horse-riding foxes bearing down on desperate looking men, amused the visitors as they waited in the lounge. The stairs creaked as feeble steps haltingly descended. Remembering that Crow had scaled several mountains in the Himalayas, this saddened Symonds. A wizened man stood framed in the doorway. A frayed plus four suit hung from his skeletal frame like a rag on a scarecrow. He had a goatee beard and tufts of white hair bristling from his otherwise bald scalp. He fixed them with a stare. What is he so startled by, wondered Symonds? That he is going to die? The Beast trotted out his ritual greeting in a quavering voice.

'How do you do? I'm John Symonds, editor of *Lilliput* magazine. This is my friend Rupert Gleadow.'

'I seem to recall hearing that name before. What was your war work?'

'Oh, you know, stuff for the ministry.' Gleadow was vague.

'Knight's black angels?'

Gleadow wondered if the gaffe was intentional. 'Same mob, different department, but I've met Major Knight on a couple of occasions. I'm demobbed now. Up to my old tricks as a lawyer.'

'I hope I will not be requiring your services. You could say I'm demobbed myself. I certainly played my part for the nation.'

'Rupert's hiding his light as usual. He's also an astrologer. Wrote a marvellous book on magic and divination. That's probably how you know of him.'

Having risen at the Beast's entrance, they resumed possession of an armchair each, while Crow lowered himself shakily onto the sofa.

'I believe there's less than one per cent of truth in astrology!' The Beast savoured the shock his opener had caused. Given that Gleadow had come to pay homage, Symonds found this a bit tactless.

'There's a bit more to it than that,' said Gleadow. 'Ever heard of Krafft?'

'Hitler's celebrated astrologer?'

'According to the press, but he probably never met the Führer.'

'My, you are well informed.'

'Krafft predicted the assassination attempt in '39.'

'As well as the attack on Russia.'

Gleadow looked surprised. 'I didn't know that.'

'Mum always seems to be the word. Perhaps I was a little harsh. I do the occasional horror for the guests here.'

'Horoscope?'

'If you met them, you'd agree I have used the appropriate term.'

Crow had a large gold brooch of the ibis-headed god of wisdom Thoth pinned to his tie. An immense gold ring hooped the third finger of his right hand. Gleadow leaned forward and peered at the hiero-glyphics engraved on it.

' "His life is in Khonsu",' he translated. 'That's the moon god of Thebes, isn't it?'

'You are erudite as well as accurate. Ankh-f-n-khonsu was a high priest of the twenty-sixth dynasty in ancient Egypt. My first incarnation.'

It struck Symonds that Crowley's preoccupations were very different from the common run of men.

'I read Egyptology at Cambridge,' said Gleadow. 'Trinity man like yourself.'

This elicited a complicit nod from the Beast.

'Pity that magic's had its day,' sighed Symonds. 'It's all atom bombs, Tupperware and rockets now.'

'That's just the window of appearances. Science and magick will unify again. What if I told you that the head of my Californian Lodge is a leading rocket scientist? By my current reckoning, magick will leap out of the shadows in the mid-1960s. I won't be around, of course.'

'Come now! You'll make it to your nineties.'

This was more flattery than fact. The Beast seemed shrivelled, his eyes glassy, his cough perennial. Having invited them to stay for lunch, he bolted to his room for a restorative boiled egg and shot of heroin.

Printed on a card on their table, the house rules entertained the visitors during lunch. Afterwards, they decided to take a stroll in the grounds. Gleadow joked they might find one of the advertised bodies hanging from a tree. Instead, they ran into Vernon in the lobby. He was wearing a large, brimmed hat and a floppy bow tie. He told them he was off to London to sell a play. They asked the title. "Venus Iscariot," he tipsily informed them.

Despite fleeting clouds, the sun was doing its best to retain contact with the Earth. They came upon Will in patched overalls, attacking a hedge with a fearsome pair of shears.

'Are you the gentlemen who've come to see Crow...I mean Mr Crowley? He's not been well. Bad chest and problems with his teeth. He was very excited that you were visiting.'

'Which room is his?'

Will pointed to a bay window ringed by ivy behind which the Logos of the Aeon was taking a nap.

An hour or so later the two visitors found themselves in the same place. Crow had sent a message: he was feeling too poorly to join them downstairs. Wrapped in a voluminous padded dressing gown, he offered them brandy. It was very good and had cost a princely ten pounds according to its provider. They discussed the end of the world. The visitors were impressed by their host's encyclopaedic knowledge of the subject, though puzzled when he informed them that the planet had been destroyed by fire in 1904. Then the Beast reached into the pocket of his gown and produced two copies of *The Book of the Law*. Handing them each one, he shuffled to the bedside table and refilled his pipe from two round tins. One contained Latakia, the other Perique, ordered on as regular basis as his followers could fund from Dunhill's in Belgravia. Both were considered too strong to be smoked on their own. The Beast had resorted to the simple expedient of mixing them together.

'I believe you "received" the book you've kindly given us,' said Gleadow.

'It was dictated to me in Cairo.'

'Just like Yeats. He believed his wife was a channel for higher powers and incorporated her spirit writing into his work,' put in Symonds.

The Beast curled his lip. 'Not a comparison I would invite. My then wife lit the spark, but Aiwass stood behind my left shoulder and recited every word.'

'He was a spirit from ancient Egypt?'

'Authentically.'

'I've read your book,' continued Gleadow. 'Very 1890s, with a dash of Nietzsche that anticipates the Nazis.'

This animated Crowley. 'I made the same connection myself when I read *Hitler's Table Talk*. The Führer clearly plagiarised me after a follower sent him my work. I should have sued. Not that I had any truck with the Black Brothers, you understand.'

'Yeats believed Christianity was dying and the new age would be ruled by a savage god,' said Symonds.

'Isn't that being borne out even as we speak! Yeats was a dishevelled, sexually incontinent versifier who set up house with the fairies. I, on the other hand, am that rough Beast, my hour come at last, slouching towards Bethlehem to be born.'

His eyes held them with the embers of a gaze as blank and pitiless as the sun.

* * *

On the train back to Victoria the two visitors leafed through their booty.

'He's not a complete fraud,' said Gleadow, 'but he doesn't know half as much about astrology as he makes out.'

'Nor about magic. He struck me as a bit pathetic. I bet he never expected to end his days on his uppers in a seaside boarding house. Where are all the gold and riches? The spells didn't work!'

'What did he mean about playing his part for the nation?'

'He pulled the same stunt after the Great War. I'm sure the Service would run a mile from someone like him.'

Gleadow wasn't so sure. 'I met some rum types when I was in it. Hey, you might make your name if you befriended him. The gutter press can't get enough. His notoriety crosses borders. Lord Haw-Haw even broadcast he should hold a black mass for victory in Westminster Abbey. Mark my words, sex and brimstone sell.'

Little realising he was sealing a Faustian bargain with himself, Symonds' eyes glistened.

Chapter Twelve
The Comintern Couple

Monday 18 to Wednesday 20 November 1946

The burgundy Wolseley Eight saloon pulled into the drive on a foggy morning. Will looked up from the log he was sawing and admired the shield-shaped grille and round projecting lamps. The burly chauffeur got out and opened a rear door. A gamine creature swathed in furs alighted, followed by a man so cadaverous he almost vanished into the folds of his forest green loden coat. The girl glided up the front steps. At the top she turned and gazed at Will a moment longer than was necessary.

'Boy, 'elp!' The chauffeur had a gruff, heavily accented voice.

Will trampled across mud and gravel to the open boot. The chauffeur jerked his thumb at two costly-looking suitcases. Will lifted them out, carried them up the steps into the hall, and then along to reception, where Johnnie was registering the new arrivals. Close to, the girl had a pixyish face with a pert nose, luminous grey eyes, and silver hair tied back into a ponytail. Johnnie handed three light green passports back to the man. They were joined by the chauffeur. Will carried the luggage up to the only suite Netherwood possessed, which was on the second floor. A favourite of adulterers, and runaway couples en route to Gretna Green, the bedroom connected via a door to a drawing room with a sofa bed. Will set the luggage down. The skinny man fumbled in his pocket for a tip and then thought better of it. He had sunken cheeks, bad teeth and round brown glasses. Will disliked him immensely.

Back at reception, Johnnie seemed very pleased.

'Vernon's terribly excited,' she said. 'Our new guest's a famous Hungarian scientist called Professor Molnar. He's going to give a talk tomorrow night for the Brain's Trust.'

'He's with his daughter?'

'Wife.' Johnnie laughed. 'Her name's Gizi.'

* * *

The chauffeur was sorting the slides in the tray alongside the projector. Professor Molnar drew on a black Sobranie cocktail cigarette. The last of the audience took their places in the three semi-circular rows Vernon and Will had arranged in the lounge. Resplendent in a torn purple velvet smoking jacket, plus fours, frayed tartan stockings and buckled shoes, Crow lounged in the front row. He had become a regular at Vernon's talks and had even given one himself just before Christmas 1945. "Magick is the art and science of causing change to occur in conformity with Will," he had begun, going on to make the occult sound far more matter of fact than the audience, including Will, expected.

'We'll have to find Will another Scarlet Woman now that Maria's gone.'

The term puzzled Vernon, who was sitting next to him. 'What is the nature of such a beast?'

'Loud, adulterous, shameless before all men.' Crow rolled the adjectives on his tongue like boiled sweets. 'Maria was a tad too prim and proper to fit the bill. There was a melancholy about her that would have touched the heartstrings of lesser men.'

'You're forgetting Will's vocation.'

'A ludicrous promise he made with himself when he was twelve! Do you really think he's going to keep to that now that the juices are flowing? The New Aeon's not going to be easy. Hitler was just a harbinger of the horrors to come. But bliss will it be in that dawn to be alive, and to be young will be very heaven. Wine, strange drugs, women, song. Excess in everything!'

'But will it lead to the palaces of wisdom? Not sure that's Will's bag.'

'Well, he can suit himself. He's barking up the Tree of Death if he wishes to manacle himself to a slave god.'

Vernon rose and made his way to the front to introduce the professor. Molnar, a respected colleague of Einstein and David Bohm, was about to generously share the latest developments in quantum physics and reveal the quirks of subatomic particles. Some of these were so bizarre they rivalled the otherworldly insights of a previous talk given by a Netherwood resident. Crow, penetrator-of-the-mysteries, basked in this salute and nodded to his admirers. The professor spoke with little accent but had the rasp of a heavy smoker.

'What I am about to explain is very difficult to grasp. You will say it defies logic and you will be right. But by a process of elimination, it is all we have left to explain how the universe comports itself on a microscopic level. I must also stress we are probably on the threshold of even more bizarre and earth-shaking discoveries.'

He nodded to the chauffeur, who strode across the room and positioned himself next to the door. With his shaven head, pitted cheeks, and ruthless eyes Farkas was the double of the Beast in his heyday.

'I want you to imagine that my chauffeur and I are one and the same. "Impossible," you object, "he is standing several metres from you." Yet in the sub-atomic world, two particles can be separate yet intricately linked simultaneously. Measurements made at widely separated locations can be correlated in ways that suggest the outcome of an event involving one determines the fate of the other.'

'As above, so below,' barked Crow.

'I beg your pardon?'

'As usual, science has stumbled on a basic tenet of magick and is now giving itself a hearty slap on the back. Congratulations on having rediscovered the secret of the ages.'

'I really do not follow you.'

'The Doctrine of Correspondences is the basis of sympathetic magic. Everything is connected. There is nothing new in what you are saying. You are standing on the shoulders of giants. Watch you don't fall off!'

'Crow, it's an honour to have the Professor with us today,' hissed Vernon.

The Beast raised his digit finger to his lips in the sign of Harpocrates, the Greek god of silence.

Farkas switched on the projector. The first slide showed spinning atoms linked by arrowed lines. Molnar explained that these atoms were waves and particles simultaneously. The most extraordinary thing was this seemed to wholly depend on whether they were observed or not. No fixed conclusion could be determined about them, only probabilities. Crow nodded vehemently. Such subjectivity was a key element of ceremonial magic.

Will sneaked a glance at Gizi. She was sitting further along the second row wearing a beige jacket with rounded shoulders and a swirling black skirt. It was the New Look, recently imported from Paris, currently provoking indignation in press and parliament, as it required forty metres of material as well as new corsets, in defiance of the austere tempo of the times. He could see she was bored.

After the talk, Will sat down to dinner with the Symonds, Crow, the professor, and his wife. Farkas intimidated Miss Clarke and other staff, eating in the old dining room beside the kitchen. The Symonds' farm supplied the ham and peas for the soup, as well as the pork that followed. Crow ate sparingly, using his fork to flatten the food into a mush that his new, ill-fitting dentures could just about cope with.

The diners were more fortunate than the rest of the country. Dire economic straits had imposed peacetime rationing even more Spartan than that during wartime. Netherwood could not escape such hardship entirely, however. Convinced that all foreigners required bread with their meals, Vernon was doing his best to slice a loaf that was hardly bigger than a bun, new regulations obliging bakers to drastically reduce the size of their creations.

'I mean what was the bloody war for? No money about! People practically starving!'

Johnnie rested her hand on her husband's arm. Vernon always seemed furious these days, a fact not unconnected with the Pernod, Calvados, and whisky he downed daily, starting usually before breakfast.

'We stopped Adolf and the Hun,' objected Crow, always eager to flash his credentials as a patriot. Realising this might offend the Hungarians, he did something quite out of character. 'I mean the Black Brothers.'

'And what did we damned well do that for? Just to take a bash at Stalin? That will be next, you mark my words. With the new weapons in the pipeline, it will be fiendish — the end of days!'

'I thought you would be happy, Vernon. Aren't we on the threshold of your socialist new Jerusalem?'

'I suppose you wish Winston was still in charge.'

'He did a lot more in the war than people realise.'

'Labour's going the right way about it with nationalisations and the welfare state, but their hands are tied. Ever since the blasted Yanks tore up the Lend-Lease agreement and left us on our uppers!'

'Every day in Hungary you have to add another 15 noughts to the forint,' said Molnar dolefully. 'People line their homes with banknotes. It's cheaper than wallpaper.'

'I read in *The Manchester Guardian* that the Russians have confiscated your gold reserves and transported whole factories to the USSR,' said Vernon. 'You're being forced to pay huge sums in war reparations.'

'Because you sided with Adolf and attacked Russia.'

'Crow!' hissed Johnnie.

'We did not have a moat like the Channel to protect us. You had your Blackshirts; we had the Arrow Cross.'

'Who've just switched uniforms and are now torturing anti-Communists instead of Jews and gypsies,' said Vernon. 'What sort of topsy-turvy world have we created?'

'One that has shattered like a globe of glass. Now we must pick up the pieces,' said Molnar.

'What was the bloody point of it all? There are millions of refugees throughout Europe. Whole nations have been uprooted and dispersed, leaving wastelands behind them,' sobbed Vernon. 'Meanwhile, conditions here are worse than in wartime. Don't get me wrong! I can accept our pitiful rations if I know it's helping Germany not starve.'

'*Parturient montes, nascetur ridiculus mus,*' declaimed Crow. 'Will, if you please.'

'The mountains are... in labour. A...ridiculous mouse will be born?'

Crow looked crestfallen. ' "You move mountains but give birth to mice". Much is promised at the outset, but little yielded at the end — an apt description of Atlee's government and our post-war world.' Crow leered at Gizi. 'Will is my protégé. I am teaching him Latin.'

'Whatever for he needs it?' Her voice was alluringly husky.

'He wants to be a priest of course. What youth, endowed with a robust constitution and fine athletic limbs, wouldn't?'

'In my country priest likes boys.'

Nobody seemed shocked.

'Will is not of that persuasion,' said Crow. 'Like the rest of his generation he is exceedingly dull and unadventurous.'

Gizi yawned.

'You have put it in a nutshell, dear girl.'

'You have classroom?'

'Yes, indeed, my quarters: Room 13. Do drop in if you're in the vicinity!'

After pudding, they broke open a bottle of Crow's cognac. When that was finished, Molnar produced a bottle of Tokaji.

'My word,' said Crow, 'last time I had this was at the Hungaria, a wonderful restaurant on Lower Regent Street.'

Vernon made a toast to world peace and the fledgling United Nations. The sweetness of the wine camouflaged its strength. Will's head was already woozy as the conversation took a metaphysical turn. The voices seemed to be coming from far away. Crow's notoriety must have preceded him, for the Professor challenged him to describe the devil. It was an impertinent question, but nobody seemed to care. They were all drunk.

'He resembles neither a particle nor a wave and is quite possibly just a probability.' The Beast smiled as though humouring a child. 'It all depends, my dear Professor, on the eye of the beholder.'

'So, everything you have experienced in your rites is subjective?'

'Just as in your experiments if I have understood you correctly. I might say the devil looks a lot like your chauffeur, or Hitler, or Stalin for that matter. Magick is something we do to ourselves. It is just convenient to assume an objective existence for a supernatural power we have raised within.'

'Then the demons ranked in their hierarchy before the Gates of Hell are all imaginary,' blurted out Will, surprising himself and everybody else.

'Just like the angels shielding heaven. "Push imagination to the point of vision, and the trick is done," as Saint William Blake of Soho put it.'

'You have confessed: your Magick is a fraud!' Molnar sounded pleased with himself.

'No more than the whirling atoms that only exist because you're imagining them, that mysteriously change form when you're not there, as you conjecture.'

Will had the strangest sensation he was hovering on the ceiling looking down. Like a wizened Mandarin, Crow was ramming home a point, his translucent yellow fingers jabbing at the sallow faced professor. Crucified by drink, Vernon was crucifying Johnnie in the process. And then there was Gizi...

* * *

A massed band of drummers was pounding away in his head. He was naked under a sheet, with the eiderdown pushed back, in a room he failed to recognise. There was blue stucco wallpaper, an art-deco wardrobe, a Persian rug and ottoman couch. Outside it was snowing. His mouth was so parched he feared his cheeks would crack if he parted his lips. There must be water somewhere. He raised himself with difficulty, swung his legs onto the floor and stood up. When his head stopped spinning, he made out the room had three doors. He approached the nearest and turned the knob.

Gizi was stretched out in an empty bathtub. Apart from a string of pearls and a pair of black boots, she was naked. Her breasts were small, with a purplish blush circling each chill-hardened nipple. The hair tangled in a V beneath her belly was darker than that of her sleeping head. He went to the washbasin and turned on the tap. Icy water gushed out. He cupped his hands and transferred some to his mouth. The noise woke her. She murmured something in her own language.

'You can't be comfortable like that,' he said.

She honked like a pig, jabbing her finger in his direction.

'You mean I snore?'

He'd never had the opportunity to find out before. What other discoveries had they made about each other? Everything after dinner was a blank.

'I'm sorry, I had far too much to drink.'

She seemed to find this funny. 'In my country man never sorry for drink. You are strange people. Help please!'

She was shivering and had goose bumps. He went round to the other side of the bath and cupped his hands under her unshaven armpits. Though she was relatively light, it took a lot of effort to lift her out. The New Look had not lied. She really had an hourglass figure, with a tiny waist, broad hips and a perfectly curved behind. She sprinted into the bedroom, leapt into bed, and pulled the eiderdown over her. He followed. She raised the corner of the covering and beckoned him to join her.

'Your husband?'

'How you say? Marriage in convenience.'

Will smiled. That sounded about right. 'Where is he?'

'Hustings.'

'And Farkas?'

'Shush, scary man. Name mean wolf.'

He slid in beside her. His body was warmer than hers as she snuggled up. She placed her digit finger against his mouth and traced the shape of his lips. She began to moan, surprising him because though he was still a novice in the game, he understood that not enough had transpired to excite such transports. Her panting grew so loud it sparked anxiety not desire. He tried to calculate the time, wondering who might be about, fearful of discovery. The connecting door swung open. Farkas was standing there, his face bent over a box camera, preparing to take a snap of Will's stricken face.

'Smile, yes please,' he said, displaying an unexpected bent for humour.

* * *

'It is such a simple thing,' murmured Molnar, 'hardly requiring any effort at all.'

Fully dressed once more, Will was sitting nervously on the edge of the bed. From the vantage of a stiff-backed chair, the professor faced him, an inevitable Sobranie wedged between his nicotine-stained fingers. Gizi sat cross-legged on the couch in her dressing gown. Farkas was leaning against the wall beside the connecting door, sphinx-like, his arms folded.

'You see, Will, we are being totally transparent. We want you to help us of your own free will,' the professor inhaled lustily and continued. 'Your teacher has a friend, a spymaster who has a habit of hiding documents in places nobody expects to find them. We think there is one we want very much in Mr Beast's room.'

'You are socialist?' said Gizi.

'Yes, Will, the wave of the future is on the march here as it is in our homeland. Will you not join us in the battle against the kings and capitalists who oppress the people?'

'Christ overturned the tables of the merchants in the temple. He said it was more difficult for a rich man to enter the kingdom of heaven than for a camel to go through the eye of a needle.'

'Bravo! That's why you must get the file for us.'

'I'm not a thief.'

'Nobody's talking about stealing. We borrow the file, make a copy, and return it. Your Mr Beast will never know. You have access to his room. Surely, he sometimes leaves you on your own. It is such a small thing to ask. Then we can destroy that regrettable photograph which could prevent you pursuing your calling.'

'Last night…?'

'Farkas and I carried you up the stairs and heaved you into bed. You slept like a baby.'

Gizi emitted a snore just to rub it in. He had never felt such misery.

Chapter Thirteen
Latin Lesson

Tuesday, 26 November 1946

Crow was at his desk, heaping so many tablespoons of sugar into his tea Will wondered why he didn't just upturn the bowl and swamp the cup with its contents. The Beast had a very sweet tooth which necessitated frequent visits to the dentist. At his behest, Will sometimes pilfered extra sugar from the larder in defiance of rationing. His reward was chocolate creams, barley sugar and walnut whips that regularly arrived in parcels from admirers. The wizened mage had received a letter along with one of them. Sipping tea, he flourished it before his pupil, who supposed it to be an extract from the bard's latest work.

'Now the imbeciles are intent on making a homunculus!'

Will was stumped. Whatever did this strange word mean? Had it been set for homework?

Crow explained. 'A child, magically created without the intercession of the male. Your Jesus was one. I wrote a book about it.'

Crow shakily rose and, going to a book tower, began peering down the titles. What he was looking for was in the second stack, fortunately near the top. He slid it out, came back and handed it to Will. Sharply rendered in feathery blue and yellow lines, the jacket bore the face of a woman with heavy-lidded eyes. A pouting child was silhouetted beside her. *Moonchild* was the title. Will was more certain than ever he was dealing with a writer whose fictions had spilled over into his waking mode. The response to his next question only served to confirm this.

'Who's trying to create this magical child?'

'Jack Parsons. He's exceedingly wild and impetuous even for my tastes. I mean just take this poem.' Crow picked up and brandished the letter again. 'He lives on "peyote, marijuana, morphine, cocaine, and exults in a madness that burns at the heart and the brain". I used to come out with ravings like that but was never that far gone. No wonder he's under investigation by the FBI and the Los Angeles Police Department! Then there's Lafayette Ron Hubbard, his new partner in magick: a science fiction writer, with little science and tons of fiction.'

It had struck Will before that "Parsons" might be a sly dig at his vocation, but the other name was so preposterous it was obviously invented. Did Crow dream up his fantasies in advance or make them up as he went along? He fished for an answer.

'Events in California are a sequel to *Moonchild*?'

'You don't need to be Sherlock Holmes to deduce it's all inspired by my book.'

'Why do they want to create a moonchild?'

Crow looked at him in feigned horror. 'You're asking me when you're hell bent on sacrificing the rest of your life to one — all that zest and passion flushed down the drain for Jesus! The moonchild's name is Babalon. He or she, for we mustn't pre-judge matters, will speed up the coming of the Aeon. But you can't accelerate things like that. It won't be for another twenty years or so that the big changes kick in. I don't suppose I'll be around — not in my present incarnation. But you will.'

'How do you make a moonchild?'

'The formula's in here,' Crow tapped the book. 'Elixirs, athanor, fluids etcetera. And you need a Scarlet Woman of course.'

That word again. Something told Will one might be found where the streetwalkers loitered outside the seedy hotels near the station.

'Sounds very Dennis Wheatley,' he said.

'Ungrateful man. Came to study under me. Ransacked my best ideas. Made a fortune. Not a shred of thanks. I haven't yet put him on the list of the accursed, but I've a good mind to.'

'So how will it end?'

Crow shrugged: 'Nothing good will come of it. Parsons is fixated on poltergeists, floating orbs, disembodied voices. There are banshees screaming outside the Lodge windows every night. Maybe Hubbard is at the root of it. He's already stolen Jack's girlfriend, that diabolical hellcat Betty.'

'Doesn't Jack mind?

'He's a Thelemite. We take things like that in our stride. Though if it were me, I'd be doing the stealing. I may burst a blood vessel when I contemplate the idiocy of those goats. Just as well Watson is taking me to a matinee at the local fleapit, followed by a trip to the chess club. Just the tonic I need!'

Herbert Frank Watson was the owner of the Ridge Stores in Saint Helen's. To general bewilderment, he had taken a shine to the King of Depravity, for whom he ran errands and arranged deliveries of heroin from Heppell & Co., the London chemist.

'What's the movie?'

'Bah, I loathe Americanisms outside of America. The film is called *The Wizard of Oz*. It seems Hollywood has finally cottoned on to me.'

In 1941 the Beast had published *Liber Oz*, a single-paged Thelemic bill of rights which, among other things, advocated killing those that thwarted the right to Do What You Will. Johnnie had tried to explain it was a kid's film, but Crow was having none of it: the coincidence was too compelling.

'No class today?' said Will brightly.

'Don't think you can get out of it so easily! What can compete with the sublime musings of the Romans?'

A rhyme often repeated by his long-suffering classmates popped into Will's head: *'Latin is a language, as dead as dead can be, it killed the ancient Romans, and now it's killing me.'*

'What utter bilge! The classics are the noblest known way of training the mind. I have prepared a sublime nugget for you to render.'

A slim volume lay open on the table. Alongside were blank sheets of paper, a Swan fountain pen and a massive Collin's dictionary. After the Beast had gone downstairs, Will examined the book. It was a collection of epigrams by the poet Martial, open at IX.67. There were only eight lines. He hoped to make short work of it.

Lascivam tota possedi nocte puellam, it began.

The first word was new to him. He checked Collin's, which gave *lascivam* as 'playful, lustful, wanton'. This was not a great deal of help as he only recognised the first adjective. Something told him the other two were out of bounds for a fledgling priest. The rest of the line was more straightforward. He quickly scribbled: *I possessed this playful girl last night.* "Possessed" bothered him. *"Puellam"* could also be translated as "slave girl". Was the poet referring to taking ownership of her? Now for the second line.

Cuius nequetias vincere nulla potest.

This was easy: *A girl whose naughty tricks are unmatched.* Perhaps the slave girl knew some conjuring tricks?

The next line also presented few problems: *We did it a thousand different ways.* It dawned on him the "it" was what he was dying to do with Maria, but he quickly evicted the thought. There were five more lines, which initially stumped him. Not so much the words, though they required frequent checking, but their meaning.

Tired of the same old thing, I proposed she play the boy.
Before I finished speaking, she said Yes.
Made bolder, I then blushed a bit and laughed,
And asked for something even dirtier.
Without batting an eyelid, the lusty girl agreed.

Did the poet want the girl to dress up as a boy? Or was a "with" missing and there was a male child in the room who the man was urging her to play with? Did they get dirty when they played? In that case, why would the writer want her to get even dirtier?

His eyes strayed to the chest.

Who really was this relic of the 1890s wreathed in tobacco fumes and the arcane? 1946 was the dawn of a new epoch of jet engines, satellites, and atom bombs. Electronic signals bounced across the globe and would soon beam down from space. How could the modern age accommodate a magician? *In that chest is something that would merit the Victoria Cross if people only knew.* But people did know, and if he didn't get it for the Hungarians, he could kiss goodbye to the seminary.

He crossed over to the chest and raised the lid. On top was strewn a silver pentagram, phials of Abramelin oil, and a pack of rainbow-coloured Golden Dawn cards used to summon magical images. Will transferred all the paraphernalia to the floor and was left with three columns of books and papers. He slid a thick manuscript from the top of the left-hand pile: *The Confessions, an Autohagiography, Volume Four* stated the typewritten top sheet. Under this was a file. He tugged it out, replacing the manuscript as he did so. The cover was stamped TOP SECRET in red and beneath, OPERATION MISTLETOE. A photograph slipped out. It was grainy and taken at night in a forest glade ringed by searchlights. In full wizard's garb, Crow was plunging a dagger into an effigy in a German uniform with a swastika armband. Looking on were Major Knight, clad in purple and silver robes, a man in naval uniform with a crooked nose, and two SS prisoners of war, who, unbeknownst to Will, were on hand to leak news of the event back to Germany. Will slipped the photo back into the file, which he slid back into its place, and pulled the one under it out. It bore the puzzling title Molnar was blackmailing him to get. It would be several hours until Crow returned. Plenty of time to find out what all the fuss was about.

Chapter Fourteen
'The Z File'

Subject: Arrival of 666 at Camp Z
Location: Mytchett Place, Mytchett, Camberley, Surrey
Sources:
1. Transcript from hidden microphones
2. Debriefing of 666, 'M', Major Foley, Major Dicks

Visitors to Camp Z frequently arrived disguised as doctors, a convenient blind, as were the darkened windows of the ambulance navigating the newly diverted road. Through these 666 glimpsed the recently excavated slit trenches, machine gun positions, and heavily patrolled barbed-wire barricades. 'M' continued with the briefing.

'Z's' only other visitor so far was Lord Simon, the Lord Chancellor, on 9 June. 'Z' had met him before the war in Germany as the lord was a leading advocate of appeasement. Ostensibly, he came to Camp Z to negotiate. In fact, his brief was the same as yours: to get as much gen out of 'Z' as possible. 'Z' trotted out his peace terms, which you've read. Lord Simon informed 'Z' the proposals would be considered at the highest level. That's where you come in. What better follow up than a visit from the most powerful figure in the land?'

The country road gave way to a heavily fortified entrance. After checking the driver's pass, the guards raised the defensive gate. Jolted by gravel, the ambulance trundled through a second barbed wire barrier lined with electric spotlights and alarm bells. It followed the curving tarmac for 200 yards and pulled up outside a mansion of striped breeze block, with a three-storey tower protruding from it. The once stylish country house had been customised for war. Tape sealed the windows to prevent bombs splintering the glass. There was a sentry box at the entrance manned by a Scots Guards who scurried to the rear of the ambulance. Swinging open the doors, he was too highly trained to display surprise at the eminent visitor who stepped out.

June had been mostly cool and unsettled, but on the twenty-first the thermometer had climbed above 86 degrees. Today, Sunday the twenty-second, was set to be even hotter. 666 was wearing a pin-stripe cotton siren suit and a Panama hat. The one-piece suit was on loan from its designer, Winston Churchill. The hat had been sourced by 'M', himself in army uniform and going under the alias "Captain King". The front porch had two pink columns with black bases on either side. A waiting guard swung the oak door open. Two of 'Z's' "Companions" were wating to receive them. The foremost was a short, round-faced man, with grey hair and spectacles. Also in army uniform, he was in fact a major in MI6.

'Foley!' said 666.

'I was wondering if you'd remember me from the days when Germany was a civilised nation.'

While running the passport office in Berlin, a traditional cover for secret service personnel when overseas, Foley had also run Crowley, passing on to Broadway information sourced from the Beast's unwitting flatmate, an Irish republican and communist agent.

'Now I'm responsible for this uninvited guest. Helping with that is Doctor Dicks.'

Got up as an army physician, the doctor was an Estonian-born MI6 psychiatrist. He had a tensely drawn face and thin lips. He nodded brusquely at the newcomers.

'You'll find 'Z' trussed up like a turkey,' Foley went on. 'Threw himself over the bannisters in the early hours last Monday. Dicks, here, bore the brunt of it.'

There was a wisp of accent as the doctor said, ''Z' summoned me to his first-floor rooms claiming he couldn't sleep. His door suddenly opened, and he rushed out in full Luftwaffe uniform. Crazed look, staring eyes, dishevelled hair. I thought he was coming for me.

Instead, he swerved, leapt over the banister, and plunged down the staircase well.'

'If his fall hadn't been broken by the handrail, he would have landed just about there.' Foley indicated the floral star at the centre of the diamond-patterned tiles. 'The handrail probably saved his life.'

'A soldier climbing the stairs drew his revolver,' said Dicks. 'I had enough wits about me to order him not to shoot.'

'Thank the good Lord!' said Foley. 'Imagine if he'd died on my watch! 'Z' fractured his left thigh. Lucky he did not do more damage to himself! I came across his type quite often in Germany, you know faddish, neurotic, prone to every psychosomatic nerve and stomach ailment under the sun. Claims to be a teetotaller and vegetarian...'

'Yet he scoffs fish and veal and demands whisky or wine on occasion,' said Dicks.' He's one of the most difficult patients I've ever had the misfortune to treat. A bundle of contradictions. On Wednesday he told me that we Companions were in the grip of a Mexican drug and were not responsible for our actions. He could see it in our eyes. Other times he claims we're feeding him that or other substances.'

666 raised a satanically coiffured eyebrow. 'Perhaps he does have second sight.'

'That's your department,' said 'M'. 'He certainly believes in it.'

'Along with astrology, ghosts and all sorts of hocus-pocus,' added Dicks. 'He has many of the behavioural quirks of paranoid schizo-phrenia. A profile study of his forehead, chin and ear line indicates sub-normal intellect. However, when I performed Raven's Progres-sive Matrices Test, a standard army measure of intelligence, he filled in columns A to D without a single mistake, placing him in the top 10 per cent.'

'I think he's putting on an act,' said Foley. 'Just as well for us. If he really were mad, we'd have to send him back to Germany under the Geneva Convention. He longs for a quack with a pendulum, healing waters, and a diet of seaweed and loganberries. Peculiar race the Germans. They prize logic and reason, yet there's a dark underbelly hungering for the weird.'

'Which is exactly why you're here, 666,' laughed 'M'. 'How's our prize specimen today?'

Dicks looked down at the daily report. 'Slept fitfully. Heat doesn't agree with him. Awake and talking to his guard until 06.50 and then dozed until 07.30. Passed urine, 18 ounces, and slept slightly better until 09.25. Received a soap and water enema. Treatment to pressure points followed. Took a late breakfast at 09.55. Continually moans about the heat, which is aggravated by the 35 pounds of weight pulling at his broken leg from the Balkan frame. Can't concentrate on reading or writing but began a small drawing of his left foot which he quickly tired of. He has that faraway look in his eyes which usually means he's homesick. Says he'd like something to occupy his mind.'

'I'll soon give him that,' declared 666. 'Did you administer…?'

Foley smiled. 'Your magical elixir? He had it a few minutes ago with his herbal tea. We told him the powder in the capsule was atropine, which he's been demanding since his suicide attempt. He's highly suspicious of the food and drink we give him, by the way. Complains it's drugged or poisoned. He may have a point.'

The psychiatrist didn't notice Foley's wry glance, as he described how Hess squirrelled away samples of food wrapped in cotton wool, with the intention of having them analysed later.

'Here,' said Foley, handing 666 the thin file he was carrying. 'Bit of background. You can read it while waiting for your Mexican potion to work.'

Flight

Sources:

1. 'Z's' letters to his wife
2. Conversations with the guard (Lieutenant Malone)
3. Royal Observer Corps radar records for the night of 10 May 1941

The North Sea is glowing with evening light. Far below, a multitude of small clouds resemble shards of ice floating on the sea. The seascape is tinged red. Then the sky is swept clean, leaving not a trace of the dense carpet of cloud forecast by the weather report. No cover spells disaster! He considers turning back, but the images that haunt him day and night will not be stilled. He is squatting in a dug-out expecting to be crushed by an enemy tank. Shells hiss overhead, mines explode, there is the deadly rattle of machine guns. He straps his gas mask on and feels he is suffocating amid the cloud of mustard gas. He is frozen, hungry, and on the verge of madness. He hears the cries of the mortally wounded. Men, blinded by gas, stagger by. This cannot be allowed to happen again. Guided by the Wotan navigational beam, which will soon direct the Luftwaffe squadrons to their London targets, he flies on.

When he nears England, providence seems to be on his side again: mist veils the seascape. Less welcome is a Spitfire on his tail. With throttle full on, he dives into the mist and shakes off his pursuer. He crosses the East Coast a little below Holy Island. Escorted by three warships in line abreast, a convoy is steering between the Farne Islands and the shore. Just after sunset he swoops low over the little town of Bamburgh, flying barely higher than the rooftops. The plane is doing 750 kilometres an hour: a terrific speed. Visibility is good. He skims over trees, cattle, and houses, waving at people in the fields. It is exhilarating. The duke is bound to be impressed by his "hedge-hopping", as the English airmen call it.

He does not bother with a map. During months of feverish planning, he has memorised the entire route. He flies up the slope of one of the Cheviots, only a few yards above the ground. The mountain range is his lodestar, then the next appears: a little dam in a narrow range of hills. His route takes him left. He is above a country estate that just might be the Duke of Hamilton's. It is shrouded in darkness. To avoid all possibility of error, he flies on to the coast, crossing at West Kilbride. Lit by the rising moon, the Firth of Clyde is calm. A pale reddish rock juts out of the water. Turning south, he swings in again over Ardrossan, picking out the railway and small lake: two key landmarks. He passes over Dungavel again. The landing lights come on, marking out the runway alongside the Kennels. As he lines up for the descent, he glances in his rear-view mirror and is shocked to find a night fighter on his tail.

He pulls the joystick and ascends to a height of 2,000 metres. He switches off the engines. Propelled by red hot cylinders, the first engine goes on spinning and humming. Eventually, it gives out. He attempts to climb out of the cockpit but when he slides the cabin roof open, the air pressure glues him to the back of the seat. He did not foresee this. With no motors running, the plane will soon plummet out of the sky. How is he to escape? He remembers being told to turn the aircraft over and allow gravity to do the rest. He pulls the joystick again as if for a semi-loop. If he slides out even a little, the pressure will snap his neck and spine. Immense centrifugal forces drain the blood from his head. He is seeing stars. He will crash very soon. He blacks out, releasing the joystick.

The plane has now completed the bottom arc of the loop and is heading vertically upwards, losing speed as it climbs. Finally, it stalls and stands on its tail, allowing the blood to flow back into his head.

He comes to, finding the cockpit is now upside down. The pointer on the speed gauge stands at zero. He flings himself out, striking his right foot hard on the tail as he plunges down. The plane hurtles past him, on course to crash. He pulls at the ripcord and is jerked about like a puppet as the parachute unfurls. He sways in the air, enveloped by mist through which the full moon relays a thin reddish light. Hitting the ground makes him black out again. He comes to with no idea where he is or what he is doing. He feels like Adam when seeing the world for the first time.

Interview

Sources:

1. Transcript from hidden microphones
2. Debriefing of 666, 'M', Major Foley, Major Dicks

Heat was making the itchiness of 'Z's' plaster-encased leg unbearable. The prospect of another visitor did little to lighten his mood. His trusting nature made him seem slow-witted, but it had eventually dawned on him that the negotiation with Lord Simon had been a ruse to winkle out his secrets. Had he badly misjudged things? He had brought peace terms so reasonable they were guaranteed to spell Churchill's downfall. *The Times*, however, a luxury permitted him after the suicide attempt, informed him that fascist fellow-travellers in the Link, the BUF and Anglo-German Fellowship had been interned under Defence Regulation 18B. Aristocratic appeasers like Wellington and Londonderry were still at liberty but discredited. A nation purportedly reeling from the unstoppable Nazi advance was instead resolute and defiant. When driven to the Tower in an unmarked ambulance soon after capture, he had been amazed how little Blitz-related damage he had seen in the streets of North-East London.

It was very simple. He had not got to the right people. He had crossed the regimented flight zones of Germany at the correct altitude; he had roared over Holland and evaded a Spitfire and dived into the mist and hedge hopped, waving at farmers toiling in their twilight fields. If he had landed at the Kennels, he would not be lying trussed up like a sacrificial lamb waiting for the "Companions" to lead him to slaughter. The war in the west would by now be over. It was such might-have-beens that were driving him crazy with regret.

The elder Haushofer's dream was a marsh light. The glorious reception at Dungavel from a beaming prince, the interview with the king, gratefully accepting his peace terms and sacking Churchill with one stroke of his mighty pen, had never transpired. There would be no triumphant return, no basking in the acclaim of an adoring Folk. Nor would a doting Führer forgive his recklessness and plant the Maria Theresia on his chest, a medal given to soldiers justified in disobeying orders. It was these realisations that had launched him over the banister. He had failed in that as well. Yet hope was not entirely spent. Lord Simon had promised his peace terms would be relayed to a higher power. As though to confirm this, the door was unlocked and lieutenant Bill Malone, the most sympathetic of his guards, entered, followed by Winston Churchill.

'You have come at last,' gasped 'Z'.

This reassured 666 his disguise was working. 'We have been at cross purposes too long. It is time to settle this bloody business once and for all.'

666's imitation of the Prime Minister's measured growl was passable, though the nasal twang would have grated on a better listener. Malone exited. There were to be no witnesses. But in a secret room in the basement, ultra-sensitive amplifiers relayed everything the microphones hidden in the room picked up to majors 'M', Foley, and Dicks. Each word was engraved onto disc, while a Hungarian stenographer also transcribed them.

'Z' was stretched out on top of a single bed, his broken leg supported by the ropes, weights, and pulleys of the Balkan frame. Beads of sweat glistened on his shaggy eyebrows and streaked his cheeks. Despite the heat, he had insisted on wearing his blue Luftwaffe jacket, which made an incongruous pairing with his striped pyjama bottoms and bare feet. Much to 'Z's' dismay, Dicks had cut away his breeches to minister to his leg.

A fan whirred ineffectually on a small table beside the bed. The temperature kept rising. 666 lowered his bulk onto an armchair, glimpsing the living room through an interconnecting door. The sombre, poorly matched furniture was typical of the house. George V and Queen Mary had once spent the night and could not wait to get away.

It was coming up to an hour since 'Z' had ingested the capsule. Parke-Davis in Chicago, 666's original supplier, had ceased extracting mescaline from peyote in 1915. Prior to that, 666 had used the drug to spike audiences at the Rites of Eleusis in the Caxton Hall and on guests at parties in London and New York. With the extract no longer available, he had fallen back on slivers of flesh cut from the top of the peyote cactus where the mescaline was most concentrated. Such buttons could be ground up and compressed into capsules. They retained their potency for decades. The Mexican drug was the closest thing 666 had found to the transformational elixir lauded in grimoires of ceremonial magic. He also prized it for intelligence work. It lowered the subject's guard, making him or her susceptible and indiscreet.

The quantity was small and should make 'Z' no more than a little nauseous. In fact, his angular face wore a look of petulance. 'They are torturing me with noises. I am so weary. Motorbikes keep me awake at night.'

666 had been briefed about this. 'There is a military police motorcyclist's school adjacent.'

'I hear strange gusts that do not beat against the window nor shake the trees.'

'That's the wind tunnel at Farnborough Aerodrome. This is a military zone. You must accept that.'

It was a bit like talking to a deaf man. 'Z' did not seem to register the answers, which he must have already heard repeatedly from Foley, but immediately moved on to the next gripe.

'My food is poisoned. My throat is getting warm after the eating. I am excitable and happy. Later dark and sad.'

This confirmed 666's suspicion that Dicks was feeding 'Z' amphetamine, a very modish drug amongst the psychiatric fraternity.

But he said: 'That sort of thing may go on in Germany, but it certainly doesn't happen here.'

'Then you are proving it to me.' 'Z' bent forward, reached into the top of the plaster where it made a recess, and pulled out a plastic bag, containing pieces of biscuit and Ryvita, sugar, and a medley of pills. 'Analyse, *bitte*!'

666 took the bag, opened it, and swallowed the contents.

'Z' squirmed, his mouth gaping in horror. 'I cannot have the guilt of this. You must be sending for the doctor.'

'I can assure you absolutely nothing will happen to me.'

'Z' shook his head in disbelief. 666 tossed the crumpled bag onto a bedside table. 'Z' began to bleat again.

'Why can I not to see the Duke of Hamilton? My flight went wrong because I did not meet the people I am supposed to. They keep me hidden from the king also. If I have but 15 minutes with him, we are ending the war. The king has promised to protect me. He will give me parole, and I will return to my wife and son. It is you, the warmonger, that prevents this.'

'I am not as you think I am,' said 666. He made a Masonic sign and was gratified by the response. 'I have more sympathy with your position than you realise. Lord Simon relayed your terms. Germany will have full sway over Eastern Europe but will withdraw from the West, including France and Holland. We will keep the Empire, except for your former colonies which will be restored to you. That all seems eminently reasonable. But we need to bring the public on side.'

'Z' was gazing at him with the devotion of a puppy. It was a look 666 had seen many times in the eyes of followers. You could pluck someone like an instrument if you knew the way to tune their heart.

'The Führer's abiding wish is to end this war with you. The East is our living space.'

'Then Hitler knew what you were doing?'

146

'Knew what I was doing? Knew what I was doing?' 'Z' laughed delightedly and thumped the mattress. '*He* was what I was doing. Even if you will be allied with the Americans, we will have such munitions and U-boats, so strong will to win that we are driving all before us. There are miracle weapons coming that will strike terror in your cities.'

'War Engines?'

It did not pay to be too direct. Confusion flickered in 'Z's' glazed eyes. By now, the drug was coursing through his system.

'Just look at the sunshine streaming in! It has the lustre of sunflowers in an Alexandrian Garden. The Sun Gun will beam death rays on your cities. Our rockets will rain fire upon your streets. The Amerika bomber will pound New York. You see now, that is why we must stop this war. Our two great white master races are like Siamese twins in blood and attitude. The Führer has told me repeatedly he will do anything to make peace. Why else did he let you escape at Dunkirk?'

'The America bomber, you say. You're preparing to attack the United States?'

'We have no intention against them. The so-called "German peril" is a pipedream. If we make peace with you now, they will be furious as they want to inherit your empire. But if they are choosing to intervene, we have no fear of them. Soon we will have more planes and U-boats than you and they combined.'

'You'll have to be a bit more precise.'

'Messerschmitt is a friend and I know all the factories and Luftwaffe commanders. Our air personnel have reached the same numbers as your entire English expeditionary force in France. They will pound you into oblivion and destroy America as well. Our U-boats will drown your fleet and convoys.'

666 snorted. 'Oh, come now! German figures about sinking British tonnage are a standing joke. Everybody jeers at them.'

'They will not laugh when the Führer is blockading your island and they starve. He does not want to. It is you who will make him.'

'But we've bombed your U-boat yard at Kiel to smithereens. The same will happen at Bremen, Hanover, Wilhelmshaven. Your submarine fleet will be destroyed.'

Hess snorted. 'Aerial photographs are high unreliable, and as for agents reports, we are having our own miserable experience of them. We have several other U-boat yards. The submarine warfare the Führer plans is not even started.'

'And the Soviets?

'The Bolsheviks are our true enemies. But if we are attacking them now, the stars forebode the same *Moscowdammerung* as Napoleon.'

The Haushofers dabbled in astrology, but they read horoscopes, not cast them. This must have come from Krafft, the mysterious seer 666 had encountered in Albrecht Haushofer's diary. He felt a twinge of professional envy at the astrologer's famous accuracy.

'The Swiss told you that?'

'You are knowing that too? Opening another front while we fight you who are almost the same Folk, deeply bonded by ancient links, will be madness! Yet Hitler cannot be mad. He is the Führer. That is the whirlpool that is dragging me under.'

'That's precisely why I'm here: to rescue you!'

He exchanged Masonic signs with 'Z'. 'Brother in the Sanctified Rite of the Gnosis, how much time do we have?'

'It is too late. Are you not understanding?'

'Let me be the judge of that. Give me the placements!'

'Mars in Pisces in opposition to Neptune.'

'Actions unclear, energy dissipated. Mercury?'

'Retrograde.'

'Unwise to initiate action. They'll get bogged down: snow, long marches, ice, death!'

'*Prezis!* That is what the Swiss was seeing. Now do you understand why I fly to Scotland.'

'Uranus?'

'Aligned with the Fixed Star Alcyone.'

The Moon?'

There was a calendar hanging on the wall beside 'Z's' bed. At his request it displayed the phases of the moon, but he did not glance at it.

'Void, in the last degree of Taurus.'

'But that is today!'

'Yes, yes, I told it is too late. If only, the king will be seeing me. I am believing in our final victory, but if the attack on Russia fails, America will swallow your Empire and the Bolsheviks will eat Europe.'

'Marxist dogma is no prescription for the long term. People need more than economics.'

'*Absolut!* But Christianity is not fitting for Germany. We need a new creed.'

666 was never one to miss a marketing opportunity.

'I believe a man called Crowley has just what you are looking for. His *The Book of the Law* provides an impeccable framework for a new religion. Any country that adopts it will rule the world.'

'I know not of that. You are feeling yourself well?'

'Never better.'

'Z' frowned. 'Then the food is not poisoning. Why do I feel myself strange? I have so much thoughts, but I do not know what they are!'

The fleur-de-lys on the dark green wallpaper bloomed and wilted. Through the window, a solitary cloud morphed into a chariot, transporting 'Z' to Alexandria. The sea foamed with white horses, the waves thudded, the seagulls screeched. The red-hot wind called the *hamsin* stung his skin. The ceaseless howling of the dogs in the desert only served to underscore the silence of the night. He was sitting with his mother on the sand as she unravelled the mystery of the great brilliant stars by giving each a name: "Betelgeuse", "Rigel", "Aldebaran". A different enigma confronted him now: the visitor with the bloated face straining forward in the armchair. Who really was this cunning man? 'Z' brushed doubt aside, flattered the Third Reich's nemesis had come to pay his respects.

A Coldstream guard pushed open and held the door ajar. Malone entered with a tray. The guard followed him in and transferred a crumpled copy of *The Times* and a slim hardback from the bed to a side table. A glimpse of the dust jacket informed 666 the book was *Three Men in a Boat*. Malone handed a bowl of soup and a spoon to 'Z'. The brawny, dark-haired lieutenant whipped out a second spoon from his pocket, scooped up some of the liquid and transferred it to his mouth. 'Very tasty,' he grinned. 'Z' grunted and lowered his own spoon into the soup. He looked down and shrieked.

'It is the Führer! I see his face. He is in rage with me.'

666 was versed in many mediums - the scrying stones of Doctor Dee; the drugged ravings of Scarlet Women - but soup was new to him. Nevertheless, he heaved himself out of the armchair, leaned over the bed and gazed down at the thin vegetable gruel as though deciphering the dark pool of the oracle.

'On the contrary, he's bursting with thanks for the immense sacrifice you've made.'

'Are you really believing so?' 'Z' gazed meekly up at him like a child.

'Look he's smiling!'

There were tears in 'Z's' eyes as he looked back. 'Yes, I see it now. He is happy that at last my mission is finding success.'

There was a handkerchief on the bed just beside the prisoner's left elbow. 666 picked it up and began dabbing the soup that had spilt onto the eiderdown. The handkerchief was made of silk and had a map inscribed upon it. Such artefacts were standard issue for spies or airmen in case they found themselves in enemy territory, he remembered. Hess was catatonic after his vision, his eyes glassy, still staring at the soup as though it would spring a further revelation. 666 held onto the handkerchief. He wanted at least one souvenir of the occasion. Malone and the guard exited, almost colliding with Foley, who in a highly agitated state rushed in, with Dicks close behind.

'The Axis armies poured across the Russian border at 3.15 a.m. today,' the major announced breathlessly. '180 divisions! The Red Army's totally unprepared and in full retreat.'

'It has started after all,' said 'Z.

Was he smiling or frowning, wondered Dicks, as he inspected 'Z's' Cro-Magnon forehead, shaggy eyebrows, sunken eyes, irregular 'buck' teeth, and receding lower jaw? Hitler's number two was a caged great ape, oozing hostility and mistrust, he concluded.

'You knew it all along, didn't you?' he snapped. 'Why couldn't you have bloody told us?'

'Steady on,' said Foley.

'It's just not good enough, men are dying in their thousands, cities are being razed, and this smug bast-'

"That's quite enough, Dicks! As a matter of fact, we had advance intelligence. You even informed Stalin himself in person back in May, didn't you, Prime Minister?'

Still gazing up at Dicks in shock, 'Z' didn't notice the wink Foley exchanged with 666.

'Then why wasn't the Kremlin prepared?' demanded Dicks.

'Because they trust nobody and thought we were feeding them lies. Hitler massed three million troops on the Russian border and hoodwinked Stalin into believing they were resting before invading England.'

'That still doesn't excuse this "missing link".'

'I begged the Führer not to do it,' screamed 'Z'. 'I told it is madness. Not now when we are fighting you.'

'But he didn't listen, did he? And why not? Because you're a bloody joke, with your water cures, star maps and ludicrous diets.'

'Dicks, I really must insist-'

Gunfire cut Foley off. Everyone looked at one another, except the man on the bed, hunched over as though trying to disappear into himself. There was the rattle of machine guns, an explosion, and muffled shouts. Foley ran to the window that overlooked the driveway.

'There's an armoured car tearing down with a truck just behind it. That's where the firing's coming from. Slow down you idiots! Christ, they've ploughed through the first barrier and are going to hit the second! Too late, they've smashed through it. Troops are spilling from the truck. Seem to be our boys, going by the uniforms, so why are they attacking us?'

Foley unclipped his holster and pulled out his service revolver. There were shouts and shooting from downstairs. 'M' appeared in the doorway with pistol drawn. Malone could be seen just behind, letting off rounds from his Webley through the steel grille on the landing. Foley yelled at him to lock the cage door. Malone reached into his breast pocket but was hit. He slumped against the mesh like a useless sack. 'M' moved alongside Foley. Both aimed their revolvers at the doorway. 'Z' straightened and gazed at 666, his face an oval of happiness.

'My Führer is not forgetting. He sends these men to liberate me.'

There was the thumping of boots on the uncarpeted stairs. Two soldiers barged through the door, wielding sub-machine guns. They wore standard British army uniforms but had an eagle on their helmets and POLAND printed in white on their red shoulder flashes. Another man lumbered in after them. He was wearing a colonel's uniform and a walrus moustache. His eyes were bloodshot, and he seemed to be drunk. He gaped at the gloomy man on the bed and the rotund figure next to him.

'What did I tell you! We've caught the buggers red-handed. Hess and Churchill slicing up Europe and selling Poland down the river. '

'You're making a grave mistake,' said Foley.

The glowering colonel walked up him and rained spittle as he bawled, 'I outrank you so just keep your bloody mouth shut! That goes for everyone else as well! We're here to make sure the Hun bastard gets his just desserts.'

'You have no authority,' boomed 666, still in character. 'This man is a state prisoner.'

'We haven't driven all this way to bandy words with traitors. Boys!'

The Polish soldiers glanced at the bed but maintained their standoff.

'The Polish community is held in very high regard in this country,' said Foley. 'For God's sake don't change that. You must respect the law.'

'That man is killer,' said the taller of the two soldiers.

'That may well be so, but it's not for you to judge him.'

'No, let him judge himself,' a hysterical voice rose from the bed. 'I have failed my country, my family and my Führer. Yes, I am guilty, guilty, guilty. Please finish what I could not do myself.'

'You see!' the colonel snorted. 'What the bloody hell are you waiting for?'

The Polish soldiers did not move.

'Damn it! If you want a job done properly, you must always do the ruddy thing yourself!'

The colonel wheeled around and took aim. The bullet hit 'Z' in the centre of his forehead. He screamed, gurgled, and fell silent. Blood gushed from the wound, growing glossy as it mingled with the sweat. A red trickle striping the ridge of his nose gave him the look of an Indian brave. The colonel grinned. 'Nobody can say I didn't fulfil the Hun bastard's last wish.' Another shot rang out. The colonel crumpled and collapsed in a heap, the back of his brain spilling onto the floor like a pile of offal on a butcher's slab. Malone crouched on the landing, smoke rising from the muzzle of his gun. The Polish soldiers slowly lowered theirs.

'Go and tell the rest of your comrades to lay down their arms!' Foley ordered the taller soldier. The one remaining had a square face and cropped fair hair. He looked like he had been hewn from concrete.

'Who is he?' said 'M', waving his revolver at the dead man.

'Colonel Hereward-Dunstan, Royal Fusiliers.'

'And you are?'

'Polish Corps 1.'

'Based?'

'Fort William, Scotland.'

'How could you let a drunk buffoon get you into this?' demanded Foley.

'Orders.'

'He had no authority-'

'You not understand. Not him...general.'

'M' looked puzzled, then enlightenment dawned. 'Sikorski?'

The soldier nodded.

'The general was on the Reception Committee,' 'M" told Foley in a hurried aside. 'He was due to be a star turn at the Kennels.'

'They've gone to extreme lengths to cover that up.'

'Parlaying with 'Z' would have looked bad to his own people and been a calamity for relations with Churchill. You realise this can never come out.' 'M' paused, deep in thought. 'We're going to need...'

'A double,' said 666.

Foley gazed at the head transfixed upon the blood-stained pillow. 'Or doppelgänger, as our poor Companion would have put it.'

* * *

Will slipped the file into his satchel and put the books and magical tools back in the chest. A few moments later, the door burst open. It was Vernon with a hunted look. He brushed past Will and made for the bottle on the chest of drawers.

'Don't mind me, old boy. Terrible thirst. Doing your prep, are you?'

Vernon plucked the cork from the cognac and hastily poured a large measure into one of the smeared balloon glasses alongside. In one gulp he drained the contents, coughed, and refreshed the glass.

'I'd offer you a snifter, but it's not really my call. Crow doesn't mind of course. I've got an open invitation to come and Do What I Will, heh, heh, whenever I like. Anyway, he gets it on tap from those Yankee fans of his. I couldn't find a drop in the house. Pernod, brandy, rum all on empty! Do you think someone's siphoning it off? There's a bloody thief about? It's not you, is it? No, you're a good lad. It would be against your religion, heh, heh. Just wish you could get all that "Jesus loves me" claptrap out of your head. You won't tell Johnnie. There's a good chap. What if I like an occasional snifter! This is such a drab and appalling time to be alive, you need something to get you through. Okay, maybe I overdo it a bit, but I can cut down.'

The door was still ajar. Crow appeared in the frame, with the beetroot face of Mr Watson just behind.

The Beast was in high dudgeon. 'Turned out that far from being a demonstration of the finer points of magick, *The Wizard of Oz* really is a kids' film!'

'With a tin robot and a talking dog,' added Watson in disgust.

'Do you have to remind me? Men of our erudition subjected to such horror! We walked out, of course, pursued by catcalls from the drooling brats crammed into the stalls. Beating all and sundry at chess was hardly compensation. Such an ordeal calls for a stiff drink.'

'Be my guest!' said Vernon, who had lost all awareness of his surroundings.

'Most kind of you,' chuckled Crow. 'Now, Will, no more burning of the midnight lamp! You'll be joining us, of course. Something tells me you have all the makings of a heroic drinker. Just like me when I chanced upon a bottle of white rum in the pantry aged twelve, glugged the lot and went and rogered the maid!'

Going to the chest of drawers, he raised the bottle until it was level with his shoulder and tilted it. Crow's aim was not as true as when he had picked up the trick while crossing Spain with his chela Victor Neuburg. There was some spillage as the stream of cognac poured down, filling first one glass and then two more. Nevertheless, his companion was full of admiration.

'How did you do that?'

'Elementary, my dear Watson,' crowed Crow.

Chapter Fifteen
Knight's Black Agents

Dolphin Square: Friday, 29 November 1946

The shops in the arcade were doing their bit. The dressmaker even had the New Look on display, though drab utility dresses lined the rails inside. The patisserie flaunted tiered wedding cakes, but it was just for show as they breached rationing restrictions. The grocer was a patriot featuring uniquely British brands: Jack Tar tinned salmon, Burdall's gravy salt, Woolton pie. Heinz sauces were also available but kept under the counter.

A corridor connected the arcade to a hallway with an art-deco lift. Will took this to the third floor of Hood House and walked along to flat 308, the address Major Knight had given him on the phone. There was a name next to the doorbell. A striking girl in a navy-blue uniform answered the door. Her dark hair was swept back into the pronounced curl of the 'Victory Roll'.

'I'm here to see Major Knight, Miss Coplestone.'

'That's not me, and he's extremely busy.'

'But I think he's expecting me.'

Her eyes grew even icier, but she told him to come in.

Another of Knight's black agents was hunched over a typewriter. She was also very attractive and gave Will a chilly glance as her colleague escorted him through the lounge. This led to a corridor lined with framed black and white photos of jazz greats. A rising farmyard stink sat oddly with the plush surroundings. The woman tapped briskly on a door. There came a muffled "come in". Knight was squatting in an armchair, feeding an infant kangaroo milk from a baby bottle.

'He says he's expected.'

'And so he is.'

'Be surprising if he wasn't...Sir.'

'Close the door behind you, Joan!'

Her hostility puzzled Will. His surroundings, however, were too bizarre to let him wonder for long. Crawling with snakes, lizards and toads, glass cases stood banked against the walls. There was a parrot on a perch who observed him haughtily and said, 'Open the door, you idiot!' A mongoose was taking a morning constitutional across the carpet. A window overlooked the courtyard below. It was surprising the two bronze dolphins leaping on the fountain were not alive as well.

The major looked up: 'I much prefer the company of animals. You know where you are with fish and fowl. People, on the other hand....Don't mind Joan, she thinks she's in love with me.'

' 'M'?'

Major Knight sighed and gently lowered the kangaroo onto the carpet. It hopped away. He returned to his desk, tossed the empty baby bottle into an open drawer, and pulled out a dossier. Gesturing for the visitor to join him, he collapsed onto a green leather sofa. Will felt the warmth of the major's thigh pressing against his as he produced a grainy black and white photograph. Molnar and Gizi were descending a gangway. Farkas was just behind them, carrying suitcases.

'Stalin dissolved the Third International three years ago, but its methods live on. The professor and his wife are what we used to call a Comintern couple. Passing themselves off as married arouses less suspicion than operating solo. He really is a professor of Physics, by the way, widely known in his field. She's a nightclub singer from Moldova. Classic Centre honey trap. Molnar's wife divorced him. Shades of *The Blue Angel*. A cliché really, but life is always imitating art. This was taken at Folkestone when their ferry docked. Gizi, not her real name, is the carrot. This one's the stick.' He tapped Farkas's bullet-shaped face. 'He was an executioner for the Arrow Cross, the Hungarian Nazis. Now he does the same for the communists. The sickle and the swastika, eh! Two sides of the proverbial coin. What did they tell you about the document?'

'Just that it's called 'The Z File'.'

'Come on, Will, that Jesus loves me stuff really hasn't stood you in good stead! You're a hopeless liar. You've read it, haven't you? You know who 'Z' is.'

Will blushed then nodded. 'Don't you mean was?'

He had scoured the newspaper section in Hastings Library for every detail of the Nuremberg Trials. It was all there in black and white. When an officer called the prisoner's name, he answered there was no such person as Hess there. "But if you are looking for Convict Number 125, then I'm your man". Göring repeatedly urged his fellow convict to reveal his "great secret". The man in the dock was an imposter. It leapt from the newsprint: the amnesia, the confusion; the inability to recognise his secretaries or his mentor, Karl Haushofer, when they were brought to his cell. The double didn't know who they were because he'd never met them before. He refused to call witnesses or admit testimony because that would expose him. He rejected supplying blood or a signature for the same reason.

'Who is the man in Spandau?'

Knight frowned. 'Look, I've grown rather fond of you, Will, so let's not go up that blind alley. You did the right thing and have saved us a great deal of bother. The stenographer at Camp Z was a Russian spy. We arrested him when he attempted to smuggle the transcript out. He was hanged for his trouble, though unfortunately not before he got word to Centre. Stalin is convinced British Intelligence lured the Deputy Führer to Scotland to negotiate an alliance in which Britain would join Germany in attacking Russia. They think 'The Z File' proves it. That's why they want it so badly.'

'Molnar said you gave the file to Crow.'

'It was Ian, actually…Fleming who did that. Someone tipped the professor off. British Intelligence is like a sieve these days. I've cried wolf so often people call me Peter. That's the real reason it's curtains for Dolphin Square. We're closing shop. I'm off to be a penpusher in Curzon Street. Smoke? Not yet, eh. Don't mind if I do?'

He went over to his desk, retrieved his pipe, crammed tobacco from a tin of Three Nuns into the bowl and lit it with the second Swan Vesta he struck.

'The war was child's play compared to what we're facing now. German Intelligence was like a fourth-division football team. The Russians, on the other hand, win the Cup every season. They'll have a sleeper in place for years. Don't seem to care how long it takes. Before you know it, they've infiltrated your entire network. I'm mulling over focusing on broadcasting in future. Much more rewarding.'

The mongoose had successfully overturned and emptied the wastepaper basket and was now curled up inside. 'Open the door, you idiot!' said the parrot. 'M' strode back to the sofa. His hand brushed Will's knee as he lowered himself. It was almost a caress.

'When you return to Hastings, put the file back where you found it. Source something the same size. You'll have to set up a handover. Not at Netherwood. Somewhere in the locality but out of the way.'

His hand sloped back to Will's knee. There was a huskier note in his voice.

'We have such a narrow view of things, wouldn't you agree? Nature's not like that. Dolphins, lions, even Japanese macaques rise above gender when it comes to physical love. Enslaved by marriage and monogamy, the longest journey as Shelley called it, it's we who are perverse.'

Will had never been kissed by a man before. To his surprise, it was not unpleasant.

Chapter Sixteen
At the Customs Station

Hastings: Sunday, 1 December 1946

Heathland and wind-sculpted trees line the clifftops east of Hastings. Ecclesbourne and Fairlight, two stream-and-spring-dotted glens, cut down to the sea. Until the early nineteenth century, the Sussex coast was a key drop off point for smugglers who met at 'The Whippings', the high cliff near Ecclesbourne. To monitor this, the coastguard built a station on a triangular level lower down, overlooking a slumped cliff of soft pink sandstone. A double-fronted customs house, with red roof and chimney, stood at a right angle to a watch house and cottages that faced the sea. The station had closed in 1908, but the buildings remained in use. Vernon Symonds rented one before acquiring Netherwood. Now, however, they were so dilapidated that nobody wanted to live in them.

It had taken Will 30 minutes to cycle from the Ridge, shooting down Old London Road and pedalling along Barley Lane. He propped his bike against the pebble-stone wall of the watch house. The vague contours of the glen climbed in gorse-covered levels to the headland. The luminous hands of his Timex sluggishly moved towards eleven thirty, the time appointed for the handover.

He heard the engine first and then saw the headlamps jerk up and down as the loose gravel of Barley Lane jolted the Wolseley. It came to a halt on the cobbles in front of him. He stood in front of the bike, clutching the A4 Manila envelope he'd pulled out of his rucksack. Leaving the engine running, Farkas got out and began to walk towards him. Will wondered if the chauffeur had come alone. A second later a searchlight in an upper window of the customs house answered his question. It silhouetted the professor and Gizi, their faces united in consternation on the back seat. The beams from more searchlights swivelled across the platform in bands of light that focused on Farkas.

'PUT YOUR HANDS ON YOUR HEAD AND KNEEL!'

No longer kind and avuncular, 'M's voice blared crisply from a megaphone. He was in the shadows that hid the entrance of the customs house. Farkas whipped a pistol out and began firing in the direction of the voice. He was met by bursts of tommy gun fire. The chauffeur spun his gun around and aimed at Will. Two bullets slammed into the wall behind the boy, making the bike bell tinkle.

Commandos were streaming from the doorways with blackened faces. Farkas scampered to the perimeter and leapt onto the low wall that overhung the cliff. A shot rang out. He wavered for a moment, raising his arms as if to surrender, then tumbled over into the maw of the sea.

A commando sprinted to the rear of the Wolseley, pulled the back door open, thrust the lever down to the locked position, and slammed the door shut. Another did the same on the other side. Gizi's head was slumped against her chest with eyes clenched shut, as though by ignoring it she could ward off the evil. Molnar was puffing furiously on his cigarette. Major Knight came out of the doorway and strode up to Will. He was in his army captain's uniform. Ever since their encounter in Dolphin Square it had been awkward.

The commandos began pushing the car towards the perimeter. Gizi turned and pressed her face against the rear window with a stricken look that Will would never erase from memory. By now, the Wolseley had reached an area where the restraining wall had crumbled away. 'M' raised the megaphone, 'EXECUTE!' The squad man-handled the car to the perimeter, where it hovered for a moment before a final shove tipped it over the edge. An outcrop tore off a wheel as the car tumbled down the cliff face and plunged into the sea. 'M' seemed happy.

'Tragic accident. Full fathom five and all that. What a riddle this will be for Centre!'

'You gave no inkling this would happen.'

'Didn't I?' 'M' seemed surprised. 'They were hostile agents of an enemy power. The chauffeur started the shooting. We have license in such circumstances. I thought that should be obvious. An operation like this can leave no traces.'

'You used me as bait.'

'It must remain hush-hush, of course, but we can reward you on the quiet. You have performed a sterling service for king and country.'

'By murder?'

'Ex-judicial execution, sanctioned by the state.'

'Those are just words. It's bloody murder. If I hadn't contacted you, they'd still be alive.'

'So Farkas could kill you instead? Believe me, that's very much what would have happened. We categorise everything: Friend or Foe, Harmless or Harmful. But nature does not work like that. Predators are her lifeblood.'

'Nature is very convenient for you. It justifies all kinds of abuse.'

Cycling home, Will realised the world, or at least his place in it, had undergone a transformation. Far from there being a benevolent destiny with best intentions at its heart, life was dark and ruthless. There was a light on in the kitchen. He found his father making cocoa.

'I couldn't sleep. Shall I make you a cup, too?'

'Dad, I've decided I'm not cut out to be a priest.'

Relief flooded Robert's face. 'Hallelujah! It's a bloody miracle.'

Chapter Seventeen
A Good World to Leave

November/December 1947

There was a tattered volume of Suetonius's *The Twelve Caesars* on the table. Will made no move to open it. Nor had he brought his usual notebook and pencils. Crow looked frail and was coughing almost incessantly. Wrapped in his soiled dressing gown, he peered across with moist, startled eyes.

'I've decided not to become a priest,' said Will.

'That's devastating news. I was relying on you to officiate at my funeral,' Crow smiled. 'And Latin? No more time for that? It's not just the preserve of priests and pederasts, you know. Prolonged marination in romance word-roots boosts your command of English and is the gateway to Italian, French and Spanish as well.'

'I want to study magick.'

Crow sucked in his cheeks, the wrinkles fanning out like cracks on a dried-up riverbed. 'I suppose people must have something: golf, pigeon fancying, drugs. Human nature abhors a vacuum. But I don't have the energy to take anybody on. I'll tell you what: Aleister will explain everything. Discover who you truly are, and all else will follow!'

'But I want practical stuff: yoga, meditation…rituals. At least, give me a reading list.'

'Study nothing: learn from life! Live fully and that will teach you more than all the books and the "Masters".' Crow jiggled his ill-fitting denture with his thumb. 'Ah Will, a few years back, I would have been keen to help, but I'm dog tired. Currently, there's nobody around in England I can think of who can train you, which I suppose is hardly a ringing endorsement of my system. The only practitioners are in California and their numbers are dwindling. But how could you get there? I've had a devil of a time trying to go myself. May I ask what has brought about this startling turnaround? Was it the terrible and mysterious accident that befell the Hungarians? Well, no matter. I suppose the road to Damascus runs in both directions. Be a good chap and top up this brandy, will you?'

His eyes strayed to the box on the table next to his bed. He grimaced.

'Heroin very rapidly becomes an unwanted guest that long out-stays its welcome. Cocaine is an express train to hell, with a few interesting stops en route. The pearl is peyote. It conveys the breath that visited you as a child.'

'The artificial means?'

'Yes, though the cactus springs from the soil and is baked by the Mexican sun. Why did the gods put such a miracle on the planet if they did not want us to use it?'

As Will made to leave, Crow tugged his sleeve and gazed up at him with his rheumy eyes. 'After I'm gone - no, no, please leave the platitudes aside! I know you hope I'll live forever, but by doing what I ask you'll help with that - I want you to get hold of something.'

Will was not so surprised to hear what it was. He asked what he should do with it. This seemed to be the most fatuous question the Beast had ever heard.

'Why, get it published, of course! Let everybody know I did my bit!'

* * *

The following morning an attractive woman in her early thirties, with luminous eyes and fair hair that darkened around the parting, walked into the front hall of Netherwood accompanied by three children. She was dressed bohemian style in a green corduroy coat, wide plaid skirt, and ankle length suede boots. Mrs Symonds emerged from the bar and her face brightened. Simultaneously, Will bounded down the stairs.

'Crow's been greatly under the weather,' said Johnnie. 'You're just the tonic he needs. Pat was with us in the spring, Will. You were away on your RAF cadet week. Will you show her up? Knock first. You better make sure he's *respectable*.'

Johnnie laughed heartily, greatly enjoying her joke. The children scrambled up the stairs ahead of their mother. The youngest, a girl, slipped on the slightly worn green carpeting.

'Someone will have an accident,' Johnnie called out. 'Leave the others with me! Just take Ataturk!'

Will followed, puzzled by the boy's name. He had wavy black hair and a freckled face. When they reached the landing, curiosity got the better of him.

'Are you relatives?'

'Ataturk is Crow's son,' Pat smiled. She had a cut-glass voice, but her tone was warm. 'His natal chart was very like the Turkish leader's, which is why we gave him the same name.'

The Beast was propped up in bed with an open *I Ching* and some yarrow stalks spread out before him on the eiderdown. He consulted the *Book of Changes* daily, even about visiting the dentist or buying a new hat. Sighting the newcomers, his face exuded an expression far removed from its usual remoteness. Will considered opening the window to release the fug of smoke, but it was chilly that Sunday, the last day of November.

'I came as soon as I heard,' said Pat.

'My little indisposition? Ah, it will pass and probably me with it. Oh, does that upset you? How good you have been to me! And Ataturk, what a splendid little fellow you are. Have you been saying your prayers?'

The boy nodded. Crow glanced at Will, relishing his astonishment.

'It does not matter who you pray to, the act's the thing. Now, Ataturk, I hope you have taken to heart the letter I sent you in May. Remember you are a descendant of Breton dukes, and must always be high-minded, generous, and noble. Live without fear and never tell a lie! Doing so means you're frightened of the person you deceived. Now, it's early days, you're...'

'Ten.'

'Quite so, but you must take Shakespeare and the Old Testament as the models for your writing style: they are the finest of all. Commit as much as possible to memory. Chess is another great tool for training the mind.'

'He knows all the moves now,' said his mother.

'So good that you could come. Just sorry you've taken all this trouble for an old log like me. Come, sit beside me for a while.'

It was a scene from Beauty and the Beast, thought Will, as the woman edged herself onto the divan. Feeling like an intruder, he slipped out into the corridor. When he reached the first-floor landing, he glimpsed a stooped, elegantly dressed woman shuffling along the lobby followed by her chauffeur. The prognosis must be bad if Lady Harris had been summoned. Will was so accustomed to the old man defying the ills of his decaying flesh that the thought distressed him.

* * *

'He's far from well, worse at least than I've ever seen him. It's the pleurisy above all that concerns me, and he does look frightfully ill and is getting weaker.'

Pat and Lady Harris were in the lounge taking afternoon tea.

'The nurse is attending to him now,' said Frieda.

'It was very good of you to hire her.'

'He wasn't being cared for properly. I hope very much it's too early to speak of this, but I'm afraid there won't be much left for you and the children.'

Pat, who was also known as Deidre, had not been lucky. She came from old Cornish stock, with several artists in the family tree, and had come out as a debutante before Queen Mary in 1933. She first met Crowley when teenage mistress of another older man, a literary agent and a spy, who was connected to the Mandrake Press that published the Beast's works. The agent died, and through Crowley she met a captain in MI6, with whom she had two children. The captain was killed on a secret mission in the war. She herself worked for a spell as a cipher clerk for the SOE in Cairo.

'We'll manage,' said Pat bravely.

'A.C. has charged Frater Saturnus and the American OTO with the raising of Ataturk.'

'There's really no need for them to go to such trouble. I'm used to fending for myself. My grandmother passed away last year and left me a tidy sum in stocks and shares. Besides, I didn't have any thought of material things when I had Ataturk.'

'One couldn't help wondering,' said Frieda.

Pat had been a striking girl of 19 when she met the Beast. He was 58, broke, with bad teeth and chronic asthma.

'I've never given a fig for security. My husband and I roamed like gypsies through Greece, Yugoslavia, the Middle East, and I never felt freer. He could never stay in one place for too long lest his cover was blown, and I'm a restless soul.'

'You first saw A.C. in court?'

'*The Laughing Torso* case. Crow believed Nina Hamnett had libelled him with her lurid account of black magic high jinks in Sicily. I was staying with a relative, a High Court judge. He thought I should see a trial as part of my education. The knives were out for A.C., but I thought the way he stood up for himself was magnificent, and funny, too. He told them Beast 666 only meant sunlight, and they should call him "Little sunshine". Didn't help a bit, of course. The judge had it in for him. The jury found against him without bothering to retire. The press used him as their whipping boy. It was horrid and so unfair. We became friends after the trial. There was no more to it than that. I went abroad and returned in '36, looked A.C. up again and we were as friendly as ever. Outside his beastly lodgings one night he took me in his arms and told me he wanted a child. I wanted one too. It wasn't easy. He had to give up drugs for three months.'

'That must have been a great sacrifice. You know, he's not so sure of himself as he was in the old days. I was doing a sketch of him earlier...,' Frieda's voice dropped. 'He said he was "perplexed".'

'That doesn't sound like him. Perplexed about what?'

'He wouldn't tell me. And the nurse heard him say, "Sometimes I hate myself". '

* * *

Illness had dogged the spring and summer of 1947, but Crow felt much worse now. The last day of November found him still bedridden, too weak to even fill his pipe. Breathing had become a trial, a racking cough its inevitable sequel, the spittoon indispensable. Yet his mind was still alert. As though projected by a magic lantern, he saw himself as a child, sitting stiffly in his starched collar as fire, damnation and apocalypse rained down from the Plymouth Brethren pulpit. Far from being repelled by the many-coloured Beast, he was tantalised. Then the dandy and poet, dripping with wealth and promise, who scaled mountains and stalked big game, sauntered into view. He had given up counting lovers and settled on nationalities instead. Now, they jostled before him, male and female, a veritable league of nations. Yet not one had done half as much for him as the free-spirited girl who now entered with his son.

'My own beloved,' he wheezed, 'your silly old bastard's on the shelf.'

Yes, he could always laugh at himself. It was a gift that people never understood. They thought he was laughing at them.

'Where's the rest of the brood?'

' Johnnie is teaching them how to bake a cake.'

'Ataturk doesn't need to be here with his sick old dad. Here, boy, squeeze my hand before you go.'

The boy leaned forward and gave his father a peck on his wizened cheek. This pleased the old man immensely.

'Completely undeserved, of course.'

Which was also an apt description of the child's existence.

'Fill my pipe, will you beloved? The tins are on the table. I was thinking of my schooldays. Could have done better the masters would say.'

'You're very hard on yourself.'

'I should have been harder. What am I leaving behind? A religion with few followers. Scores of books that nobody reads. Scandal! Infamy! It all seems pointless.'

'I read your poetry to Ataturk.'

'Is it any good?' he demanded in a quavering voice. 'Is it any good?'

His head slumped back, and he slipped into oblivion. Johnnie and Will looked in on him later, as did Vernon, who toasted his comatose guest with a shot of his own brandy. In the evening the doctor arrived, examined him, and declared no more could be done.

Nothing stirred as the first of December dawned. There was no wind. The leaden sky was still. A great silence had descended. A few moments before eleven, Crow's eyes blinked open. He looked at Pat and whispered, "So, you're here…and not afraid." He died on the hour with Pat the only witness. At the moment of his passing, the curtains billowed in and there was a peal of thunder. She took this to mean the gods had received him. Now there was no part of him that was not of them. The doctor gave the cause of death as bronchitis and heart congestion.

* * *

In clear breach of the Merchandise Marks Act, Room 13 still reeked of the perfume of immortality. Nearly three years of superhuman smoking had stained every surface yellow brown. Strips of Sellotape and rusting nails had further contributed to the wall's decline. The furniture was blackened and chipped by burns. Vernon would bill Crow's estate the considerable sum of £70 for extensive redecoration and refurbishment. Sadly, the Beast died bankrupt.

Will looked in again that evening. Crow was propped up in bed. Pat had arranged his hands, so his palms were upturned in Salute to the Sun. His eyes were open. They did not appear startled anymore. Will went over to the chest, raised the lid, and gazed at the tools of magic. He started transferring them to the floor, wondering as he came to books and manuscripts what lay in store for work that would be of interest to nobody other than collectors of curios and the bizarre. He placed one too many books on the pile he was making so it toppled over, obliging him to get to his knees to retrieve a slim volume that had tumbled under the bed. He glimpsed something else under the frame. He reached in, pulled out the object and removed the silk handkerchief it was wrapped in. He was holding a brass strongbox. He flipped the clasp, raised the lid, and whistled. There were enough bank notes to set up a business or go around the world.

The wad was so thick it was difficult to cram it all into the top of his overalls. He imagined himself counting the money in his room, indulging in the exquisite torment of deciding whether to return it or not. He closed the box, shoved it under the bed, pushed the handkerchief into his pocket and repacked the chest. The door opened and Major Knight stood silhouetted in the frame. He glanced at Will and then scanned the room with a professional eye.

'Haven't you forgotten something?'

Will had not closed the chest. He hurriedly lowered the lid, turned and faced the major, never sure if he were Friend or Foe.

'Crow wanted me to take 'The Z File'. He thought it was something people should know about, but it isn't here.'

Knight pursed his lips. 'After that nasty business with Centre we intended to remove it ourselves, but Crow forestalled us. He sent it to America.'

This amazed Will. 'Then he really does have followers over there?'

'Yes. Quite a few at one point.'

'I thought they just existed in his head.'

'You even met one: the U.S. commander, the day of the children's party.'

The spymaster strolled over to the table. Crow's plum-coloured velvet jacket was draped over the chair. Knight emptied the pockets. There was a wallet, from which Knight extracted a visiting card engraved with the legend Sir Aleister Crowley, a letter, and a parchment folded into a square. Knight opened it and gazed at the extravagantly looped letters.

'The wording is Enochian. A complex language Ian once proposed we use as a cipher. This is a talisman, consecrated to great treasure, marinated without doubt in the Beast's fluids. Care to touch? Squeamish, eh.'

Knight inserted the magic square back into the wallet. Then he unfolded the letter. 'It's from The Director of Naval Intelligence. It's inviting Crow to the Admiralty for an interview just after the war started. Crow took great pride in our line of work.'

'I'll leave you with him.'

'Thanks. I'd appreciate a few last moments with the old boy.'

Will went to the door but found he could not go through with it. He retraced his steps, removed the wad from his overalls and placed it on the table. Knight, who had extracted confessions from the

Soviet spies at the Woolwich Arsenal and Tyler Kent, the Nazi mole at the American embassy, hadn't had to do a thing. He seemed pleased.

'It was money he was keeping aside to publish more books. Frieda Harris wanted him to spend it on his health, but he was very single-minded when it came to his literary pursuits. His principle in that regard would come as a surprise to many.' Knight leaned forward, peeled off the top note and handed it to Will. 'A keepsake. He'd have no objection, I'm sure.'

* * *

Crow was cremated on Friday the fifth, as cold and dismal a December day as Johnnie and Will, who followed the coffin on its journey from Hastings to Brighton Cemetery, could remember.

The service was held at 2.45 pm. There were fifteen mourners, several of whom Will recognised from Netherwood: John Symonds, Frieda Harris, Pat and Ataturk, and a tall, fiery man called Louis Umfreville Wilkinson, an author and Crow's oldest and most stead-fast friend. Carrying a selection of Crow's works, he strode to the rostrum and read in a stirring voice what Crow had ordained for the Last Ritual. Hunched over their notebooks in the back pews, the reporters were greatly roused on hearing the 'Hymn to Pan', accompanied by cries of 'Io Pan' and 'Do what thou wilt' from a congregation of dishevelled bohemians, sadly lacking in haircuts. Lurid headlines scandalised readers the next day with news of the black magic goings-on. Brighton Council made a firm undertaking never to permit such a blasphemous event again.

Pat threw a spray of red roses onto the coffin as it made its way to the flames. As the mourners filed out, someone muttered, 'Perhaps now that he's safely dead, I'll write his biography.' Wilkinson, who was just behind the speaker, said, 'Ah, what do you mean by *safely*?'

On the drive back to Netherwood, Johnnie and Wilkinson talked about Fleet Street's coverage. The *Daily Express* had led the pillorying: "Black Magician Crowley Dies: The Wickedest Man in Britain". Others expressed relief at the end of "Awful Aleister" and made a damning judgment on the efficacy of Ruthvah: "Mystic's Potion to Prolong Life Fails". A further spate of headlines ensued when Crow's doctor died within 24 hours of his patient. This was widely viewed as the result of a curse the Beast had put on him for prescribing insufficient amounts of heroin.

'I always felt there was a melancholy about him,' said Wilkinson. 'Latterly, this element grew much stronger: he became almost endearing. He knew he had not achieved what he wanted. He was a bogeyman, a figure of notoriety not fame, to be mocked and spat at. I tended him when he was ill. After he inscribed a book, saying I had saved "his worthless life". His vanity, which at times transformed him into a despot, was in full retreat.'

'I liked him,' said Johnnie. 'He was great fun.'

A flash of lightning lit up the rain-drenched road ahead. It was followed a second later by the rumble of thunder.

'Just the send-off the old boy would have wanted,' said Wilkinson.

Part III
Pasadena 1952

Chapter Eighteen
Pioneers

Saturday, 7 June 1952

'Anyone see you come in?' demanded Jack Parsons fretfully.

They were on the first floor of the coach house of the old Cruikshank estate. The war had wrought great changes on Millionaire's Row as this wealthy part of Pasadena was known. The estate's tall white mansion had been demolished like many in the area, the land subdivided and fenced in, and soulless condominiums erected. Even the sky had changed. Formerly an intense blue, it was now hazy with smog that obscured the San Gabriel Mountains on the skyline. Will told Jack he hadn't noticed anyone loitering around the house or on the lawns of the French-style manor house across the street.

'What is it you say you do?'

'I'm a trainee flying boat engineer,' explained Will. 'I delayed national service to study music but...'

'It caught up with you in the end. Things like that always do.'

'It's just 18 months, and I've been lucky. I'm on a six-month secondment to the U.S. navy base at San Diego, learning all about Catalina PBY, the best flying boat ever built.'

'Yeah, I've seen those beauties in the bay. They're huge.'

'They won't be around for much longer. Before the war it was far easier to touch down on water than land, but thousands of runways have been built. Those, and the jet engine, will soon make flying boats a thing of the past.'

'I'm sort of an engineer myself. Rockets are my thing. Rockets are the future. That's what you should get into.'

Beneath a tangle of black curly hair, Jack Parsons possessed the thin moustache and chiselled good looks of a movie star. Yet his face was transitioning to florid and his torso to fat. His eyes had the same startled expression as Crow's, making Will wonder just what the pair of them had witnessed. Jack had been easy to track down. He was in the phone book. It had only needed two words, 'Crow' and 'Netherwood', to elicit an enthusiastic invitation to visit when he was next on leave, as Will was this weekend.

'I don't think the British Navy's got round to rockets yet.'

'It was like that here when we started out. People thought we were crazy, but the war's changed everything. You wouldn't believe the crowds when they rolled a pair of captured V2s through Pasadena train station on an open flatbed rail car. In '49 they mounted a WAC Corporal on the nose of one of them things and launched it to a height of 244 miles. Next, destination moon! Werner Von Braun is working for us. We were pen pals before the war, but I'm not sure what to make of him now.'

'I don't think Will came all the way out here to talk rockets, honey. Besides, you won't be able to play with your fuels and propellants when we're in Mexico.'

Parsons' wife, Cameron, had the husky voice of a chain-smoker and slant green eyes. Her cropped bronze-red hair was cut into a fringe and worn bunched over the ears, giving her the look of a satanic Joan of Arc.

Jack snorted. 'That won't matter. I'll have all the grass, peyote, and tequila a man could want. I won't be leaving San Miguel for a mighty long time.'

San Miguel de Allende was the current Mecca on the boho map, a magnet for artists as well as veterans, who found the army pensions provided by the G.I. Bill bought heaps of fiesta. Cameron had relished the town and was taking Jack back with her.

'Now tell us all about the Beast,' she said. 'I was in Paris and planning on visiting him. Such a drag he passed.'

Will described Crow's life at Netherwood and the offbeat courage he had displayed in the face of infamy and decrepitude.

'Sounds like you've been bitten by the bug,' said Jack. 'It's a one-way street, son. Not sure I'd recommend it. You better stay for dinner.'

They ate ribs washed down with rosé, both new to Will. He was dazzled by the plenty of America, the malls brimming with mega-sized cartons of breakfast cereal and mammoth jars of peanut butter; such a contrast to the frugal shores he had left behind. They followed with waffles and ice cream. Cameron produced a tightly rolled one-skin reefer which she took a few hits from and offered to Will.

'Lesson number one,' she said.

'Aw, come on!' said Jack, noting Will's reluctance. 'All that reefer madness stuff is bullshit. I can happily go without grass if it's not around, but as it's here...' He lunged for the reefer, took a few deep puffs, held the smoke in his lungs, and insisted Will take it.

The harsh smoke burnt his throat and impelled a fit of coughing. When this was spent, Cameron encouraged him to take another puff. The faces of his hosts became more complex, the man's melding with Cameron's portrait of him dominating the room: a dark angel exulting in the fall. The artist herself resembled a witch, her mouth wide and scarlet as she announced, 'It's all about freedom.'

'And poetry and vision, and the derangement of the senses, Io Pan! This calls for Lesson number two: a Khayyám Kontest!'

Jack bustled off to the kitchen and returned with a tray of glasses and two bottles. One held Pernod, the other sweet French wine. He filled two small tumblers with the former, and two wine glasses with the Sauternes, handing Will one of each.

'You dig the Rubáiyát?'

Like many of his generation, Will's father knew the Fitzgerald translation by heart and had used it to train his son's voice.

'Ok, the rules are simple. Drink the Pernod, recite a verse, chase with Sauternes!'

It was a heady mixture of two highly sugary alcohols. Will gave up after four verses, but Jack continued exuberantly until he correctly pronounced "Jamshyd" and "Kaikobád" in verse nine. All the while, Cameron was plying them with weed. At one point she went to the window, pulled up the blind and peered outside.

'Someone's under that magnolia tree.'

'Feds?' said Jack, propelling himself onto his feet and going over and joining her. 'Naw, trick of the light, sweetheart. I told you they're done with me.'

A few minutes later, he was struck by an idea. 'Know what a Joshua tree is? Nope! Well, I'm going to show you.'

Jack's battered open Packard was parked in the drive alongside the jeep Will had driven from San Diego. The door on the passenger side was held on by wire so Will had to clamber over. Jack himself slid into the driver's seat.

'We'll just wait a little while,' he said. 'If there are any Feds around, that should flush them out. Nothing like taking them on a wild goose chase to the desert.' He saw Will's incomprehension. 'FBI,' he explained. 'They see commies under every bed, ours included. They've wiretapped and tailed me more times than I care to remember. My security clearance has been revoked until the end of days, meaning I can't work with rockets no more. Cameron's paranoid and thinks they're still snooping. That's why we're going down Mexico way. Too much heat!'

He grinned, reversed, and backed out slowly, maintaining the same snail speed as he negotiated the serpentine lane. Such caution was out of character, but wise given the state he was in. It stayed lush and warm, the stars flickering gamely through the haze. At the end of the lane, they turned into Orange Grove Avenue.

'That's 1003, formerly the Agape Lodge.' Jack indicated a cluster of featureless condominiums. 'It was a beautiful, palatial mansion. They knocked it down as soon as I sold. Millionaire's Row? More like

Poverty of the Imagination Gulch. I posted ads for artists, anarchists, dreamers, eccentrics. I got a fortune teller, the newshound who broke the Black Dahlia case, a crazy avant-garde German actor, and a woman who'd been mistress of all the famous men in France. Jane Wolfe was our earth mother. A star of silent movies, she was with A.C. in Sicily. Bob Heinlein, the sci-fi writer, dropped by all the time. Hey, you should meet my galaxy! They're still around.'

Arroyo Seco, the parched strip of land that buffered Pasadena from Los Angeles, hurtled towards them. Jack was driving faster now and more recklessly. There were few cars on the road, fewer houses.

'Last time I came out here was with Hubbard, Lafayette Ron, you dig? Must have heard about him from A.C., right? He wangled the proceeds of the sale of 1003 out of me. Stole my girl Betty as well, but I've schooled myself not to nurse a grudge. Very bad karma! Boy, is Ron minting it now! His book on Dianetics is a national bestseller. He's invented an e-meter that audits you for 600 bucks. If you keep paying, you go clear and are cured of bad eyesight and a stammer. Probably makes your pecker longer too. Ron really has the gift of the gab.'

'Crow said he cheated you.'

'Ah, you gotta hand it to him. His gig is perfect for our times. It's as streamlined as computers, satellites, and science fiction. In fact, it is science fiction. With A.C. it was like the Middle Ages: all those weird gods and rituals. "Do what thou wilt!' Is that marketing speak? Who's gonna follow someone calling themselves Baphomet? I tried telling him, but he just shot back about all the famous cats he'd hung out with.'

'Sorry?'

Jack glanced at him; one eyebrow quizzically raised. 'Wow, we really speak a different language. "Hanging out" means spending time with somebody. A.C. was the 1890s, that was always the trouble.'

Will felt obscurely hurt on the Beast's behalf. 'A biography came out last year. It's been doing quite well.'

'*The Great Beast*? Yeah, did you see the blurb? "No deed too hideous, no sin too evil…": prime grade bullshit! Who's gonna take him seriously now except absolute freaks, which I guess includes your driver, and possibly yourself?'

Will felt a wave of nausea rise from his stomach. He told Jack, who pulled over. He climbed out of the car and made for a clump of bushes. Before he got there, technicolour vomit spurted from his mouth and drenched the sandy ground. He was sick repeatedly. Illuminated by the neon light on the sidewalk, the vomit gushed out in rainbow hues. It seemed every gram of foreign matter in his system was being expelled.

'That'll teach you to mess with Omar!' Jack slapped himself on the forehead. 'Jeez, I've just remembered. Cameron crushed up some peyote buttons from San Miguel and put them in the Pernod.'

It was the crown of the Mexican cactus that Crow had spiked Hess with.

'What will happen to me?' croaked Will in alarm.

'Oh, you'll feel a little rough for an hour or so. But when it kicks in, you'll find lesson number three a humdinger. Enjoy the ride!'

The nausea passed to be replaced by a lingering headache and drowsiness. Only a growing dread of the inscrutable man racing the Packard kept him alert. Jack expertly tapped an unfiltered Camel out of its soft pack, scooped it up with his lips, then fired it up with a Zippo he took from the dashboard. Macabre speculations about their destination inflamed Will's imagination.

After passing the last dwelling on their route - a rundown shack - miles of featureless dunes whizzed past until a turning came up ahead on their left. Jack veered off, and they rattled down a dirt track. He braked to a stop at a point above which two massive power lines intersected. Jack got out of the car, went round to the boot, and took out two robes, one of which he tossed to Will. Overhead, the sagging cables droned like Buddhist monks.

'Probably a little large for you,' Jack grinned. 'It was made for Hubbard.'

'You came out here with him?'

'Yeah, plenty. It was here I summoned an elemental, and, lo and behold, Cameron showed up the next day. I make rockets but I know there are enough megatons to blow up the planet. We need to radically alter our ways if we're gonna survive. That's why I raised Babalon: to bring on the New Aeon.'

'There's debris on those boulders over there.'

'In my previous life this was our firing range. That's what's left of the rockets we launched. That rusted metal hulk was our viewing platform. Come on, we gotta scale that dune!'

There was a twisted tree at the foot of it, its tilting branches terminating in spiky crowns of vegetation. 'This is the Joshua tree,' said Jack. 'Aptly named from our point of view, considering we're here to speak the language of Enoch, another patriarch. Hey, what's up with you? You seem riveted.'

'I've never seen stars like this.'

'The desert sky is the darkest on Earth. When it's this spangled, man, you can hear the music of the spheres. Somewhere up there old Doctor Dee is plucking his celestial harp. Where do you reckon that is? Betelgeuse? Sirius? Wow, man, you're really gone! Hang out here and stargaze. Join me when you're ready.'

Jack scrambled nimbly up a dune and disappeared over the crest. Will stayed below transfixed. He was in the belly of the universe. A lung filled with cosmic wind bounded Ursa Major. Another billowed like a sail south of Cassiopeia. At the centre of the triangle of Camelopardalis, the heart thumped. Everything was linked. Everything was sentient. The stars were huge reasoning machines, messaging fire. Each grain of sand beneath his feet contained worlds without limit. It was this he had been hunting since childhood: the ecstatic breath visiting him now. This was the philosopher's stone, the grail, the miraculous they were all in search of. There was a boulder beside him. It straightened and stood up. It was Crow, cowled like a monk in red robes.

'The Khabs is in the Khu, not the Khu in the Khabs,' he wheezed.

'Whatever does that mean?'

'Why must you always badger me? Jack will explain everything. He will give you what you seek.'

Will started running up the dune, his feet slipping on the grains of sand they displaced. Jack was at the top, hieratically holding a black circular obsidian mirror out before him. Will repeated the phrase he had heard; the 'Khabs' and 'Khu' felt like solids, hovering in the desert air.

'In ancient Egyptian "Khabs" signifies star and "Khu" spirit,' Jack explained. 'It means light infuses the spirit, not the other way round.'

Will was so glad he had met this man who now freed one hand to trace a pentagram in the air, while mouthing an invocation in Enochian. Four watchtowers appeared upon the desert, each with an angel shining on its battlements. A windstorm blew up, refashioning the dunes and propelling stinging sand that made them shield their eyes.

'That was the trouble with A.C.,' said the crazed man next to him, 'he did not go far enough. In his deepest heart he was an old reactionary, hidebound by the very conventions he loved to break. Witchcraft, voodoo, even Satanism are all tools there to be used.'

'What if there really is a soul, and that soul can be damned?'

'Man, where are *you* coming from?'

'My mother died giving birth to me. She was a Catholic. My father had me raised as one to honour her. It made sense for a while. I was even going to become a priest.'

'Heaven and hell are just ciphers for realms of the imagination. It's all within yourself. You can live any narrative you want. Look into the slate!'

There was just blackness on the smooth surface. This morphed to grey that cleared like mist to reveal an angel standing beside a slanted marble table on which the 21 letters of the Enochian alphabet were inscribed within a square.

'I wish to interrogate the spirit of my father,' entreated Jack.

The angel, who had a solemn face and colossal wings, began tapping letters with a wand. Jack mouthed the words they formed.

'We must go down. He is waiting for us there.'

They retraced their steps until they reached the boulder. Apart from clumps of cacti and the skull of an antelope, there was nothing. Jack kept chanting, but without result. The wind began to subside.

'I've already seen him,' said Will, explaining how the boulder had transformed into the dead mage.

Jack was cut up about this. He had lost his own father early on. Crowley was the closest surrogate he'd found. Both were raised to be spoilt, wealthy, and bored, which might account for their shared predilection for the dark.

'He won't appear again tonight,' groaned Jack. 'Why you, not me?'

'He said you would give me what I seek.'

'If it's Cameron, take her. She gives freely. Fidelity is slavery. Love cannot be owned. Jealousy is an abomination.'

It was the party line.

'Crow sent you a file a few years back.'

'Oh, that old thing. There was no magick in it, just stuff about the war. I wondered what I was supposed to do with it. It's yours if you want it.'

They made it back to the coach house a little after dawn. Will was due back at the San Diego base that evening. He needed rest before the two-hour drive, but his mind was still dazzled by peyote. Contrasted with the intricate greens of the surrounding vegetation and the vivid blues of the sky, the grey and black of drills and duties seemed ludicrous. He wished he could just "hang out", here in Pasadena. In no mood to sleep, Jack put Charlie Parker on the turntable. This roused Cameron, who clad in a loose purple robe, joined them, lounging on the sofa as she skinned up.

'Get far, hon?'

'Further than is permitted,' smirked Jack. 'We made it to the desert and Will saw A.C.!'

'Wow, and you didn't?'

Jack looked sheepish. 'I guess the old boy is hiding from me.'

'Or you from him. You may still get your chance. Folks are saying there's a shaven-headed cat in Little Venice who's the spitting image of the Beast. What did he say to you, Will?'

'That Jack would give me what I seek.'

Cameron's top lip brushed the lower. She flashed the tip of her tongue.

'Will wants some old file A.C. sent me a while back,' said her husband. 'Hey, I never asked what you needed it for?'

'A memento,' said Will.

'Yeah, I understand. Sometimes I reread his letters. You look like you're gonna collapse. Spare room's through there if you need to crash.'

There was a stack of Cameron's canvases in one corner and a single bed. The colours eddying round the room showed little sign of dwindling; nor did the new sense of self. The world was too vital and magical for sleep, but he drifted off when he was sure he wouldn't and dreamt Cameron was straddling him. One pear-shaped breast projected from her robe, swaying back and forth with her gyrations. Her over-ripe lips stayed shut, but he could hear her voice, coming from the sitting room where she and Jack were bickering.

It was early afternoon when he re-joined them. Jack fried three eggs, bacon, and pancakes for him, and he drank a lot of coffee.

'Any more leave coming up?' asked Cameron.

'Yes, the week after next.'

'We're leaving for San Miguel on the eighteenth. You could come for supper the night before. Stay over if you like and see us off.'

'Yeah, you can meet our galaxy. I'll invite Jane and Bob. It will really be a send-off.'

Will reminded Jack about the file.

'I had a look but drew a blank. It must be below.'

Will glanced at his watch as they went downstairs: it was three twenty-seven. If he reached base a minute after six, he would be put on a charge. On the ground floor he was disheartened to see papers, books, and magazines heaped on almost every surface as well as on the floor. Jack began rummaging, flinging objects to one side, so new mounds even messier than the ones before started rising like anthills. The ground floor was formerly a laundry. There was a boiler in one corner and a large cast-iron wash tub in front of it. Phials and Bunsen burners lined the work benches. Jack used these for his temporary job at the Bermite Powder Company, developing pyrotechnics and explosives for the motion picture industry. It was almost five to four.

'Jeez, I'm sorry,' sighed Jack. 'I'll have it for you next time. That's a definite! We must respect the Beast's undying wish.'

Chapter Nineteen
Jack Blows It

Tuesday, 17 June 1952

Just after five in the afternoon, Will was driving up Orange Grove Avenue when he glimpsed the Beast at the wheel of a Chevrolet, thundering past in the opposite direction. Just as it dawned on him the shaven headed man was Farkas, a tremendous blast ripped across the trimmed lawns, closely followed by another. He turned off the road and followed the bends of the drive. Smoke was wreathing the coach house ahead. He pulled up and vaulted out of the jeep. Papers lay scattered like confetti over the driveway. He bent down and picked up the torn cover of *Astounding Science Fiction* which featured a scantily clad girl straddling a rocket. Scrawled equations, chemical formulae, cabbalistic symbols, and fragments of Enochian covered other scraps, but there was no sign of 'The Z File'. The Hungarian must have taken it.

One garage door swung on its hinges. The others had been blown off. Will went through into the house. The acrid fumes were slowly dispersing. Even so his eyes began to sting. The back wall had exploded outwards, the vacant square framing a greenhouse twenty-five feet away in which every pane of glass had shattered. Stripped from the side wall, broken plaster rose in mounds on the floor, criss-crossed by timber beams that had collapsed from the ceiling. A blackened hole took up the centre where the floor had been. The air reeked of chemicals. Will sneezed and wiped away the forming tears.

A young man and older woman were trying to heave away a wash tub that had wedged against the wall after being ripped from its fitting. Will joined them. Together, they managed to push it to one side. There was a body crushed beneath it. Puddles of blood ringed Jack's head, torso and unnaturally bent, shattered leg. Will and the man dragged him to the wall and propped him up. His shoes were shredded, his shirt scorched, the right sleeve empty. Will saw a blackened stub ringed by ash a few feet away. It was all that was left of the rocketman's arm. Jack's face now formed two distinct halves: the slack, expressionless left-hand side, and the right, from which the skin had peeled, leaving white jawbone and teeth exposed. The eye on that side seemed to be missing, or completely caked by blood and sinew. Miraculously, his other eye fluttered open and he groaned.

A second man was coming down from the first-floor apartment. He paused on the stairs and shouted across that the police and fire services were on their way. Along with the young actor crouching beside Will, he had recently taken over the first-floor lease, while Jack kept the ground floor for his work.

'Jack was working on a rush job and seemed a little flustered,' said the actor. 'I told him not to blow us all up. He just grinned. Said not to worry.'

The dying man was struggling to tell them something. They could not make it out. The woman, who was the mother of the actor's boyfriend, began to make her way up the stairs. She did not want the soup she was making to boil over. Will bent his ear so close to Jack's mouth he had to wash flecks of blood off after. Jack sounded oddly pleased: 'My father the Beast was here. You see, you're not the only one he visits!'

Mostly broken, vials, flasks, test tubes, and bottles with blackened glass littered the floor. Hypodermic needles spilled out of an upturned trash can. Will and his companion exchanged a look. 'Better move them before the cops get here,' the actor said. They swept up the needles and gingerly dropped them into a trash bag. A siren alarmed the woodpeckers and finches outside. They fluttered squawking around the magnolia trees.

The actor went outside and talked to the police. Then he took his own car and drove to 424 Arroyo Terrace, two miles to the north. Cameron and Jack had been staying there with Jack's mother, who was taking care of the house for the summer. The actor wanted to find Cameron, but only the mother was at home. He told her the news and left. Mother and son were very close. She began drinking heavily. Later that day, she took an overdose of Nembutal that killed her.

Cameron had been doing some last-minute shopping for Mexico. She drove back to the coach house to pick up Jack. By now it was teeming with cops and reporters. The open Packard was pulling a trailer. Reporters pulled back the tarpaulin and peered inside. There were canvases, paints, archery gear, fencing foils, and a record player. Cameron emerged from the car, causing a stir with her scarlet presence.

'I am an artist. He was a chemist.' The past tense rendered her momentarily mute. 'We were supposed to leave for Mexico earlier today, but the studio contacted him with a rush job. He said a few dollars more couldn't hurt. Goes a long way in San Miguel.'

A burly reporter in a porkpie hat took out his notebook. 'The police are saying it's an accident. He must have dropped something when he was tinkering with the explosives, and boom!'

'Jack could be wild and reckless but when it came to his work, he was always very safety conscious.'

'Maybe he was in a hurry, mam. Just couldn't wait for the fiesta to start.'

There was a well of laughter despite the occasion.

'Your husband testified as an expert witness against a corrupt cop who was paroled last week. Any connection?'

Cameron peered at the new speaker, a skinny reporter with horn-rimmed glasses. 'Jack had history,' she said.

'What about the Israelis, mam?' demanded another newshound. 'Word is they wanted to recruit him for their rocket programme.'

'Jack was a very talented engineer. Sure, we were considering Tel Aviv after Mexico.'

'Then he could have been a target for the Soviets. They sure as hell don't like anyone working for the new Jewish state. Let alone a rocketman!'

This gave Will pause. Perhaps 'The Z File' was old news as far as the Russians were concerned, and Farkas was on a mission more in tune with his murderous skills. Cameron spotted Will on the fringes of the crowd and called him over. 'Will you come to the hospital?' she said.

Dazzled by flashing bulbs, she steered the Packard through the throng and accelerated up the winding lane.

'Whatever brought you here?' she said.

'You invited me for dinner.'

'Oh Jeez, honey, we switched days and clean forgot about your visit. Things have been frantic with all the packing. How lousy of us not to let you know! You saw him? He was in a bad way? Like when we get to the hospital, they'll tell me he's a goner?'

'He was alive when the ambulance left.'

'Jack's been handling explosives since his teens. Worst that ever happened was a minor burn or two. But he always said he'd be blown away.'

'By his own hand?'

'Oh, he loved himself too much for that. You heard those reporters. I'm surprised they didn't ask about Hubbard, who claims he was working for Naval Intelligence all along. Rescued a girl and broke up the black magic ring he'd infiltrated. What a hero! Then there's the FBI. When they revoked his clearances, Jack was sure they were out to get him. Like I said, he had history.'

She looked directly at Will. 'Hey, you don't seem that shook up yourself! What's your take on this?'

Part IV
London 1965

Chapter Twenty
Year Zero

Thursday, 8 April 1965

Everybody's hair was getting longer. Ginger Baker's was tangling into a red fuzz, framing his sucked in cheeks, pinned eyes and nicotine-veneered teeth. It was a face that threatened to eat you and your kids for breakfast. They'd just listened to 'Play with Fire', the B-side of the Rolling Stones' current number one, 'The Last Time', and Baker was having none of it.

'The tossers couldn't play black blues to save their lives. Now they've gone all psycho wiv fairy 'arpsichords an all.'

'Psy-che-delic,' corrected Alexis Korner, in his gravelly, well-spoken voice. With his afro hair, cool shades, and full lips he appeared to be part black. In fact, he was a Paris-born melange of Austrian Jew, Greek and Turkish.

'Psy-fuckin'-cho! I'm amazed Charlie don't roll over and die of shame.'

Before migrating to the Stones, Charlie Watts had been Baker's replacement in Korner's Blues Incorporated. Korner smiled indulgently and passed the joint. The sweet pungency of red Lebanese enveloped the living room of his fusty flat. A television, with the volume turned down, was showing 'Juke Box Jury' in direct line of sight of Jack Bruce, sprawled on the sofa.

'I thought the harpsichord was pretty cool,' said Bruce in his lilting Scottish burr.

'That's because you're a fuckin' cellist who moonlights playin' R & B!'

Bruce gazed with stoned serenity at his bandmate.

There was a ring at the front door. Nico, Korner's son, peered through the peephole and turned the latch. The newcomer tottered into the room in Cuban-heeled Chelsea boots, a black cloak, and striped hipsters that were too tight for his pudgy frame. He had dark penetrating eyes, a bloated face, and a Fu Man Chu moustache. He knew everyone except Will.

'Meet the soundman,' growled Korner. 'Will, this is Graham Bond.'

'I 'ope 'e's a *sound* man,' Baker spat out, glaring at his neighbour.

'He's not a sound, man, he's a man, man.'

Bruce was out of his gourd. The others were just out of their heads.

'Do what thou wilt,' said Bond in his estuary voice.

Will recoiled, too shocked to do anything other than reply: 'Love is the Law.'

It was Bond's turn to look startled. They faced each other like boxers about to exchange blows.

'You dig A.C.?' said Bond.

'Dig him? I knew him.'

'You knew my dad?'

Bond had landed the knock-out punch.

The musician was a Barnardo boy, born in Essex in 1937, the same year the Beast had sired an illegitimate son in the county. That he and that boy were one and the same was Bond's inescapable conclusion. Will remembered Jack Parsons, and wondered how many offspring the Beast had spawned, now roaming the planet in search of Dad.

'Gram, we need to 'ave a catch up,' said Baker, rising from his chair and hustling Bond out to the bathroom.

Nico came in and demanded a quid from his dad.

'Think I'm made of bread, man? What's it for?'

It was six thirty. The gritty police drama 'Z Cars' was playing on the flickering black-and-white screen. In an hour or so, Nico was due to hook up with 'H' and 'Trippie Dickie' in the ticket hall at Notting Hill Gate tube station. They would pool info about happenings in shabby flats in Gate and Grove, before making off for one. Korner pulled a red note from the chest pocket of his corduroy shirt, tossed the ten shillings at his son, and took a glug of Bulgarian plonk.

Bond and Baker re-emerged with glistening eyes and sprightly movements. They would remain fired up for all of ten minutes. Bond grabbed a Muddy Waters' album from the stack next to the record player, placed it on his lap and commenced crumbling black crystal-speckled Nepalese Temple Ball into golden Three Castles tobacco.

'Can't you feel it happening, man?' he said. 'Year Zero! Everything's in flux. Full speed ahead to the New Aeon. He knew, didn't he? The Crowned and Conquering Child. The Beast dug it long before anybody else!'

'Crowley was a creep,' muttered Baker.

'Yeah, if you believe Symonds. He sensationalised and belittled the Holy Guru. He spat and trampled on Sacred Magick. Just wait till karma catches up with him. Have you tried LSD, man?'

Courtesy of a professor of physics at Imperial College, Will had. He agreed it was remarkable.

'Thelema in a nutshell.'

'Give us a toke, Alexis!' demanded Baker.

Korner took three rapid puffs, held the smoke down, then broke into a racking cough. He proffered the joint as though offering a peace pipe, which in a sense it was.

Eighteen months before, Baker, Bond and Bruce had abandoned Blues Incorporated to form The Graham Bond ORGANisation. Korner had been a bit put out, but his band was a revolving door, arguably the launchpad of the Rolling Stones, Free and Led Zeppelin. Korner was inured to the phenomenal success enjoyed by musicians who had thrived under his tutelage in the blues, hitherto a backwater. It was a feat of humility that Graham Bond would prove far less agile at making.

Bond and Baker were starting to nod off. Both were registered addicts and received pure high-grade British pharmaceutical heroin on prescription, for which they queued at midnight outside the Boots all-night chemist in Piccadilly Circus. Baker's addiction stemmed from the late 1950s when he had convinced himself that heroin, a staple of the scene, fuelled his virtuoso jazz drumming. Bond had only recently tipped over into the abyss, following a divorce and a sequence of personal crises that would continue to dog him. Korner's jeopardy was much greater. Allowing premises to be used for smoking cannabis had just been criminalised and the penalties were draconian.

'Smack!' he muttered with distaste, gazing at the sleeping beauties.

'You're a pillock who surrounds himself with talent just so 'e can look cool,' murmured Baker, without unshuttering an eyelid.

Three hours later, Will's practised fingers were twiddling the knobs and levering the slides on the mixing desk, while he checked that the tape reels on the four-track were revolving smoothly. A crowd of heaving souls were crammed into Klooks Kleek, a gritty music venue in West Hampstead. It had been a storming set of jazz-infused rhythm and blues and had all the makings of an excellent live album. A pioneer in his introduction of the mellotron, Bond was creating a hybrid of Bach and the blues on 'Wade in the Water'. A berserk Baker thrashed at the drums. Bruce hammered the bass, producing a wild proliferation of notes. "You're too fuckin' busy!" Baker yelled. Will wondered if the tape had picked that up.

The next number, the Baker-penned 'Camels and Elephants', featured a lengthy drum solo. Bruce joined in about halfway through, keeping time with Baker's trademark double-bass drums. At first the Scotsman hung back, but soon his booming notes began to take over. Highly sensitive to volume - if to little else - Baker raised his drumsticks above his head and hurled them at the bassist. "It will be a knife next time," he shrieked as he vaulted from his stool and laid into his bandmate. With his trademark goatee jutting out, Dick Heckstall-Smith, the saxophonist, helped Bond part the feuding bandmates. The crowd booed and catcalled. Other than Baker shoving Heckstall-Smith's cap off his head, there was little damage. No live record, however, would see the light of day. There was a sour mood in the van on the way back to Shepherd's Bush, where the gear was stored. Reluctant to end the night on such a downer, Will hailed a black cab and went to Soho.

* * *

A tiny lift in the foyer of 7 Leicester Place accessed the Ad Lib, a club above the Prince Charles Theatre. Will pressed the fourth-floor call button. The doors began to close, but two Beatles jammed them apart, squeezing in followed by their wives. All giggling, they seemed to on the verge of hysterics. Will wondered if his face was dirty or flies undone. The laughter was not directed at him, however. Judging from their glazed, illuminated eyes, the Fab Two and their consorts were in a highly altered state. As the lift began to ascend, the cackling evaporated, replaced by panic.

'This lift's on fire!' shrieked George.

'And we're going to hell,' howled John.

'We'd be going down for that.'

'Then it's your Woody.' John seemed surprised to find he was also smoking, in his case a Gauloise Bleue.

'The Bismarck's sinking!' contributed John's wife Cynthia, who was wearing large granny glasses with blue lenses.

'What's that up there then, all red and crackling?' said George.

'Definitely flames,' responded John.

All four started screaming. Will felt obliged to intervene.

'It's a red light actually.'

This did not have the required effect. In a neat reversal of the established order, the lift door opened on two screaming Beatles and their squealing wives. The Ad Lib was a cavernous space, sound-proofed by fur that lined the oak-panelled walls. The club's dim lighting rendered the low tables, chandeliers, and faux-leather banquettes as shadowy shapes. Behind a grand piano stacked with record decks, DJ Teddy was playing imported American soul and R & B, the only genres deemed sufficiently "cool". The clientele included a sprinkling of Stones, Who and Pretty Things, two famous cockney photographers, models, actors, dealers, and career criminals.

John had a reputation for blowing up if crossed. A path was quickly cleared as he swayed towards the private table reserved for the sole use of the Beatles. It was in an alcove, with a large window overlooking the tiled roofs of Soho. Bystanders were amazed by John's affable manner, though this was easily outshone by George, beaming at them like a man in love.

'Mind if I come to?' said Will.

'Do your own thing, man,' grinned George, coining the alternative society's take on "Do what thou wilt".

Will followed a little sheepishly. He did not want to be looked on as a groupie. There was a definite hierarchy in the club and the Beatles were at the apex. The nascent counterculture was feudal. Musicians exercised droit de seigneur after every gig. The serfs stood and gaped from the bar. Ringo was already sitting at the table. The two couples shook with barely suppressed laughter at the sight of him.

'Have you been at the wacky baccy?' the drummer demanded in his deadpan way.

'No, wack,' said George. 'It's better than that. I'm seeing God.'

'Do say hello from me.' John put on his upper-class voice, transforming the vowels into strangulated parodies of themselves.

'I love everybody.' George surveyed the dim surroundings with kaleidoscope eyes. 'I want to hug and kiss them all.'

'I hear the Krays are in tonight. Not sure they'd dig that,' said Ringo.

'Ronnie might,' said John.

'Who's the fella?'

'I'm Will. I was in Studio Three at Abbey Road while you were in Studio Two.'

'You're a bit long in the tooth to be a rocker,' said George.

'I'm a sound engineer.'

'Who were you recording?'

Will mentioned an American singer with a reputation for being a firebrand.

'He's a nutter,' said John.

'Did he have a revolver?' demanded George.

'I meant the fella barging through the woolybacks in our direction,' corrected Ringo. 'He's making a right commotion.'

'That's our wicked dentist,' said George.

'They're letting any riff-raff in these days. He's a very groovy tooth fairy, though.'

The man was turned out in check hipsters with a wide belt, a shirt with floral prints, and a brown Carnaby leather jacket. His name was John Riley, a south Londoner who had trained in cosmetic dentistry in Chicago and set up a flourishing Harley Street practice. Known as dentist to the stars, many of the crowns and bridges in the club owed their existence to him.

'I see you're keeping him to yourselves,' said Ringo.

'Who'd want to keep a dentist?' said John.

'A dentist keeper,' suggested George.

John Riley's florid face was steeped in anxiety, which melted at the sight of them.

'Glad to see you got here safe and sound, boys.'

'Shapeshift and crystal fashion,' said John.

This reduced he and George to hysterics. Their cackling lasted long enough for Ringo to drain his scotch and coke, stub out his Rothmans, glance up at Will and say, 'Are they always like this?'

'It was quite a journey wasn't it, John?'

'I'll say, George. Marshmallow trees. Grenadine skies.'

'We came by mini,' said his wife, surprising John who thought they had journeyed by submarine. 'The Bismarck is sinking! A man of your standing shouldn't do things like that.'

'Yes, you're a very naughty dentist and I'm not flashing my molars at you ever again,' said John.

'Or my wisdom teeth,' said George. 'I need as much of that as possible.'

'Look, boys, I'm sorry. I thought it would be fun.'

Riley was referring to the LSD he'd spiked their coffee with after dinner in his Bayswater flat. He gazed forlornly at Cynthia and Pattie's brilliant veneers, making his farewell. His practice was painless. He shot patients up with Valium beforehand. Not only was he the catalyst for 'Doctor Robert', but he was also...

'Tomorrow never knows,' said Ringo.

'We're quite aware of what sort of fun you had in mind, you dirty perv,' said John.

'But we forgive you,' said George, 'cos we love you.'

There was a free seat at the table. Will asked if he could sit there.

'Only if you don't talk,' said John.

Chapter Twenty-One
Soho Haunt

Friday, 9 April 1965

The voluptuous Italian film star Gina Lollobrigida opened the Moka Bar in Frith Street in 1953. Compared to the watery concoction of inferior grains and chicory available hitherto, the frothy espresso dispensed by the gleaming new Gaggia machine was both revolution and revelation. Coffee bars soon proliferated throughout Soho. French students frequented Les Enfants Terrible. Politicos dawdled for hours in The Partisan over a single coffee and Chairman Mao's *Little Red Book* until it went broke. Beats in black polo necks and sunglasses hung out at The Picasso, spouting ersatz-Kerouac and Ginsberg to Françoise-Hardy lookalikes, flaunting mini-skirts and the pill.

Will's usual haunt was the 2i's, named after the two Iranian founders. Tommy Steele, Cliff Richard and the Shadows, Vince Taylor and the Playboys had all launched careers from the foot-high stage with its battered piano in the basement. Feeling the aftermath of too many whiskies and cokes the night before, the neon lit interior, with its linoleum floors, Formica tables and stainless-steel fittings, made him nauseous. The cool, white-walled interior of the Heaven and HELL next door seemed far more soothing.

He had left the Ad Lib just as it was getting light, turning up his collar in the crisp Soho dawn, while a dustcart trundled by to a chorus of clattering lids as the bins were collected. After snatching a few hours restless sleep at his studio in Maida Vale, he had returned to the scene of the crime. Working girls were already touting for business on the chequerboard of streets. Garlic reeked from the market, where barrow boys were flogging fruit and veg at knockdown prices.

Will took a sip of frothy coffee from his transparent Pyrex cup. A pair of strippers were trotting past the red-lit sex shops on the other side of Old Compton Street. The girls carried little suitcases holding costumes they would discard faster than the paint peeling from the walls of the grubby basements they worked in. A spotty youth, puffing greedily on Player's hit new brand No. 6, came next, wheeling a handcart loaded with film cans. He brushed past a pipe-smoking figure in a Harris Tweed jacket, moss green cords and brown trilby, peering into a shop window. The man glanced round. He was in his sixties, stooped, with silver hair. The nose was the give-away. Will abandoned his espresso and rushed across the street. Passing Act One, Scene 1, usually a haunt of actors, he glimpsed a surly looking Brian Jones lounging in the back with puffy eyes and trademark helmet of blond hair. The man in the trilby was looking at a display of girlie, nudist, and weightlifting magazines, and green-bound Olympia Press erotica, *Lolita* and *Naked Lunch*.

'They cater for every taste,' said Will.

The startled pipe-smoker wheeled round.

'Long time since anyone crept up on me like that. Must be losing my touch.' The voice was as warm and avuncular as ever, though a little hoarse. He nodded at the display. 'Curiosity got the better of me.'

'Major Knight.'

'Oh, do call me Max. Military titles don't seem very "with it" these days. Had to see the quack. Thought I'd take a stroll. Must be getting on for twenty years since we last met. I suppose my limb gave me away.' He tapped his nose with one finger.

'They do a very good espresso across the road.'

'I'm an Orange Pekoe man myself, but coffee's all the rage. I could give it a whirl.'

They crossed back to the bar. Will ordered another coffee, paid the ninepence, and bore it to the major.

'So, this is where it all happens. Not much sign of hell.'

'Oh, that's downstairs. Want to take a look?'

Knight smiled. 'As long as it doesn't mean taking up residence.'

'Let's not get ahead of ourselves,' said Will, immediately regretting it.

A giant devil's mouth at the bottom of the stairs admitted them into a cavern. The walls and ceiling were black, lit by red-eyed demon masks. There was nobody else there.

Knight took in their surroundings, still smiling. 'Crow would have been in his element. One of his crankier schemes was for a Bar 666 with the skulls of goats and spooky lighting. Very like this in fact.'

'There's another place, Le Macabre in Meard Street, where patrons sit on coffins and use candlelit skulls for ashtrays.'

'The Gargoyle club was in Meard Street: huge mirrors, artists, tipsy dukes and debutantes. Went there a couple of times with Crow. He mellowed in Netherwood, you know. I think he grew tired of shocking people. After he died, *Time* said the world of 1947 shrugged its shoulders and moved on, but I notice his name cropping up more and more lately.'

'It's a real shame his war work's never seen the light of day. That might change the way people look at him.'

Knight shifted uncomfortably. 'He sent the file to America, as I told you.'

'I know. I went to look for it.'

Will described his visit to Pasadena and his belief the Soviets might now be in possession of Parson's copy. He wondered why they had not made more of it.

Knight appraised him steadily. 'Despite our best efforts to persuade him, Admiral Godfrey, Ian's boss, vetoed the idea of 666 interviewing Hess. 'The Z File' is a fake.'

Will had never considered this. 'What about the stenographer who was hanged?'

'Sorry, old chap. Sometimes a dash of fiction is expedient.'

'You weren't in Surrey on 22 June 1941?'

'I was in Dolphin Square. I recall it vividly. After all, it was probably the turning point of the war. Joan Miller - the pretty assistant who didn't like you - ran in and told me the Germans had attacked Russia. Not a big surprise. There'd been reams of advance intel.'

'So, the man in Spandau...'

'Really is Rudolf Hess.'

'Then why is he still refusing to see his family? And what about the amnesia?'

'He faked the memory-loss at Nuremburg, but it may well be genuine by now. After all, he's in his seventies. He doesn't want to see his family because he's too proud or too ashamed. Face it, Will! He's a crank. Obsessive. Quirky. That's why he made the flight in the first place.'

'A surgeon in Spandau couldn't find the scar where Hess was shot in the First World War.'

A man in possession of all the secrets, Knight kept smiling. 'The doctor was looking in the wrong place. '

'I still find it difficult to believe the file's invented.'

Knight pulled his pipe out of his pocket and tapped it against the wall. A shower of ash floated down.

'The day after he lunched with the Beast, Ian went to the States with Admiral Godfrey via Portugal to help set up what became the CIA. When he returned to England, he still regretted our plan had come to nothing. Being Ian, he decided to pretend that it had. He concocted 'The Z File', with the intention of bamboozling the Germans and the Russians. Even if Centre did get its hands on the file in 1952, it was irrelevant. It was a new era, remember: the Cold War.'

'But Stalin still controlled Russia, and Churchill was prime minister again.'

'Any mole in British Intelligence could have told Centre the file was bogus. Besides, Stalin was dying and Churchill senile. We came across Farkas again, by the way. He played a key role in suppressing the uprising in Hungary in '56. A very nasty piece of work. Are you sure it was the file he was after?'

Will recalled Cameron's encounter with the newsmen.

'He may have been trying to stop Jack Parsons working for the Israelis.'

Knight nodded vehemently. 'There's your answer. The Soviets are ruthless when it comes to protecting their own interests.'

'And we aren't?'

The spymaster's eyes grew hooded.

'We have to be.'

'Are there any copies?'

Knight shrugged. 'Broadway's files are sealed for the duration. Intelligence of the highest sensitivity is transferred to Royal Archives at Windsor Castle that remains classified in perpetuity.'

'Like 'The Z File'.'

'Which, as I keep reminding you, was black propaganda spawned by Ian's over-ripe imagination. Besides, Crow's getting more than enough attention these days in books and magazines, even on the radio.'

'Music, too, and film.'

When they were back upstairs, Will recounted the night he had seen *Inauguration of the Pleasure Dome* at the ICA. Kenneth Anger, the filmmaker, had created a 38-minute hallucinogenic cavalcade in which extravagantly costumed amateurs played gods and goddesses. Before a turbaned image of Crowley, Cameron smoked reefer. Everything about her was scarlet, from her cropped hair to her glistening lips, and there was a curl to her mouth that was unalloyed evil. Will had got goosebumps at how closely the single breast jutting from her shawl resembled that in his lucid dream in Pasadena. He described how Lady Frieda Harris had rebuked Anger in the foyer after the screening. She had called his creation a disease not a film, a work of absolute filth that ought to be suppressed, a rank disservice to the memory of the Beast. Anger had thrown down the present she had given him on arrival and stormed off.

'I think I'd have sided with Lady Frieda,' said the major, sucking on his pipe. 'Crow wasn't the only draw, you know. It was an age-old belief in numinous existences, in angels, and devils as well: something more than the run of the mill, of which we all get an inkling. I used to find some of it a bit far-fetched — the Aeon, for example.'

'Look at my generation! There really does seem to be a changing of the guard.'

'Yes, your generation. The Soviets are rubbing their hands at the sight of all you ban-the-bombers. You're not the first, you know. The jazz scene was a revelation when I was in New York in 1918. We'd had the Great War. It was "never again". Everyone was looking to remodel the world.'

'Still playing?'

'Hardly, and all's quiet on the wireless front, I'm afraid. Everything's television these days. I was offered a dog food commercial but thought it a bit off. I did do a couple of Peter Scott nature programmes, but the BBC concluded I'm not cut out for location work and talking to the camera. No flair for "improv".'

'Improvisation?'

'That's the ticket. You seem fluent in the lingo.'

'I do a bit of session work at Broadcasting House.'

'So, you're still at it. That's very good.'

'I'm more into the engineering side. I help produce records and do the sound at gigs...I mean concerts.'

'We called them "gigs" in the Twenties.'

'I played in a few bands but as far as being a pop star goes, I'm past it.'

'God doesn't age catch up with us! You seem a mere stripling to me. I find music these days a terrible racket, but my father's generation said the same about jazz. Very kind of you to invite me. This coffee certainly carries a kick.'

The major rose.

'Far to go?'

'Camberley. Leafy suburbs and all that. Feel free to visit. My number's in the book.' He glanced at his watch. 'Fascinating programme on the wireless after tea. Must get home.'

Back in his Maida Vale flat, Will checked the *Radio Times*. On the Home Service there was a competition for bands called *Challenging Brass*, on the Light Programme, a radio newsreel and sports review. That just left the Third Programme, which was featuring a broadcast about a German poet. This did not sound very promising until Will read the poet had been mixed up with Rudolf Hess. If Beth didn't pass by, he'd give it a shot. Then he remembered she was on a Cornish beach, waiting for the sun. Beth dropped in and out of his life like a yoyo, smoking his hash, strumming his guitar, leafing through his copy of *Melody Maker*. 1965 was a free for all, with the emphasis firmly on "free". Just before seven he turned on the radio. It was tuned to Radio Luxembourg. The strident opening chords of the Yardbird's current hit 'For Your Love' blasted from the speaker. He twiddled the knob until he found the frequency.

Chapter Twenty-Two
The Sonneteer of Moabit

Announcer: 'Our programme tonight focuses on the diary Albrecht Haushofer kept from December 1944 to April 1945. Haushofer is remembered as the principal adviser of Rudolf Hess and the author of a remarkable sonnet sequence composed in the prison of Moabit in Berlin. Arrested during *Aktion Hess*, the crackdown sparked by the Deputy Führer's flight to Scotland, Haushofer was held by the Gestapo for two months. As the Nazi regime still prized his connections with the British, he was released and allowed to continue as a professor at Berlin University.

'Over the next three years, Haushofer was a key player in the resistance. After the failure of Count Stauffenberg's assassination attempt in July 1944, he went into hiding in the Alpine Partnachalm region where his family had a lodge. The Gestapo captured him on 7 December. Allied officers removed the diaries of Haushofer and his father from the lodge in May 1945. Their whereabouts since then is unknown. However, in November last year, the diary Haushofer kept in Moabit was discovered in the prison archives. The new light it casts on the Hess affair will be of particular interest to historians. The poet Michael Hamburger translated the diary. The actor Richard Burton reads it for us tonight.'

Monday 11th December 1944

From the poorly jointed window of my cell, I see the prisoners trudging around a yard that radiates from the conical control tower. The convicts' faces are as grey as the pocked walls that brood over them. Their hopelessness reminds me of Van Gogh's painting of a prison exercise yard I saw in Moscow. Moabit is constructed like a five-pointed star but is lucky for nobody. Even the guards, formerly well-fed farm boys from villages east of the Danube now obliterated, are furtive, scrawny, and secretly anxious about their fate. There is no future for them either. They are prisoners just like us. The overseer in the yard alone is exultant. In his stiff uniform and shiny jackboots, he scurries to and fro, cuffing one straggler, kicking the next. Why is he so ecstatic? Doesn't he realise his days are also numbered? There are planes in the distance. Bombs are falling. The explosions are getting louder every day.

Tuesday 12th December 1944

I made a count of the time I spent hiding: four months and thirteen days. I could have swum the Rhine to Switzerland or accepted the offer of a friendly innkeeper who wanted to hide me in a cave and then guide me across the Alps. But I did not want to abandon my homeland. I was sure the Americans would come soon, or the British. They are probably there now, but too late for me.

My father disowned me for my part in the resistance. The Gestapo interned him in Dachau. They threatened my mother with deportation to Theresienstadt - the transit ghetto in Czechoslovakia where they process Jews for the death camps - if she did not give me up. She had no idea where I was, nor did the Gestapo until five days ago they searched the farm of the woman who was sheltering me. One of them climbed the ladder to the hayloft and spied vapour rising from the bales under which I was hiding. How gleefully he hauled me out in my soiled green hunting coat, with my hair dangling to my shoulders and a flowing beard! I'm cropped and shaved now. If it had not been so cold that day...but it is winter, and we all must breathe.

Thursday 14th December 1944

Apparently, I am receiving special treatment. A skeletal Jesuit whispered as much to me in the yard. I wondered what he was talking about. It almost made me angry. They handcuff my hands in front of my stomach by day - making it a trial to write this - and behind my back at night. They chain my legs to the wall beside the bed. The lamp stays on all night, except during air raids when they cover it with a cloth. But I still have my fingernails and teeth, which many trudging the circle lack. I have been given a notebook, pencils, books, and yesterday's newspaper — unimaginable luxuries. At Gestapo headquarters on Prinz-Albrecht-Strasse, the interrogators are bewilderingly civil. They seem almost embarrassed by the muffled screams coming from the basement.

Is Hitler considering using my contacts with the British to cut a deal? In my play *Sulla* the Greek sage Zosias refuses to become foreign minister to the Tyrant. Would I display such courage? Hitler hiring me is my greatest fear, that, or a visit from the SS Rollkommando extermination squad. Genghis Khan commanded his Mongol hordes to exempt thinkers and artists from the pyramid of skulls they raised in conquered cities. Today we are far more egalitarian. Life is National Socialist, but death a democrat. All skulls are equal!

Saturday 16th December 1944

There is a purpose to the notebook after all. Today the Gestapo instructed me to set down my political views and the best means of getting a reasonable deal with the Allies. Rats! A sinking ship! We failed to wrest the rudder out of their hands and soon the sea will engulf us.

Tuesday 19th December 1944

The guards carried in a new cellmate on a stretcher yesterday evening and heaved him onto the other bunk. He is very ill. His coughing kept me awake. I lost a lot of weight while on the run and several kilos more since being here. The food is atrocious. A thin gruel heralded at noon by a bell, like those lepers use to warn of their approach. Then, shortly after dusk, watery stew speckled with drowned flies served with maggoty rye bread. But I am in the pink of health compared to my cellmate. His cheeks are so hollow they seem about to cave in. He sweats constantly despite the cold. There is something strangely familiar about his haughty features and burning black eyes.

Wednesday 20th December 1944

My new cellmate spoke for the first time this afternoon. The moment I heard that sneering tone I realised it was Krafft. I told him to be careful. The Gestapo must have placed him here for a reason and have certainly bugged the cell. But he is as headstrong as old and spoke as if we were chatting over coffee in the Tiergarten. Like me, he was first arrested during *Aktion Hess* in June '41. The Gestapo rounded up all the candidates for his *Who's Who of Border Science* - clairvoyants, irido-diagnosticians, nature healers, mediums, astrologers, telepathists, soothsayers, diviners. Their pernicious doctrines were blamed for inspiring Hitler's beloved comrade-in-arms to make his lunatic flight. Eventually, most were released. But not Krafft. In confinement, he was put to work for Goebbels. The bogus horoscopes and fake prophecies he was forced to churn out so disgusted him that he refused to produce any more. He is an oxymoron made flesh: a Nazi man of principle. After that he was dragged from gaol to concentration camp and back to gaol. He was even here in Moabit before.

It was February 1943. The prison was full of young soldiers who had deserted on the Eastern Front. There was, amazingly, a carnival atmosphere Krafft told me. All day they were singing, swapping jokes, and laughing, even though they were going to be shot. They considered Moabit a paradise compared to Russia. The rations were better, and you only had to stand against a wall once and be killed, whereas at the front there was no end to the suffering before you died. Confined in an underground cell designed for 12 with 50 others, Krafft was less delighted with his new home. He is surprised how much better his conditions are this time.

I told him he was a beneficiary of my good fortune. Krafft, who is deaf to irony, looked puzzled. Then he came out with something that really shocked me. The report I have been asked to compose is for Himmler not Hitler. The SS boss is looking for an escape route and wants to make peace with the Allies. His master is still resolute. Hitler is building the pyre on which he will fling himself and be consumed. But "faithful Heinrich" is inching away from the flames.

Friday 22nd December 1944

This afternoon I asked Krafft what the stars held in store. He said Uranus rules the Third Reich as it does him, making their fates synonymous. The war ending in '43 would have brought victory. As things stand, Germany is doomed, and we with it. You don't have to be an astrologer to realise that!

Sunday 24th December 1944

Is my cellmate an impostor? Incredibly, Krafft showed sympathy for his fellow man and enquired about my life since Hess flew to Scotland. I described how I was escorted by armed guard to Berchtesgaden and ordered to write a report on the peace party at Westminster - *English Connections and the Possibility of Utilising Them* — on the *Führer-Maschine*, a typewriter with outsize lettering Hitler can read without glasses. The Tribune summoned me that evening. He was in the field grey uniform he has worn since assuming command of the Wehrmacht. I expected a tantrum, but these blow up with the unpredictability of hurricanes. Even when my father's proposed redrawing of the frontiers of Europe angered him, he just walked out stony-faced and silent. In private he is stiff yet cordial. This time was no different — at least at the outset.

Krafft wondered if the Führer knew what Hess was up to. The Deputy Reichsführer was not a man of cunning like Göring or Speer, I responded. The Führer may have caught an inkling of the plan via a throwaway remark but not so as to forbid it. On that evening, two days after Hess's flight, Hitler was downcast and filled with suppressed rage. How was he supposed to explain his deputy's futile peace-overture to the Italians and the Japanese, or reassure the Wehrmacht whose morale had taken a battering? Hess's act was a terrible admission of weakness.

'I have given orders for the madman to be shot if he returns! Thank God I made Göring next in line. A talk with the Air *Reichsmarschall* is bracing, like bathing in steel. With Hess you are floating on the Dead Sea. You neither sink nor swim. You get nowhere, he is so stubborn.' He peered at me gloomily. 'Will counts for far more than the number of tanks or divisions you possess. Hess never understood that. Where, I ask myself, did his muddled objections originate? Am I looking at their author, the Cassandro who fed his craven doubts? Ever since Mussolini came into my compartment on the Führer train and complained of your urging him to make me more moderate, I've kept my eye on you. Trying to teach me about TERRITORY just like your father, were you, Haushofer? You always were a bird of ill omen. Ribbentrop wanted me to lock you up for deviationism, but I let Hess convince me that we needed a doomsayer in our midst to balance things. Is he here to protect you now? I don't think so. The crazy fool, with his pacifist delusions, is in England, spilling my secrets even as we speak.'

I supposed he was in full tantrum mode now. During speeches, a sort of hypnosis possesses him, transforming him into a clairvoyant or medicine man. You can almost hear the shamanic drum. After-wards, he is exhausted and just sits down, once more a simple and pleasant seeming man. It was like that now. He had the look of a rag that all the water had been squeezed out of.

'Like you, I am an artist not a warrior or even a politician,' he said. 'I do not want to turn Germany into a vast barracks. I will only do so if forced. Once this business is over, I will roam through Italy as an unknown painter.'

The Gestapo kept me for two months. "Gestapo-Müller" - to distinguish him from the SS general with the same surname - interrogated me. The Gestapo chief is short and thickset with a peasant's square head, razor-thin lips and piercing brown eyes. "Intellectuals should be sent down a coal mine and blown up," was his shock opener. Naturally, I feared where this might lead, but it turned out he only wanted to dictate how often I might write and teach.

They tried it on of course. I had left my map briefcase in an anteroom. On my return I found it crammed with communist pamphlets. I quickly discarded them. The Gestapo officer who searched me on the way out looked quite miffed. The upshot was I was allowed to resume my lecturing. "Because of your connections with the English," said Krafft. I know this very well and hate myself for it. Yet he who constantly spits at himself becomes worthless.

Monday 25th December 1944

One of the sentinels played the violin this morning. The music briefly banished the heavy pounding of the munitions factory and the distant screech of rails as a train goes by. Krafft dismissed the playing as artless, but Mozart, who composed the melody, would have approved. The desolate wailing of a siren cut it off. A little later we heard the rarest of things, church bells, and remembered what this day was for.

Friday 29th December 1944

Krafft badgered me to divulge the true reason for Hess's flight. It was for this, of course, he had been planted in the cell. Stupidly, I told him.

'To bring peace with England so we would be free to conquer Russia.'

'And dropping in on an obscure Scottish duke would end the war?'

'Not so obscure,' I countered. 'Hamilton was Lord Steward of the British king's household and an intimate of Churchill. Besides...' I felt goaded. There seems so little left to lose. I blurted out what I'd kept back since 1941. 'Douglo was just the middleman. There was someone far higher up waiting for Hess in Scotland. If they had met,

I might still be making maps, and you casting horoscopes, with your good Dutch frau frying bratwurst in the kitchen. But Hess crashed. Every attempt to end this accursed war has been doomed from the outset!'

Saturday 30th December 1944

They hauled Krafft out first thing this morning. He was delirious and dripping with fever. I protested to the guards. He should be taken to the sick bay. Shortly after, the Gestapo hauled me off to Prinz-Albrecht-Strasse. They seemed more purposeful than usual, rigid in the black Mercedes sedan. We passed buildings with their façades blown out. Families are still living in them, swathed in overcoats and scarves as they huddle at tables, squabbling over scraps amid the debris. Then there are no houses at all, just acres of bombed out wasteland. At Gestapo HQ there is no way back after the guard waves you through: the doors have no handles on the inside. Usually, I am bustled up the grand staircase beside the grand arched windows that insanely give the place the feeling of a cathedral. This time I was dragged down to the basement: the land of unmuffled screams.

They bellowed at me to provide the names of Hess's Reception Committee. My immunity has expired, and they were eager to get started on pliers and blowtorch. I saved them the trouble and told them what they wanted. What does it matter now? The man Douglo shielded is dead as is any chance of a negotiated peace. I asked what had happened to Krafft. One of my persecutors, a languid and very beautiful young man with blond waved hair, pencilled eyebrows, and make-up on his lips and cheeks, muttered "Oranienburg". It is a town on the river Havel, about half an hour's drive due north of Berlin. It boasts - the irony will kill me - one of the first shrines of the Thousand Year Reich — a concentration camp set up in 1933.

Wednesday 10th January 1945

Interrogations again. They seem tired of the Hess affair; even the July

20 Plot does not animate them as it once did. Most of the conspirators are dead by now, hanged with piano wire from meat hooks on the Führer's express instruction. They must realise they have squeezed everything out of me. "You are too good at your job," I told the Gestapo. "I have nothing more to give you." The officer in make-up whispered that Krafft died, while being transferred to Buchenwald.

Friday 12th January 1945

I can't get the conspirators out of my head - Stauffenburg, the Wednesday Society, the schoolkids of the White Rose — all dogged by bad luck or failure of the will. In December 1942, they arrested Horst Heilman, the student who the Luftwaffe lieutenant had asked me to take on. Heilmann was only nineteen, sweet-tempered, idealistic, though I did not agree with him that communism was the cure for Hitler. He spied for the Red Orchestra, a European-wide network of Soviet agents, so called because the operators of the clandestine transmitters were nicknamed "pianists". Nevertheless, the Berlin branch also fed information to the Allies, helped Jews and members of the resistance escape, documented war crimes, and fomented dissent with their rebel pamphlets.

In July 1942, the Gestapo deciphered the Orchestra's wireless telegraphy codes. They found a Moscow-Centre transmission triggered by a breakdown of the radio links which gave the repairman the addresses of the three transmitters in Berlin. Heilman, ironically, was a technician in the *Funkabwehr*, the counterintelligence organisation charged with hunting down the transmitters. He handled the very print-out that betrayed his friends. His attempt to warn the others failed. More than a 100 were rounded up, including many I had met in Altenburger Allee on Carnival Monday. The lady of the masks was one. After secret trials, the executioner, in his frock coat, white gloves, and polished top hat, dispatched them. They hanged the valiant Luftwaffe lieutenant and beheaded Libertas, his wife. The

Führer was outraged that a segment of high society had turned against him and commanded that their defiance be erased forever more from the records. But you learn a lot in prison. A survivor of the Orchestra told me of their fate.

Sunday 14th January 1945

After the Gestapo released me, I tried to steer clear of trouble. But I ran into Admiral Canaris at Prince Hohenlohe's estate in Baden-Württemburg. Stubby man, salt and pepper crop, honourable, vacillating. The Admiral did not come across as German at all, or Greek as he first believed, but of Italian ancestry as he volubly denounced Hitler. But I outdid him. "Scum!" we both agreed.

We drank Riesling and paced the castle battlements. His two dachshunds were lapping at his heels. He doted on the animals, happy to discuss their health for hours. He told me he had compiled a secret dossier of the atrocities in Poland. He revealed he had a channel to 'Control', the head of MI6, via his mistress in Vienna whose sister was married to 'C's' brother.

We tiptoed around the solution. You could assassinate the Führer, but who was waiting in the wings? Himmler, or "iron-hearted" Heydrich? Better that Hitler was forced into exile on a Bavarian mountaintop, like Napoleon on Saint Helena. That would bring principled generals that had sworn the Hitler oath, such as Rommel, on side. The Allies put paid to the idea in January 1943 when they insisted surrender must be unconditional. After that I lost all faith in assassination or putsch. Like a malignant forest fire, Nazism must burn itself out. Look, the embers are barely glowing! Soon they must expire.

Thursday 18th January 1945

Gestapo-Müller was waiting for me today at Prinz-Albrecht-Strasse. His drooping eyelids still have their nervous twitch. In his heavy Bavarian accent, he demanded my views on the feasibility of an

Armistice. I informed him that, given my current circumstances, I was out of touch and embarked on a rant against the folly of Ribbentrop, who told Hitler that Britain and France would roll over and accept our invasion of Poland, just as they had done with Czechoslovakia. I had told the Führer the opposite. "What a pity the Tribune didn't listen to you!" sighed the official who had told me Krafft was dead. He was wearing no make-up, presumably because his boss was there. Müller told me that Hitler had been nonplussed when he learned who was really waiting for Hess in Scotland. The Gestapo chief drummed his stubby fingers on the table. Why had I stayed dumb about this when the Führer had quizzed me about the English peace party? Yet there still seems to be no order for my elimination.

Müller told me a strange rumour. Hess had been killed in 1941. The circumstances were unclear, but to prevent reprisals against allied prisoners of war and preserve their reputation, the British had substituted a double. My shock told him that this was new to me. And my father? He had corresponded with Hess. Had he noticed any tell-tale signs that the letter-writer was not who he seemed? I could only shrug. The prospect of defeat is loosening tongues. At the end of our interview, Müller told me Hitler compromises too much. Stalin is more ruthless and gets things done. It turns out that the Gestapo chief is a great admirer of the Soviet secret police.

Tuesday 27th February 1945

I've been churning out sonnets like mad. Fifty-seven now, written in iambic pentameters, covering just four sheets of paper in the same miniscule lettering I am writing this. Will anybody read them? My brother Heinz is also here in Moabit. He was rounded up after last year's failed plot. He never travelled abroad or dined at the tables of the great. He ploughed his fields and led a blameless life. I hope he sees his clever, courageous wife again and his beloved children. I picture us all during a family holiday in Partnachalm. Bombs are falling everywhere these days, but I like to think our wooden lodge will survive, snug in the mountains, whose rugged flanks more usually shield it from blizzards.

Monday 16th April 1945

The bombardment of Berlin has begun. We can hear the Russian guns getting closer. It has taken hundreds of years to build this city. Yet its monuments, churches, department stores, bars, galleries will be smashed to smithereens in seconds. Troy is buried under layers of graves and dust. In Petra there are steps leading nowhere, in Carthage, a ruined temple and single archway. What will be left of us?

Tuesday 17th April 1945

Last night Annemarie came to me in dream in all her boyish beauty. She had avoided me for so long and was perfect, without a single bruise. She was so close that this time I thought she would say "Yes". The stars blazed in the heavens just as when we parted for the first time. She asked if I had healed. When I woke, I thought she was still with me. I had to remind myself that the androgynous girl, who thought nothing of driving overland to Persia, had been killed by a fall from a bicycle on a Swiss country lane. Her grave is in Engadin. She loved Klara Mann, the writer's daughter, not me.

Wednesday 18th April 1945

One carpet of bombs after another thundering down. Behind prison bars, we are rapt observers, computing their deadly path. Who amongst us does not hope they will survive?

Thursday 19th April 1945

Russian shellfire. A direct hit on Moabit. We are moved to the cellars. My new cellmate is Herbert Kosney, a communist. He was condemned to death by a civil court but because he is a soldier the sentence must be upheld by a military tribunal. The hearing is set for Saturday.

Friday 20th April 1945

Confusion, panic, mayhem! Such welcome guests. There are only six SS guards left in the entire prison and they keep dashing off for news. Their comrades have been replaced by customs officers, redeployed now there are no frontiers left to guard. For the main part they are kindly fellows who seem uneasy with their duties. Some prisoners have been released, and we hear more will follow, but it seems entirely random. Herbert took me to visit his brother Kurt, who is a few cells away. He has fixed up a primitive radio. We listened to the BBC and learnt the Russians are slowly but methodically burning their way towards Unter den Linden and Kurfürstendamm, demolishing every house in their path.

Saturday 21st April 1945

Herbert's trial has been abandoned. The judges ran away from approaching Russian shell fire. There is indescribable confusion. This evening they told us to pack what belongings we have and ready ourselves for release. Can it be true? Will I really see the lush green meadows and silver-grey mountains again? I have found Herbert to be an agreeable fellow. I gave him my loaf of pumpernickel.'

Announcer: 'On Sunday, 22 April 1945, twenty-one men are freed from Moabit. Those remaining expect to receive the same treatment. That night this seems to be confirmed when the guards assemble two groups of eight men and march them from the cellars to collect their personal belongings. The prisoners are high-ranking soldiers, Abwehr officers, distinguished lawyers, industrialists, and priests. They return to their cells to gather up what little clothing they have. Herbert Kosney, the principal source for what follows, helps Albrecht pack.

'The guards marshal the two groups in the prison yard, where they receive the rest of their valuables: watches, rings, cigarette lighters, wallets. They sign receipts and fill in forms stating they have been released. The prison commander informs them this will happen immediately. "You'll soon see your wife," murmurs the kind-hearted customs officer guarding Kosney.

'The prisoners are herded through a darkened passage towards the exit. A flashlight is switched on. SS Sondercommandos stand ranked on either side, gripping machine guns. Thirty-five or so blank faces peer out from beneath steel helmets. Many are still in their teens. They march the prisoners out into the street. The sky is blackish grey. Rain beats down. The SS commander bellows at them that they are being transported by train to another prison and will be shot if they try to escape. They march down Lehrter Strasse and halt on the corner where it meets Invalid Strasse. The commander orders them to throw their recently returned belongings into a waiting truck. The grotesque mixture of brutal arbitrariness and bureaucracy strikes Kosney as trademark Nazism.

'The SS turn towards the bombed-out Ulap Exhibition Site. "We're taking a shortcut," a sergeant says. Nobody knows if the double meaning is intentional or not. As they blunder across the debris, the prisoners realise this is not the way to Potsdam station. The SS herd the prisoners into the ruins of the huge structure. It is piled with rubble and pitted with bomb craters. Albrecht's group is marched to the left, the other to the right.

'The SS force the prisoners up against a wall. Kosney glances at Haushofer. His face is expressionless. A voice says, "It won't take long". The commander shouts, "Ready!". "Ready," the SS chant. A volley of shots mows the prisoners down. On the ground but still conscious, Kosney feels a warm stream of blood flowing down his face and neck. The bullet has entered the back of his neck and come out under his eye.

'Gestapo-Müller has ordered the executions at Hitler's urging. There are to be no survivors. The SS commander walks up to a prostrate body, shines a torch into the man's face, and fires a revolver into his head. He repeats this with the others until he comes to Kosney. "This pig is dead," he snarls like a cartoon Nazi and grinds his boot into the prisoner's face. There is whimpering nearby rapidly terminated by two shots. The sound of footsteps fades as the SS march away.

'The bullet has passed through Kosney's turned-up coat collar, and the folded prison towel wrapped around his neck. He tries to stem the bleeding by tightening the towel and pressing his handkerchief to the cheek wound. He is drenched by rain, but it feels refreshing. He staggers off in the direction of his home. After evading a patrol and encountering a passer-by on a bicycle, who is not a Good Samaritan, he reaches Hagenauer Strasse at 3.15 a.m. Two hours have elapsed since the executions. His brother and wife are there. Kosney's wounds are too grave for them to minister to.

'Several days later he comes to in a public hospital. He finds a bloodied piece of bread in his coat pocket — the pumpernickel Albrecht has gifted him. He manages to get word to the dead diplomat's brother. After being freed by the Russians, Heinz Haushofer finds Albrecht's body at the exhibition site on 12 May. His brother is clutching five sheets of paper which bear in miniscule handwriting the 79 poems Albrecht has composed in prison. A rare testament to light that glimmered in the blackness of the Third Reich, the Allies rapidly publish them. *The Moabit Sonnets* appear in occupied Berlin on New Year's Day, 1946.'

Chapter Twenty-Three
The Secret of the Bug Hotel

Saturday, 15 May 1965

Surprisingly, there was a Maxwell Knight in the telephone directory. Will toyed with the idea of contacting him, but instead Knight himself rang in early May. "We never did get round to playing together," the major said. "Why don't you come over for a drink? Do bring your guitar as well!" Will took an early afternoon train from Charing Cross. His hair was shoulder-length, his eyes dilated, his stance loping. He was every inch a dedicated follower of fashion in a dark green Regency jacket, a frilly shirt, and mauve, elastic-sided boots. The day turned warm, with temperatures in the high 60s. He was perspiring by the time he reached Knight's suburban terraced house. He had a handkerchief in the pocket of his tweed hipsters but did not use it. It was the one draped over the strongbox beneath Crow's death bed, now designed to make another sweat.

In London the Beautiful People were hailing the Age of Aquarius, but they numbered about three thousand in total. In the rest of the country life was little altered since the 1950s. The sitting room Knight ushered him into was subdued and apologetic: lime green floral wallpaper, a sandy carpet smudged with brown squares, a faux-flame radiator, a pipe rack on the mantelpiece, with tins of tobacco strewn like lifelines throughout the room. A fish tank bubbled near the door. A blue-feathered Amazon parrot puffed out its chest on a perch by the bow window.

'You'll have whisky?' Knight poured two generous measures from a bottle of supermarket scotch on the sideboard. He added a dash of water to one from a Toby jug and peered enquiringly at Will. 'You're looking a bit hot and sticky. Why don't I give you water in a separate glass? The whisky's blended I'm afraid. I retired ten years ago. Bit silly really as it meant forfeiting a good slice of the pension, but to tell the truth I was out of step, a relic. Thought the BBC would keep us going, but that seems to be drying up. They pay far less than people imagine.'

'I listened to that programme.'

'Oh, which one was that, dear boy? Haushofer's diary? Didn't Burton do it justice? Reminded me just what a riddle Hess was. He drafted laws against the Jews yet tried to prevent the worst outrages of pogroms like the Night of Broken Glass. If he hadn't been so in thrall to Hitler, you might almost consider him a decent cove. Certainly, a notch above the rest of the crew who were appalling gangsters, really. Yet he's the one rotting in Spandau. Fascinating about the Swiss astrologer as well. How did he always get it right? And Müller, the Gestapo chief! Little wonder he spoke so highly of the Soviets. He was a Russian asset, which is why he was one of the very few high-ranking Nazis to escape Berlin. He may well be in Moscow as we speak, drowning his sorrows in vodka, just like Kim Philby.'

A key turned. There was bustling in the hallway. A woman poked her head around the door. She had permed hair and a hearty face.

'Susi! I thought you were at the vicarage preparing for the fête. This is Will, an old friend. More your generation than mine in fact.'

Susi was Knight's third wife. His first had killed herself. Rumour, inevitably, implicated the Beast. The likelier cause, however, was the major's inability to consummate the marriage. His second wife simply left for the same reason. Susi had met Knight on the rebound from a relationship in which she discovered heterosexual intercourse disgusted her. Having that in common was fortuitous. Less so was Knight's cruelty. She smiled, but there was a hunted look in her eyes.

'I bought some chops for our supper. They need to go in the fridge.'

'Yes, you do that. Then run along. That's a good girl.'

223

Knight visibly relaxed as the front door closed to Will's consternation. He had not come for a replay of their sticky encounter in Dolphin Square.

'Snifter please, Jerome,' the major said.

This was a cue for the parrot to mimic the squeaking of a corkscrew, the pop as the cork came out, and the gurgling of a drink being poured.

Will smiled. 'That's a neat trick.'

'Not a lot for a fellow to do around here,' sighed Knight, topping up their glasses. 'Now I think it's time for our little jam. Don't look so surprised! That's another term whose pedigree stretches back to the Jazz Age. The problem with your generation is you think you've reinvented the wheel. Sorry, that was uncalled for! It's very good of you to indulge an old man's whim.'

Knight had positioned two straight-backed chairs in front of the fireplace. Will hung his jacket over the back of one, sat down and unlocked the case.

'Not a jazz guitar I'm afraid,' he said, lifting out the Gibson semi-acoustic.

'Oh, it looks just the ticket. I thought we'd kick off with a bit of Sidney Bechet. The Frogs called him "God" when he moved to Paris. I think that's pretty accurate. Absolute hero of mine! He blew me away in New York. Do you know who the very serious man sitting next to me at Carnegie Hall was? Harpo Marx! We shot the breeze, as the Yanks say, in the interval.'

A record player stood on a table in the corner. Knight went over, flipped through the albums stacked beside it and selected one. The cover featured a black clarinet player with cropped grey hair alongside *Gone French* printed in blue. Knight slid the record out of its sleeve, placed it on the turntable and lowered the needle. A slinky melody vibrated from the speaker.

'Takes me back to California,' said Will.

'Glad you know it, old boy. "Petite fleur"— big hit in '52.'

A saxophone and clarinet stood propped on stands against the wall. Knight lifted the clarinet and wiped away the dust with a yellow cloth.

'Just the tune to blow the cobwebs away. It's in G.'

Will strummed along, adjusting the tuning as he played. The chord progression was conventional. He had picked it up by the time Knight raised the needle from the vinyl.

'Now, it's our turn,' the major said, beaming.

There were a few miffed notes, but he blew competently enough, beating time with his foot on the brass fire fender as Will laid down the rhythm.

'God, it's good to do this again. Fancy a chaser? Let me fetch you one from the kitchen!' Knight bounced out and returned with two frothy glasses of Whitbread pale ale. 'Shall we try something more up-tempo? This one's in G again.'

He launched into a sprightly version of "Saint Louis Blues", a straight 12 bar blues with a Latin American 16 bar segment. A quieter interlude buffered the two sections, during which Knight lowered the clarinet and tapped the beat out with his foot, as Will carried the tune. When it was time for the clarinet to come back in, however, the major let the instrument slide to the floor and clutched his chest. Will stopped playing. Fighting for breath, Knight removed a small spray bottle from the pocket of his yellow waistcoat and squirted its contents into his mouth. After a couple of minutes, he began to breathe more easily.

'Sorry, old boy, spot of angina. Blasted nuisance! Could you pour another whisky? The quack says it keeps the veins open. Who am I to argue?'

Will took the bottle from the sideboard and topped up their glasses.

'That spray's a miracle. This helps too, of course.' He clinked his glass against Will's. 'Queen and country and all that!'

They sipped the scotch in silence. Will wondered if this was the right moment to produce the handkerchief, but the major forestalled him by suggesting a tour of the premises. The house had very little to recommend it. Will was on guard again.

A flight of stairs led up to separate bedrooms. Passing these and the kitchen, they came to a pantry. Knight opened the door, releasing a claustrophobic stench of old straw, dead flies, and feeds. Muted blue light played on glass cases, Petri dishes, and trays of insect specimens that lined the shelves. Affixed to the wall, a two-bar electric fire was stoking up the heat.

Knight grinned. ' 'C' had a blue light just like this outside his office. Welcome to the bug hotel!'

They had finished off more than a third of the bottle, with the major downing most of it. His voice was slightly slurred. Will hoped he was a good drunk.

'Insects aren't my thing,' he said.

'Pity! They are the most fascinating creatures on the planet. Consider a termite colony or beehive: miracles of ingenuity and design.'

He went in, gesturing to Will to follow. The chirping of cicadas, the hissing of snakes, the stridulation of grasshoppers, and, most unexpectedly, laughter greeted them.

'The Southern leopard frog is the joker,' Knight said. 'The spring peeper clucks like a chicken, the green tree fog of Arkansas quacks like a goose. Sadly, I have neither. Nature is an accomplished mimic. I sometimes wonder if she's laughing at us.'

A black Shaw Walker filing cabinet stood at the centre of the facing wall. The major approached, Will followed. A livid green snake coiled around a branch in a case alongside; a fist-sized black spider swayed on its web. The major fumbled for a key in the pocket of his

Tattersall shirt, unlocked and pulled out the top drawer of the cabinet. It was lined with suspension files. Knight started flipping through them until, with an 'ah', he lifted one out and placed it on top of the cabinet. Raising one flap, he pulled out a typescript. *The Frightened Face of Nature* was typed on a white label glued to the cover.

'My publisher won't touch this with a barge pole. Says it's too controversial. I don't suppose you've got any contacts in that line. Sorry to ask, old boy, but it's a matter of life and death, and not just ours. Most of the wildlife on Earth will have disappeared by the next century. We launch rockets, bounce pictures off satellites, fly to Australia in 30 hours, but we can't seem to stop destroying the planet. This a warning of the catastrophe ahead if we don't change our ways.'

'The only publishers I know are music ones.'

Knight sighed. 'The young these days strike me as completely bonkers, but they do genuinely seem to want to save the world. I'm sure they'd be receptive.'

The major was very close. Brylcreem layered his slicked back hair into metallic strands. An oversight of the razor had left clumps of stubble interspersed with the broken veins on his cheek. His hands were trembling as he put the typescript back, dislodging the file. He moved to bend down, but the sudden action made him grimace. Will crouched down in his stead and began reuniting the file with the typescript, a few letters in faded envelopes, and a black and white photograph.

Two men were standing in the foreground. One wore a braided cap and an RAF uniform, the other was in army battledress. A woman in ATS khaki was hunched over a wireless receiver in a background that also featured hospital beds, with heart monitors and oxygen tanks stacked alongside. Will recognised the man in the cap from the pictures Maria was always collecting.

'That's the Duke of Kent.'

Knight whistled. 'My word, I'm surprised someone of your generation would clock that.'

Will straightened, the file in one hand and the photo in the other. Knight shifted uncomfortably and reached out to take them.

'It looks like a hospital. Was it taken during the war?'

The corner of the major's mouth had developed a twitch that Will had never noticed before.

'I really can't say, old thing.'

'Crow believed the goal was to find out who you truly are. You've been in hiding from that your whole life.'

'That's what the game does to you. Truth becomes elusive. It's like one of those dreams where you wake up only to find you're in another.'

Will had meant another sort of concealment. He remembered John Lennon's plangent nasal baritone coming over the intercom at Abbey Road with a Dylanesque song called 'You've Got to Hide your Love Away'. A Studio Two hand told him it was about somebody close to the boys who was in the closet and regularly beaten up by rough trade.

'You overstepped the mark,' he said.

'We had to eliminate them. You've no idea how dangerous-'

'I meant by what you did to me.'

'Did I, dear boy? Secrets get very hard to bear. The love that dare not speak its name and all that. Perhaps I picked up the wrong signals and thought I could share them with you.'

'You owe it to me to do that now.'

'Your generation expects everything on a platter: orange juice, college grants, state secrets! I'm sorry, you don't deserve that. The quack says I've only got eighteen months, maybe two years, if I'm lucky.'

'Even more reason to come clean.'

'This is a very nasty business, Will. People get damaged or wiped out. Take Sikorski, the Polish general. You read about him, didn't you? His plane crashed a few moments after take-off from Gibraltar in 1943. The cause has never been explained.'

Will thought again of Maria's scrapbook.

'The same thing happened the year before to the Duke of Kent,' he said. 'I worked with some of the flight crew. They couldn't understand why his flying boat was off course and over land. The S.25 Short Sunderland Mark III was an excellent plane. Visibility was good, the pilots experienced, yet they crashed in the Highlands.'

'Coincidence,' said the major.

'Crow told me there's no such thing.'

Knight emitted a protracted sigh. 'I'd give all this a wide berth if I were you!'

'What is the Reception Committee?

'You're not listening, are you, Will?'

'It had to be covered up, didn't it? Were Kent and Sikorski killed because they were on it?'

'The men in the photo are waiting for a very important visitor whose identity I can't reveal.'

'I think we've got beyond that now.'

'Oh, have it your own way! Let's call him "Jonathan". In five minutes, the men go to the landing strip outside. Jonathan lines his plane up with the runway but overshoots and flies on.'

'He's confused?'

'He's been flying for several hours and Pervitin - a very strong amphetamine that was standard issue for the enemy - is beginning to wear off. But that's not the reason. A night fighter is on his tail. Jonathan bales out and is captured. No peace is concluded.'

'And if it had been?'

'The Blitz is raging, invasion seems imminent, the country is at its lowest ebb. Imagine if news breaks that the king's youngest brother and the Führer's deputy have hammered out a treaty which guarantees Britain's independence and empire for years to come!'

'And the man with the stuck-up face? He has three pips on his shoulder-strap. He's an army captain, right?'

'Don't you think you've heard enough for one day?'

'Do you want to leave more loose ends like the *Frightened Face of Nature*?'

Knight lit his pipe and took a deep draw, the fumes overlaying the palette of other smells. 'An army captain's uniform was standard issue for MI5 during operations. We'll call the man "Anthony". Like me he's a major. Back in '43 a mole I had embedded in the CPGB was slung out. Anthony was the only one who could have tipped the Reds off. I raised a stink but as usual nobody wanted to know. "Stalin's on our side," they said, "and besides, Anthony's terribly well connected". It didn't catch up with him until a year ago. An American agent revealed during vetting that Anthony had tried to recruit him for Moscow Centre.'

'So he's been nabbed.'

Knight smiled wryly. 'The authorities saw fit to grant him immunity from prosecution. He retains his elevated position at Buckingham Palace.'

'The Establishment takes care of its own.'

'Not usually when it comes to treason, but Anthony knows where the royal skeletons are buried. In 1946 he went to Germany and burnt a trove of incriminating letters on behalf of the king. He made copies, however. These confirmed to his Moscow controllers that the royal family was implicated in Jonathan's arrival. That's why the Soviets have resisted all attempts to free him. If his mission had resulted in a treaty, Hitler would have had carte blanche to smash the USSR.'

The pipe had gone out. Knight tapped it against the edge of the cabinet, getting ready for a refill.

'In his starry-eyed way, Jonathan saw himself as a chivalrous knight who could not betray a king. Three days after his capture, Prince George visited him clandestinely near Edinburgh and swore him to silence. Fine fellow the duke, by the way. I often saw him letting his hair down in the Gargoyle. He wore too many rings and bangles, for my taste, and his perfume reeked, but God was he original!'

A key turned in the latch. There was a subdued commotion in the hallway. Knight frowned, took the photo, and dropped it into the file, which he returned to the drawer, pushing it shut and locking it.

'I'd got wind of the Reception Committee from 'C', who'd got it from Canaris. One of the ATS girls at the Kennels was ours. She took the photo. The girl must have found the secret burdensome as well because she spilled the beans to a reporter. The Macmillan government slapped a D-Notice on the story, suppressing it. Nobody will give you the time of day if you come out with anything either.'

They emerged dishevelled from the bug hotel with sweat-streaked faces and patches of shirt glued to skin. Susi was outside the kitchen, frowning.

'Just terrifying our guest with the tarantulas, my love.'

She looked at Will coldly.

'I think you better go,' she said.

* * *

Doctor Beeching's axe had done little to improve the railways. The London train was more than 20 minutes late. Will lit a Sweet Afton in the compartment. The other occupant was a dowdily dressed woman with a careworn face.

'If you're going to smoke, can you at least pull the window down a bit?'

He did so, struck by the familiarity that lingered even after her voice had faded. He scrutinised her more closely, searching beneath the palimpsest of lines for the relics of youth.

'I beg your pardon!' Her voice rose sharply.

'I'm sorry, but don't we - I mean didn't we - know each other?'

Her eyes searched him, like a telescope investigating the stars, gazing back in time.

'Will!'

'That's right, Maria.'

'Whatever were you doing in Camberley?'

'Oh, just visiting a...'

He was stumped. Friend? Acquaintance? Molester? It hardly mattered: she wasn't listening. The years had not been good. She was maid to a prostitute who worked out of a flat in Greek Street.

'My mother's in a home in Basingstoke. I go every Friday. Don't know why I bother really. She hardly knows who I am.'

A tear negotiated the faded acne scars. Will pulled out the handkerchief. Burdened with a greater revelation, there had seemed little point in confronting the major. As Maria dabbed her face, she noticed the map finely worked on the silk: the railway line, the hills, the small lake. Hess's alias was stitched at the bottom.

'Who is Hauptmann Alfred Horn?' she demanded.

Will sighed. 'A conflicted man who loved the wrong person too much.'

'Oh, I know all about that,' she said.

The End

Dramatis Personae

Blunt, Sir Anthony (1907-1983). MI5 major and leading art historian who became Surveyor of the Queen's Pictures. Exposed as a Russian spy in 1964, the Establishment shielded him, not least because of secret missions he undertook to Germany in 1945 at the behest of George VI. At the prompting of Margaret Thatcher, he was publicly exposed in 1979.

Bond, Graham (1937-1974). Rock/blues vocalist and musician considered one of the pioneers of the English rhythm and blues boom of the 1960s. He grew obsessed with magick and Aleister Crowley, believing he was the magician's son. Plagued by drug addiction, with his finances and personal life in chaos, he threw himself under a tube train at Finsbury Park station on 8 May 1974.

Burckhardt, Carl J. (1891-1974). Swiss diplomat and historian who was president of the International Committee of the Red Cross during World War II. Despite the organisation's neutrality, he was heavily involved in brokering peace and met with Albrecht Haushofer to this end.

Butler, E.M. (1885-1959). Professor of German at Cambridge University from 1945 onwards, Eliza Marian Butler wrote several books, including some on magic. She seemed to glean little from her interview with Crowley and in *The Myth of the Magus* (CUP, 1947) confined herself to making a few disparaging remarks about him.

Cameron, Marjorie (1922-1995). American artist, poet, actress and occultist who used the mononym, Cameron, professionally. After her husband Jack Parson's death, she appeared in several art-house films. In recent years, there has been increasing recognition of her painting. (See *Wormwood Star* by Spencer Kansa — Mandrake of Oxford, 2014).

Canaris, Admiral (1887-1945). Chief of German Military Intelligence, the Abwehr, from 1935 to 1944, Wilhelm Franz Canaris initially supported Hitler but horrified by Nazi atrocities became an opponent of the regime. There is some evidence he fed information to Sir Stewart Menzies, the head of MI6, known as 'C', including a warning of Hess's mission. Condemned by Hitler after the July plot, Canaris was led to the gallows naked and hanged in a barbaric fashion by the SS on 9 April 1945.

Churchill, Winston (1874-1965). Conservative Prime Minister from 1940 to 1945 and again from 1951 to 1955. Churchill was initially dubious when the Duke of Hamilton arrived with news of the Deputy Reichsführer's capture and went off to see a Marx Brothers' film. In his *History of the Second World War* (Cassell, London, 1948), Churchill views Hess as a "medical not a criminal case" who atoned for the moral guilt of supporting Hitler by a "completely devoted and frantic act of lunatic benevolence". Intriguingly, he describes Hess's motive as an attempt "to get at the heart of Britain and make its king believe how Hitler felt towards it".

Crowley, Aleister (1875-1947). English occultist, mountaineer, writer, painter, and ceremonial magician who founded the religion of Thelema. After a long association with various branches of the secret service, Crowley was invited for an interview by the Naval Intelligence Division at the outset of World War Two and subsequently offered to help crack Hess. Imitating Churchill in dress and in manner, he was delighted when he chanced upon the prime minister's tobacco supplier and could pose with the same brand of cigar. Dying in obscurity, Crowley leapt into the limelight in the 1960s when the Beatles featured him on the cover of Sergeant Pepper. A man of great erudition and originality, with some unsavoury habits, he remains - to the discomfort of some - a cultural icon. (See biographies and related works by Phil Baker, Martin Booth, Tobias Churton, Richard Kaczynski, Gary Lachman, Marco Pasi, Richard B. Spence, Lawrence Sutin, John Symonds).

Dee, John (1527-1608). English mathematician, astrologer, spy, alchemist and magician, Doctor Dee was court astronomer and advisor to Elizabeth I. In 1582 he met Edward Kelley who became his "scryer" or crystal-gazer, the channel for several books dictated by angels in a complex angelic language called Enochian. Dee's investigations into angel magic were continued by Crowley and Victor Neuburg at Bou Saada in the Algerian desert in 1909, Jack Parsons and Lafayette Ron Hubbard in the Californian desert in 1946, and Timothy Leary and Brian Barritt again at Bou Saada in 1971.

Fleming, Ian Lancaster (1908-1964). Born into a wealthy family, Fleming had several jobs before becoming a writer. While working for Britain's Naval Intelligence Division during the Second World War, he reputedly concocted a magical attack on the Nazi high command called Operation Mistletoe with Crowley and Maxwell Knight. He also gave serious consideration to the Beast's offer to interview Hess. Rosa Lewis claimed Crowley and Fleming ate together at the Cavendish Hotel. Fleming based Le Chiffre, the villain in the first James Bond story, *Casino Royale*, on Crowley.

Foley, Frank (1884-1958). Major Francis "Frank" Edward Foley was a British Secret Intelligence Officer who was responsible for questioning Rudolf Hess at Camp Z (Mytchett Place). He went on to coordinate a network of double agents, the Double Cross - "XX" - System. In 2004, an entry in a diary belonging to Foley's widow turned up that disclosed his covert trip to Lisbon in January 1941 and the part it played in luring Hess to Scotland. His saving the lives of at least 10,000 Jews, while passport control officer in Berlin, resulted in posthumous official recognition in the UK and Israel as a British Hero of the Holocaust and a Righteous Among the Nations.

Fortune, Dion (1890-1946). Violet Firth met Crowley when he attended a lecture she gave in London. Much of the subsequent correspondence between them was lost after John Symonds sent it to the USA where Charles Manson and his "Family" stole it along with other relics of the Beast. (See Janice Chapman. *The Quest for Dion Fortune* - Red Wheel/Weiser, 1993). As Dion Fortune, she was an inspirational writer and teacher, who died of leukaemia in 1946, a year after her first visit to Netherwood. She is buried in Glastonbury, near the mystical colony she founded at Chalice Orchard, whose members conducted a magical Battle of Britain against the Nazis during the Second World War.

Hamilton, Duke of (1903-1973). Prior to the Second World War, Douglas Douglas-Hamilton was a convinced appeaser and member of the Anglo-German Fellowship. There are anomalies in Hamilton's behaviour that indicate Hess's arrival did not come as a total shock. He did nothing to hinder the transit of Hess's Messerschmitt-110 when in charge of RAF Turnhouse, nor did he make any move to visit Hess on the night of his capture, though the Deputy Reichsführer demanded to see him. According to *spartacus-educational.com*, Hamilton's diary records several meetings with the Duke of Kent during the early part of 1941. Elizabeth Byrd, who worked as a secretary for Hamilton's brother, Lord Malcolm Douglas-Hamilton, claims her employer told her that Hamilton took the "flak for the whole Hess affair in order to protect others even higher up the social scale". Byrd added that "he (Lord Malcolm) had strongly hinted that the cover-up was necessary to protect the reputations of members of the Royal Family". This gives added weight to Albrecht Haushofer's remark, "you — and your friends in high places" (letter to Hamilton on 23 September 1940). Hamilton was reported as being deeply unhappy with the Hess affair, feeling he had been ill-treated throughout.

Harris, Lady Frieda (1877-1962). The Thoth Tarot the artist created with Crowley did not finally appear until seven years after her death. She retained a lifelong interest in the esoteric. After Crowley's death, she studied Gurdjieff and Eastern mysticism, dying in Srinagar in India. (See Deja Whitehouse's YouTube presentation: 'Frieda Harris and the Divine Giraffe').

Haushofer, **Albrecht (1903-1945).** Professor of political philosophy and map making at Berlin University, poet, playwright, diplomat, adviser to the foreign ministry, and key member of the resistance. Annemarie Schwarzenbach, the girlfriend who rejected him, was a Swiss lesbian writer, photographer and morphine addict who died after a bicycle accident in 1942. Haushofer met Douglas Hamilton at the Berlin Olympics in 1936 and described him as his "closest friend". He stayed with him at Dungavel House and used him as a conduit in his manoeuvring for peace. Their friendship was the key driver of Hess's flight. Despite this, it is almost certain that Hess gave no warning of his mission to Albrecht or his father Karl. (See *The Truth About Rudolf Hess* by James Douglas-Hamilton — Frontline Books, 2016).

Haushofer, Karl (1869-1946). A German general, professor, geographer and politician, his geopolitical ideas, in particular *Lebensraum* ("living space"), were instrumental in fuelling Hitler's territorial ambitions. Allied black propaganda gave rise to the myth that Haushofer was a magician who played a Rasputin-like role in Hitler's life. While he did spend several years in Japan and was prone to prophetic dreams, there is very little evidence for this. Haushofer never joined the Nazi party and opposed antisemitism. He believed Hitler had fundamentally misunderstood the geo-political ideas he had taught him and would eventually fall out with him. On 11 March 1946, Karl Haushofer and his half-Jewish wife Martha took poison under a willow tree half a mile from their house. He left instructions that no marker or memorial should be erected on or near his grave. There should be no obituary or epitaph. His last wish was to be "forgotten and forgotten".

Hess, **Rudolf Walter Richard (1894-1987).** Born in Alexandria to a wealthy merchant family, Hess served in the German Army in the First World War. He met Hitler in July 1920 and was the Nazi leader's closest friend and confidant. In 1933 he became Deputy Führer. Sentenced to life imprisonment by the Nuremberg Tribunal, he was the sole inmate of Berlin's Spandau prison from 1966 until his death. Unable to find any evidence of the severe wounds Hess had sustained in the First World War, Hugh Thomas, a surgeon who attended him, popularised the notion that the prisoner was a double. Many questions remain about Hess's flight to Scotland, not least because a great number of the relevant files are incomplete or missing. As Peter Padfield puts it in *Hess, Hitler and Churchill* (Icon Books — 2014), "In Hess's case the open files have been extensively 'weeded'…We can only guess at the number of complete files that remain closed to the public or that have actually been destroyed…The absence of these vital documents provides every opportunity for conjecture". Hess died in 1987. The official cause was suicide. As with much else, his death was dogged by too many anomalies to make such a verdict certain.

Hitler, Adolf (1889-1945). Austrian-born dictator of Germany from 1933 to 1945. Karlheinz Pintsch, Hess's adjutant, handed Hitler an explanatory letter from his boss the morning after the flight. According to him, Hitler received the news calmly, indicating collusion.

Moreover, Hess's peace overture occurred by "prior arrangement with the English". Pintsch, however, was a prisoner of the Soviets at the time and that was exactly what Stalin wanted to hear. It is far more likely that Hitler's astonishment and fury were genuine, and he was not in the know. Several witnesses attest to this, including Albert Speer, who described the Nazi leader's "inarticulate and almost animal outcry" of rage.

Hoare, Sir Samuel (1880-1959). The first Viscount Templewood was a senior British Conservative statesman who served in Conservative and National governments of the 1920s and 1930s. He was an arch-appeaser and one of the architects of Chamberlain's Munich accord with Hitler. After Churchill became prime minister, Hoare was sent to Spain as Ambassador and played an important role in shoring up Franco's neutrality. He was considered a focal point for peace overtures and was, consequently, in contact with Albrecht Haushofer. There are indications that Hoare was playing a double game and acting at Churchill's behest.

Hubbard, L. Ron (1911-1986). Lafayette Ronald Hubbard was an American naval officer, science fiction writer, and founder of the Church of Scientology. With Jack Parsons he performed the Babalon Working from January to March 1946. Subsequently, Parsons claimed to have been defrauded by Hubbard, who took his life savings as well as Parson's girlfriend Sara Northrup, known as "Betty", to the East Coast to buy yachts. Years later the Church of Scientology claimed that Hubbard was working undercover for Naval Intelligence to infiltrate and destroy Parsons' black magic cult. In a lecture recorded in 1952, Hubbard discusses occult magic of the Middle Ages and recommends Crowley's Magick in Theory and Practice, describing its deceased author as "my very good friend".

Kent, Duke of (1902-1942). Prince George was the fourth son of George V. After a youth marked by bisexuality and drug addiction, he settled into a more conventional mode when he married the Greek Princess Marina. Like his mother, Queen Mary of Teck, and his brother, the Duke of Windsor, he was an enthusiastic advocate of appeasement and conspired with his German cousin, Prince Philipp of Hesse, to prevent the Second World War. On the night of 9 May 1941, he was at RAF Sumburgh in the Shetlands, and on 11 May at Balmoral in Scotland. His whereabouts on 10 May are unknown. According to Lynn Picknett, Clive Prince and Stephen Prior, the authors of *Double Standards* (Sphere, 2002), he was at Dungavel waiting for Hess. An ATS girl also claimed to have been present but the news report concerning this was suppressed. Kent was killed when the flying boat officially taking him to Iceland crashed into Eagle's Rock in the Scottish Highlands on 25 August 1942. Why a plane designed to fly over water was above land is just one of many unexplained mysteries surrounding the disaster.

Knight, Maxwell (1900-1968). Charles Henry Maxwell Knight OBE was a British spymaster, naturalist, and broadcaster who started his career in the navy. He was head of security for the British Fascisti and then joined the secret service in 1925, rising to head section B(5)b of MI5, with a mandate to infiltrate agents into homegrown fascist and communist groups. He retained a lifelong fascination with the natural world, becoming "Uncle Max", a popular children's broadcaster and author on the subject. He was also fascinated by the occult. In *The Man Who Was M* (Harper Collins: 1986), Anthony Masters writes, "Knight told his nephew, Harry Smith, that he and Dennis Wheatley went to Crowley's occult ceremonies to research black magic for Wheatley's books…They jointly applied to Crowley as novices, and he accepted them as pupils." Joan Miller, Knight's assistant, found a photo of Crowley among his belongings which she tore up. Miller was infatuated with Knight and began living with him. She came to believe this was a cover for his homosexuality that she exposed in a memoir that was published posthumously in Ireland in 1986, despite the best efforts of MI5 to have it banned. An associate of Ian Fleming, Knight is a leading candidate for 'M' – his actual mononym – in the Bond books.

Krafft, Karl Ernst (1900-1945). The Swiss-born astrologer rose to prominence in the Third Reich when he successfully foretold the assassination attempt against Hitler in November 1939. This was just one of several remarkably accurate predictions he made. Subsequently, he was employed by Goebbels to produce doctored prophecies of Nostradamus. British Intelligence grew convinced he was the Führer's soothsayer. They used their own astrologer, Louis De Wohl, to match the horoscopes Krafft was casting in the belief they were dictating German strategy. In fact, there is no evidence Krafft ever met Hitler. After the Deputy Reichsführer's capture, Krafft was one of many German occultists detained during *Aktion Hess* and fell into disfavour. He died on 8 January 1945 en route to Buchenwald concentration camp. (See *Urania's Children: The Strange World of the Astrologers* by Ellic Howe — William Kimber, 1967).

Müller, Heinrich (1900-date of death unknown). A police official and senior member of the SS, Müller ran the Gestapo, the main instrument of internal Third Reich terror, and was heavily implicated in the holocaust. Last seen in the *Führerbunker* in Berlin on 1 May 1945, rumours persist that he was a Soviet asset who was translated to Moscow.

Nostradamus, Michel de (1503-1566). French astrologer, physician, apothecary, and seer, credited with predicting the French revolution, the rise of Napoleon and Hitler etc. The ambiguous nature of his prophecies readily invites widely differing interpretations. This allowed both Allies and Axis to use him in black propaganda during the Second World War.

Parsons, Jack Whiteside (1914-1952). Pioneering rocket scientist who from 1942 onwards headed the Californian branch of Crowley's Ordo Templi Orientis (OTO). In 1946, he conducted the Babalon Working, a series of rituals intended to invoke the Thelemic goddess Babalon and usher in a new age. He was convinced this resulted in the appearance of Marjorie Cameron whom he married in 1946. During McCarthyism, he was accused of espionage and could no longer work in rocketry. The police ruled the explosion that killed him at his home in Pasadena in 1952 an accident, though Cameron maintained he was murdered. Apart from the impact of his posthumously published libertarian and occult writings, he is regarded as one of the most important figures in the history of the U.S. space programme. A crater on the dark side of the moon bears his name. (See *Strange Angel* by George Pendle — W & N, 2006).

Philipp, Prince of Hesse (1896-1980). Head of the Electoral House of Hesse from 1940 to 1980 and early adherent of Nazism, Philipp became Hitler's art dealer. The Prince married an Italian princess and acted as Hitler's private emissary to Mussolini and Pope Pius XII. In the spring of 1943, he fell out of favour after delivering an honest assessment of the military situation in Italy and was sent to a concentration camp. He survived the war.

Schulze-Boysen, Harro (1909-1942). A Luftwaffe officer and publicist whose anti-Nazi convictions led him to become the leader of the German branch of the Red Orchestra, a European-wide Soviet spy ring. He recruited over 100 others, including his wife, Libertas. He was in contact with Albrecht Haushofer, who, at Schulze-Boysen's behest, took on his student Horst Heilmann as well as attending a party at his flat. Almost all the members of the Red Orchestra were captured and executed. On 22 December 1942 Schulze-Boysen was hanged and Libertas guillotined. (See *The Red Orchestra* by Giles Perrault — Schocken Books, 1989 & *The Infiltrators* by Norman Ohler — Atlantic Books, London, 2020).

Sikorski, Wladyslaw (1881-1943). Politician and military leader who was prime minister of the Polish government-in-exile and Commander-in-Chief of the Polish armed forces during the Second World War. Sikorski was a frequent guest at the Duke of Kent's home and offered him the crown of Poland. He flew back from the United States the day after Hess's capture, landing at Prestwick Airport, a forty-minute drive from Dungavel. An entry for 7 July 1941 in the diary of Guy Liddell, wartime head of British counter-intelligence, outlines a Polish plot to attack Camp Z and kill Hess, ostensibly for vengeance and to forestall the British signing up to German peace plans. An MI5 file apparently describes a gun battle at the camp between soldiers guarding Hess and Polish troops. On 4 July 1943, a plane carrying Sikorski crashed into the sea immediately after take-off from Gibraltar, killing everyone except the pilot. Allegations of sabotage variously blame the Russians, the British and the Nazis.

Stalin, Joseph Vissarionovich (1878-1953). A Georgian-born revolutionary, who led the Soviet Union from 1924 until his death, Stalin refused to believe Hitler was going to invade Russia even when the evidence turned from a trickle to a flood. He displayed a similar obstinacy in maintaining that Hess flew to Scotland in collusion with British Intelligence. When Churchill flatly denied this, Stalin declared his own spies keep secrets from him as well.

Symonds, John (1914-2006). An English novelist, playwright and writer of children's books, Symonds was Crowley's literary executor along with Kenneth Grant. His biography, *The Great Beast* (Rider, 1951), put Crowley on the map but its disapproving tone jarred with those who took a more charitable view of the magician. Through an accident of geography - we lived in the same street - I got to know Symonds when in my teens. He did little to hide his hostility to Crowley and would describe helping the Beast inject heroin with repugnance. He seemed horrified by Crowley's adoption as a prophet of drug and sexual licence in the 1960s. In my view Symonds' own contribution to this troubled him, as did the fact that Crowley had become a Bermuda Triangle in which his own work was in danger of being lost.

Symonds, Vernon (1899-1962). A man of left-wing views who nursed a lifelong fascination with the theatre. In 1935 Vernon married Ellen Kathleen Johnson aka "Johnnie" (1903-87). Soon after they bought run-down Netherwood and transformed it into a bohemian boarding house. While a guest, Crowley gave Latin tutorials to the Symonds' nephew Roland, who went on to become a priest, a fact transmogrified in the present work. In 1949 the Symonds sold up and ran a clinic for alcoholics, Vernon being a convert to AA and Christianity after his own battle with drink, of which he left an account called *Goodbye to Bacchus*. (See *Netherwood: Last Resort of Aleister Crowley* by Antony Clayton — Accumulator Press, 2012).

Wheatley, Dennis Yeats (1897-1977). A prolific author who became one of the world's best-selling writers from the 1930s through to the 1960s. He met Crowley while researching his black magic novel, *The Devil Rides Out*, and was also an associate of Maxwell Knight and Ian Fleming. (See *The Devil is a Gentleman: The Life and Times of Dennis Wheatley* by Phil Baker — Dedalus, 2009).

Wilkinson, Louis Umfreville (1881-1966). British author, lecturer and biographer remembered for his association with literary figures of the day, in particular the Powys brothers. Using the pen name Louis Marlow, he produced novels, essays, and biographical works, including *Seven Friends*, which contains a portrait of Crowley. Unusually, given the Beast's tendency to fall out with people, he and Crowley maintained a close friendship from their first meeting in 1907 to the Beast's death in 1947.

Further Reading

Aleister Crowley MI5

Richard C McNeff

ISBN: 978-1-914153-02-0

Mandrake of Oxford

A sinister Soho encounter with Aleister Crowley in June 1936 launches Dylan Thomas on an absorbing adventure in company with his first editor, Victor Neuburg, the Beast's lapsed apprentice. Neuburg confronts the terrifying magick of his youth and something even more perilous — an MI5 plot to avert the Abdication. *Aleister Crowley MI5* is an exhilarating work of biographical fiction with a bedrock of fact at its core.

'Brilliantly researched, ... an astonishing read, a 24-hour snapshot of the seedy underground life of artists, poets, prostitutes, spies and royalty of mid-Thirties London, all revolving around the fading powerhouse that was the Great Beast.' — *Fortean Times*

'McNeff's book is so different from anything you usually find on a bookshelf that it should perhaps be a compulsory purchase.'— *The Independent on Sunday*

'Probably the finest modern novel featuring Aleister Crowley.'— *Lashtal.com*

'A swaggering romp of a novel. Plot by Buchan; characters by Beardsley; setting Art Deco — difficult to better that.' — *Wormwood*

'Aleister Crowley, mountaineer, mage and magician, has been the basis for a number of fictional characters — Somerset Maugham's Oliver Haddo, M. R. James' Karswell, Anthony Powell's Scorpio Murtlock, Dennis Wheatley's Mocata and even Ian Fleming's Le Chiffre in the first James Bond story, *Casino Royale*. Rarely has he appeared in fiction as himself. Here, in a highly researched story based upon his relationship with his acolyte, Victor Neuburg, he is himself in all his occult and charismatic glory - a manipulative, overbearing, bizarre yet compelling character. Fiction could hardly have invented him: he is a gift of a character to any novelist and Richard C McNeff has accepted him, unwrapped the parcel and given him his head. — Martin Booth (Author of *A Magick Life: a biography of Aleister Crowley*)

'A very clever idea, fleshed out with wit and style and an excellent sense of the times.' — *Silverstar*

Note on the Author

Richard C McNeff was born in London but lived all over Britain when a child as his father, also called Richard, was a repertory theatre actor who subsequently went into film and television. His mother, Lynne Munn, was a Liverpool-born poet and artist. His father's eldest brother, Samuel Valentine McNeff, was a wartime major in MI6. After studying English at Sussex University, Richard lived and worked in Barcelona, Amsterdam, the Basque Country, Ibiza, and Baku. He is also the author of *With Barry Flanagan: Travels through Time and Spain* (the Lilliput Press), a memoir that grew out of curating shows for the internationally recognised sculptor. He has contributed to the *Guardian, Fortean Times,* and *Boulevard Magenta.* He divides his time between London and Andalucía.

www.richardmcneff.co.uk

Printed in the USA
CPSIA information can be obtained
at www.ICGtesting.com
LVHW012005051023
760026LV00024B/48/J